SWORD ART ONLINE
16
EKI KAWAHARA ABEC BEE-PEE
SWORD ART ONLINE
licization Exploding

"First Division, draw swords and prepare for battle!"

Fanatio § Vice Commander, Heaven-Piercing Blade

"I betrayed... your expectations of me..."

Eldrie § Frostscale Whip

"It's all right. Don't be worried."

"Commander...meaning Vecta, god of darkness."

Bercouli § Commander, Time-Splitting Sword

Integrity Knights

"Crush them!!"

"We're going to pay our respects to these Integrity Knights!"

Iskahn § Tenth champion of the pugilists guild

"You must capture that knight, the Priestess of Light, unharmed."

Dark God Vecta § Emperor

"Damnable humans!!"

Lilpilin § Chief of the orcs

Invasion Army

"His head will soon belong to Shibori."

Shibori § Flatland goblin chief

Dee Eye Ell § Chancellor of the dark mages guild

"I will eliminate all five Integrity Knights without fail."

"I see that look on your face, boy. It says, 'But you're a goblin…'"

Kosogi § Mountain goblin chief

"Lady…
Stacia…?"
Tiese § Trainee
"You worked a miracle
and saved my life."
Ronie § Trainee
"No way…You gotta be
kidding me."
Vassago § Dark knight

"Take me to where Kirito is."
Asuna § Goddess of creation

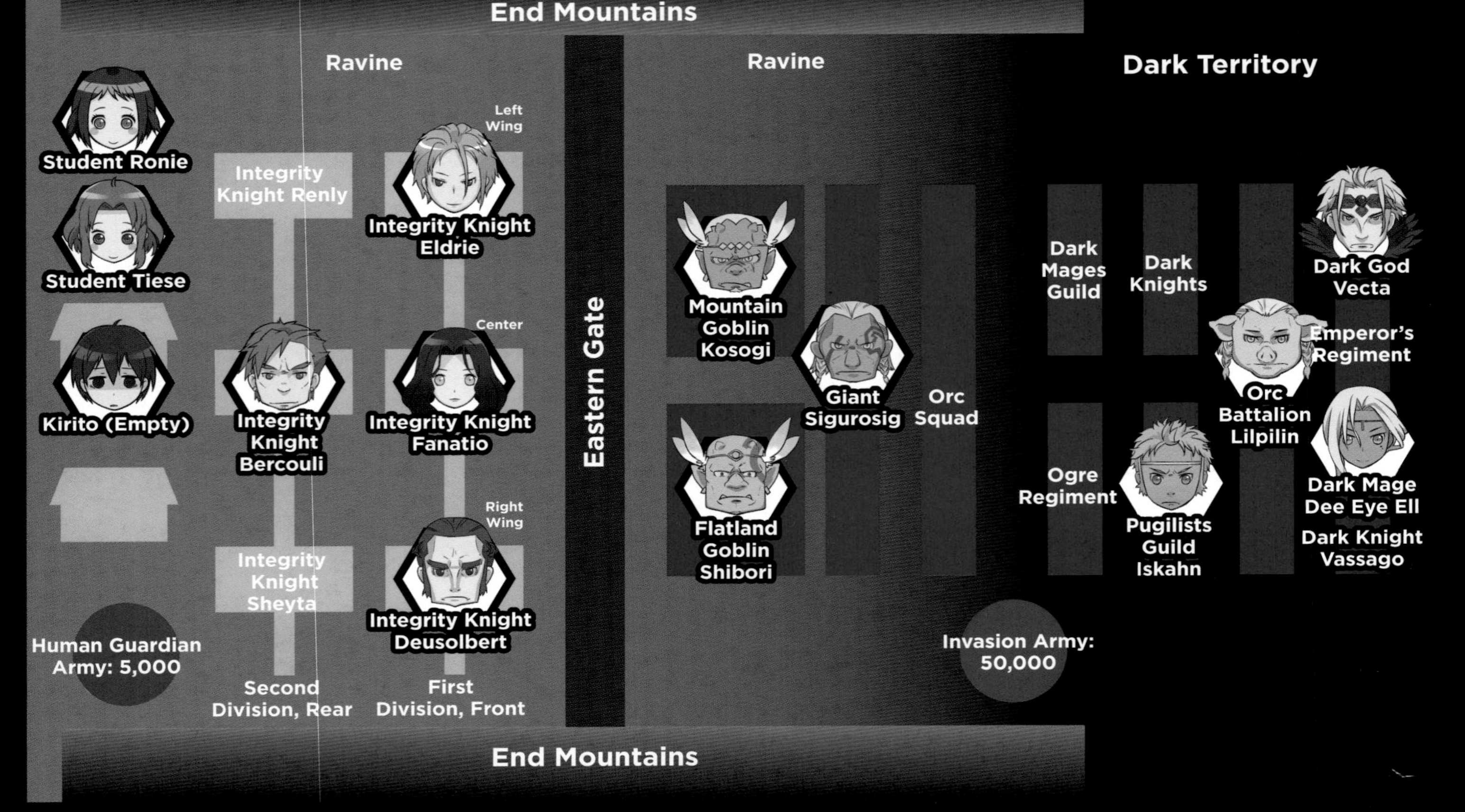

Battle for the Underworld Status Map

Illustration: Tatsuya Kurusu

VOLUME 16

Reki Kawahara

abec

bee-pee

NEW YORK

SWORD ART ONLINE, Volume 16: ALICIZATION EXPLODING
REKI KAWAHARA

Translation by Stephen Paul
Cover art by abec

Yen On
1290 Avenue of the Americas
New York, NY 10104

Visit us at yenpress.com
facebook.com/yenpress
twitter.com/yenpress
yenpress.tumblr.com
instagram.com/yenpress

First Yen On Edition: May 2019

Yen On is an imprint of Yen Press, LLC.
The Yen On name and logo are trademarks of Yen Press, LLC.

The publisher is not responsible for websites (or their content) that are not owned by the publisher.

Library of Congress Cataloging-in-Publication Data
Names: Kawahara, Reki, author. | Abec, 1985– illustrator. | Paul, Stephen, translator.
Title: Sword art online / Reki Kawahara, abec ; translation, Stephen Paul.
Description: First Yen On edition. | New York, NY : Yen On, 2014–
Identifiers: LCCN 2014001175 | ISBN 9780316371247 (v. 1 : pbk.) |
ISBN 9780316376815 (v. 2 : pbk.) | ISBN 9780316296427 (v. 3 : pbk.) |
ISBN 9780316296434 (v. 4 : pbk.) | ISBN 9780316296441 (v. 5 : pbk.) |
ISBN 9780316296458 (v. 6 : pbk.) | ISBN 9780316390408 (v. 7 : pbk.) |
ISBN 9780316390415 (v. 8 : pbk.) | ISBN 9780316390422 (v. 9 : pbk.) |
ISBN 9780316390439 (v. 10 : pbk.) | ISBN 9780316390446 (v. 11 : pbk.) |
ISBN 9780316390453 (v. 12 : pbk.) | ISBN 9780316390460 (v. 13 : pbk.) |
ISBN 9780316390484 (v. 14 : pbk.) | ISBN 9780316390491 (v. 15 : pbk.) |
ISBN 9781975304188 (v. 16 : pbk.)
Subjects: CYAC: Science fiction. | BISAC: FICTION / Science Fiction / Adventure.
Classification: pz7.K1755Ain 2014 | DDC [Fic]—dc23
LC record available at https://lccn.loc.gov/2014001175

ISBNs: 978-1-9753-0418-8 (paperback)
978-1-9753-5696-5 (ebook)

10 9 8 7 6 5 4 3 2

LSC-C

Printed in the United States of America

"THIS MIGHT BE A GAME, BUT IT'S NOT SOMETHING YOU PLAY."

—Akihiko Kayaba, *Sword Art Online* programmer

Reki Kawahara

abec

bee-pee

CHAPTER EIGHTEEN

BATTLE FOR THE UNDERWORLD, SIX PM, NOVEMBER 7TH, 380 HE

The last rays of Solus dyed the great gate that separated two worlds the color of blood.

That massive structure built by gods, the Eastern Gate, which had for three hundred years separated the human world and the dark world, was about to fall.

As the five thousand members of the Human Guardian Army and the fifty thousand of the invading forces watched in silence, the very last drop of the seemingly endless life span of the gate was spent. In its final moment, the structure let out a bellow like the death throes of some gargantuan beast.

The rumble that ensued rippled from Centoria in the west to the imperial city of Obsidia in the east, causing all the residents of the Underworld to look to the sky for the reason for that booming thunder.

A few seconds later, a single fissure ran down the center of the three-hundred-mel gate. Brilliant light poured from the inside, burning the eyes of the soldiers stationed on either side of it.

The fissure spread and branched as it reached every corner of the great gate, and as it went, the light followed like a shining net. On either side of the gate appeared enormous, burning sacred letters.

But out of the entire battlefield, only two people understood the meaning of the words *final stress test.*

The letters hung there, burning, until the flames ran out.

At that moment, there was a flash of light that shone all the way to the heavens, and the top of the Eastern Gate began to crumble.

1

"Whoa..."

It was difficult for Vassago Casals to contain his sense of wonder as he leaned over the railing of the command vehicle. "Final stress test, huh? This should put Hollywood movies to shame. Forget the AI, Bro—let's scoop this image-generation package! We could start a VFX studio and rule the entire industry."

Despite the attention-grabbing spectacle unfolding before him, Gabriel Miller replied coldly, "Unfortunately, we cannot save these visuals to any medium. Nothing in this world is generated by polygon models. It's a very exclusive show, available only to those connected to The Soul Translator."

The Eastern Gate was now only half standing, the rest of it churned into an infinite pile of rubble. The roaring and vibration of it all was tremendous, but the cavalcade of rock flashed and melted away into nothing before it hit the ground, meaning the remains of the colossal structure would not block the ravine.

Gabriel swung his black fur cape open as he stood up from his throne, which was fixed to the roof of the command vehicle. He walked toward a large skull that had been installed by one of his ten lords of darkness, the chancellor of the dark mages guild, Dee Eye Ell.

The skull, which rested on a small table, was a magical artifact with the power to transmit voices. If he spoke into this "master" skull, his voice would come out of the "slave" skulls each of his generals possessed. It didn't live up to the multichannel communication system in a Stryker armored vehicle, but it was much better than giving orders that had to be personally relayed.

Gabriel stared down into the blank sockets of the skull and summoned the cold gravitas appropriate for the god of darkness and emperor of the Dark Territory, Vecta.

"Soldiers of the dark empire! The time you have long awaited is nigh! Kill all that lies before you while you yet live! Take all that is ripe for the taking! *Plunder!!*"

From here and there among the lines of infantry, roars and bellows of excitement arose, loud enough to drown out the collapsing of the gate. Swarms of scimitars and spears glinted bloodred in the setting sun.

The First Regiment of the Dark Territory's army was thirteen thousand strong, consisting of five thousand mountain goblins, five thousand flatland goblins, two thousand orcs, and one thousand giants. This would be the first group to charge ahead and elicit a strategic response from the enemy.

As the player in this war game, Gabriel thrust his raised arm forward, giving his first command.

"First Regiment—forward march!!"

Leading the five thousand goblins of the invading army's First Regiment of the right wing was a new chief named Kosogi. He was one of the seventeen sons of Hagashi, the previous chieftain, who'd died in the violent rebellion of General Shasta.

Of all the chiefs to ever rule the tribe, Hagashi was praised for being especially cruel and greedy. His son Kosogi had inherited that streak from him, but he also hid an intelligence behind his hideous features that was unbecoming of his kind.

5

Kosogi, who would be twenty this year, had spent over five years pondering a very serious topic: Of the five tribes of darkness—human, giant, ogre, orc, and goblin—why was it assumed that the goblins must always come last?

They were the smallest and weakest members of the tribes, that was true. But that was why they had such great numbers: to overcome that individual weakness. In fact, in the ancient Age of Blood and Iron, the goblins were a force equal to the orcs and black Iums—as they referred to humankind—when they fought head-to-head.

The chaos came to an end when the tribes tired of slaughter, leading to a peace treaty. In that treaty, the goblin leaders earned seats in the highest body of the land of darkness, the Council of Ten. But in reality, they were not treated as equals by their peers; the mountain and flatland goblins were given only the thin, barren wastes in the north as their new land, which wasn't nearly fertile enough for them to grow crops and hunt creatures in large enough quantities to support their population. Their children were constantly starving, and the elderly did not last long.

In other words, the chiefs of the other tribes had betrayed them.

They had pushed the goblins, whose greatest asset was their plentiful numbers, into a spacious but barren stretch of land to keep their population under control. Ever since, the goblins had been dedicated solely to the drive for survival and could not nurture any civilization. They could not send their children to train at facilities designed to develop them, as the black Iums did; they were reduced to sending them down the river on boats simply to reduce the number of mouths to feed. And they knew the fate awaiting those children when they washed up in the territory of other peoples.

If they had rich land and ample resources instead, they could outfit their kind with fine steel weapons and armor, rather than the crude cast-iron scimitars and armor plates they used now.

They could eat heartily to stockpile their life and could learn how to fight and strategize in battle. They might even grow to understand the dark arts that the black Iums had sole control over now.

No one would dare call the goblins a lower race then.

Kosogi's father had always been tormented by an inferiority complex toward the black Iums, driven by hatred and jealousy, but he hadn't had the smarts to consider what he might do about it. The only thing his feeble mind could imagine was earning glory in the great upcoming war and the recognition of Emperor Vecta.

It was madness. What glory could they seize when this formation was taken into account?

It must have been the dark mage chancellor who had put the idea into the emperor's head. The woman had suggested giving the goblins the "honor of the first spear," putting them at the head of the pack to be useful sacrifices. And while the goblins fell to those legendary demons of the human realm, the Integrity Knights, she and her mages would reap the glory of burning their foes from a safe distance.

Well, we shall see about that.

On the other hand, an order could not be disobeyed. The newly descended Emperor Vecta had shrugged off the attack of General Shasta, the mighty warrior who'd killed the two goblin chiefs and the head of the assassins guild without a scratch. The emperor was all-powerful, and it was law in the land of darkness that the powerful must be obeyed.

But that black Ium woman was different. Kosogi was now one of the ten lords, meaning, in theory, he was of equal standing with her. He was under no obligation to bend the knee to that scheming vixen's machinations.

The goblins' orders were quite simple: lead the invasion's charge and wipe out the enemy forces. That was it—there was nothing about maintaining the front line until the mages could rain down fire from the rear. That was where he could take advantage of the human woman's scheme.

Just before the gate fell, Kosogi took his trusted captains aside and gave them special orders. When the slave skulls they'd been given rattled their jaws and delivered the emperor's command to march, he slipped a hand under his armor and pulled out the small orb he'd had ready for this moment. The other captains would be doing the same thing.

The mass of rock that was once the Eastern Gate roared, crumbled, and disappeared in a show of light. The gaping valley that extended before them gave way to campfires and the gleam of metal armaments in the distance.

It was the defensive army of the white Iums.

Beyond them, he could see the rich lands, endless resources, and labor sources that would help the mountain goblins relive their glory days.

They would not be sacrificial pawns. That role would go to the flatland goblins, who had tragically earned another fool of a chief, and the even stupider orcs.

Kosogi clenched the orb in his left hand, raised the thick mountain knife in his right, and roared, "Follow my lead and stay close, all of you!! *Chaaaaarge!!*"

"First Division, draw swords and prepare for battle! Priests, begin incanting healing arts!"

So trumpeted Fanatio Synthesis Two, vice commander of the Human Guardian Army, her voice crisp and loud in the dusk.

Her command was met with a chorus of swords sliding in harmony from their sheaths. The few campfires behind them were reflected in the steel, causing it to glow red.

There was a rumbling roar approaching from the space where the Eastern Gate had just been standing.

Quick goblin footsteps. Longer orc strides. The booming hammer of giant feet. And atop this rhythmic cavalcade was a curtain of bellows at full throttle. It was the roar of the beast called war, a sound that no human being in this world had ever heard before.

Just three hundred guards stood at the front defensive line, two hundred mels from the gate, and it was all they could do to bravely maintain their ground. It was a wonder that the formation didn't break down and give way to mad retreat before the enemy even arrived. None of these soldiers had ever seen war or even been in a life-or-death battle before.

The only thing that kept them at their stations was the sight of a trio of Integrity Knights standing apart at the front of the defensive line.

On the left wing was Eldrie Synthesis Thirty-One with the Frostscale Whip.

In the center stood the commander of the unit, Fanatio Synthesis Two, with her Heaven-Piercing Blade.

On the right wing was Deusolbert Synthesis Seven with the Conflagration Bow.

These three knights, their armor shining beautifully in the dark, planted their feet on the ground and awaited the coming enemy without budging.

There was dread in their hearts, too. They at least had battle experience, but nearly all of it was merely one-on-one fights against dark knights. Vice Commander Fanatio did not have any experience fighting against a full army, and neither did Bercouli Synthesis One, the commander of the Integrity Knights, who was leading the Second Division in the rear.

On top of that, there was no longer an administrator who ruled over the Human Empire's Axiom Church. The absolute justice that the Church once stood for was long gone.

The final defense for the knights preparing for battle was, ironically, the one emotion that should have been destroyed by the Synthesis Ritual.

* * *

As Deusolbert Synthesis Seven boldly awaited the arrival of the enemy, he brushed the ancient band on his left ring finger with his free hand. One of the oldest Integrity Knights, he had spent over a century maintaining order in the northern reaches of the realm.

He had fought off invaders who attempted to cross the End Mountains from the Dark Territory. He had eliminated large magical beasts when they appeared within his range of protection. On rare occasions, he had even apprehended people who had violated the Taboo Index. He had long since given up wondering why he was given these duties; he simply believed that he was indeed a knight summoned from the celestial realm, and he gave not a single thought to the personal lives and society of the people he protected.

But in his quieter moments, Deusolbert was tormented by a strange dream that he always experienced at the break of dawn.

A small, pale hand, so white the skin seemed clear. A simple silver ring that glinted on its finger.

The hand brushed his hair, touched his cheek, and shook his shoulder.

There was a soft, gentle whisper: *Wake up, dear. It's morning...*

Deusolbert never told anyone about the dream. He suspected that if the prime senator learned of it, he would use sacred arts to cut it from his mind. He did not want to lose the dream—because from the moment he awoke as a knight, he, too, had worn a silver ring of the same make as the one on the delicate hand in the dream.

Was the dream a memory of the celestial world? If he completed his duty as a knight down here and was allowed to return above, would he see that hand and hear that voice again?

For many, many years, Deusolbert had harbored this question—this hope—deep in his heart.

Until the great incident that shook Central Cathedral half a year ago.

Two young men, rebels against the church, invaded the

cathedral. Deusolbert made use of his Perfect Weapon Control art and still lost. The black-haired youngster used sword techniques he'd never seen before to break through the Conflagration Bow's flames, and when the fight was over, he said something that was impossible to believe.

The Integrity Knights had not been summoned from Heaven. They were ordinary mortals born here, whose memories had been stolen so they could be remade as knights, nothing more.

The idea that Administrator, the pontifex of the Axiom Church and the embodiment of supreme virtue, absolute order, and complete justice, was involved in such underhanded methods to deceive her knights was simply impossible to accept. But those young men had dispatched Vice Commander Fanatio, Commander Bercouli, and Prime Senator Chudelkin and then reached the top floor of Central Cathedral to defeat even the glorious Administrator herself. Surely their blades would not be infused with so much power if they were mere disgruntled rebels.

In fact, he understood when he first fought them. It was clear from their forthright, honest combat that there was no lie to their statements.

That would mean that the owner of the little hand in his dreams was not in the celestial realm but was born a human on Earth. When Deusolbert understood this truth, he did something he had never done before as a knight: He clutched his ring to his chest and wept.

For he knew that unlike the Integrity Knights, the life of a mortal person would be depleted at no more than seventy years. And thus, he would never again meet the person who called him "dear" in his dreams.

But still, he heeded the summons of Commander Bercouli in reporting to the battlefield. He would fight to protect the world in which he and the owner of that little hand had lived, no matter how long ago it had been.

In other words, the source of Bercouli Synthesis Seven's strength, that which made him capable of holding his ground before the charge of an invading army, was the power of the one emotion that should have been erased from his mind: love.

And though he could not have known it, Fanatio and Eldrie stood in the same place, motivated to fight by their own loved ones.

Deusolbert pulled his hand away from the ring and drew four steel arrows from the huge quiver he had planted faceup on the ground. He nocked them all in an array on his holy weapon, the Conflagration Bow.

His Perfect Weapon Control cast was already nearly complete. The others were putting a lot of faith in this skill, but Deusolbert's greatest technique was not meant for close combat. The Integrity Knight took a deep breath, preparing to take half of his trusty bow's life in one go, and uttered the final code.

"Enhance Armament!"

An enormous wave of crimson flames shot from the bronze greatbow, shining bright red against the armor of the approaching invaders, who were now just two hundred mels away. His four arrows nocked on the string took on scarlet flames of their own.

"I am Integrity Knight Deusolbert Synthesis Seven! I shall burn the bones of those who stand before me into dust upon the wind!!"

Though he didn't remember it, eight years ago he had introduced himself in a similar way when apprehending a little girl from a remote northern village. But with his thick steel helmet off, his voice was now rich and vibrant and full of life.

At the farthest possible distance, his fingers released the bowstring.

Four lines of fire shot out in a scattered formation with a tremendous boom.

The very first casualties of the war that would eventually be known as the Battle for the Underworld were a group of flatland goblin infantry soldiers charging along the left side of the ravine.

The new chief of the flatland goblins, Shibori, was not as

intelligent as Kosogi of the mountain goblins and had only his size and strength to boast of. So he had no strategy to counteract the overwhelming single-combat advantage of the Integrity Knights and simply sent his five thousand warriors forward in an unthinking, suicidal charge.

Deusolbert's four flaming arrows pierced the tightly packed flatland goblin horde head-on, giving them maximal effect. The first round of arrows instantly burned forty-two goblins at once and struck panic into those who stood just around the unlucky victims. But as there had been no order to their advance in the first place, the majority of the bloodthirsty combatants stepped right over their charred companions and thrust aside the frightened ones in a mad, undisciplined rush.

Deusolbert then nocked another four arrows on the Conflagration Bow. This time he did not spread them out, but shot them in a tight bundle.

A great spear of holy fire landed in the center of the goblin force and erupted, blasting screeching victims high into the air. This brought down at least fifty more, but it did not stop their advance.

Nor would it. Behind the formations of goblins were two thousand orcs and a thousand giants, creatures who were many times bigger than the little goblins and who would easily stomp them into shreds if they got in the way.

The flatland goblins, like the mountain goblins, felt fury and disgrace at their widely derided and highly exploited status as the smallest and lowest of the races, but unlike Chief Kosogi, they had no idea how to counteract it. They channeled that frustration into hatred for the inhabitants of the fertile Human Empire, the future slaves destined to be the new bottom of the totem pole, whom they styled "white Iums."

Chief Shibori swung a crude battle-ax with burly, un-goblinlike arms and screamed, "Kill the archer first! Surround him, slice him, strike him, crush him!!"

"Yaaaaah!! Kill!! Kill!! *Kill!!*"

The roars spread through five thousand throats.

Deusolbert absorbed all that fury and bloodlust without a word, unleashing a third volley. This, too, turned over fifty goblins into ash, but the enemy charge did not stop.

When the span between them had shrunk to fifty mels, he stifled the Conflagration Bow's flames and switched to normal shooting. He pulled arrows from the quiver with abandon and loosed them without taking time to aim. Each arrow pierced at least two or three goblins in its flight.

Swordsmen with blades drawn rushed up to flank Deusolbert on either side. "Protect the knight! Keep their blades away from him!!" shouted a young man-at-arms captain who couldn't have been more than twenty years old. He steadied a two-handed greatsword before him, the weapon nicked and dented from fierce training—but its tip trembled.

Deusolbert wanted to tell him to back down, to protect himself. Even with the strict tutoring of the knights, he knew it was unlikely that the young town guards had the mentality needed to do battle in blood.

Instead, he held that breath and replied, "Many thanks. Take my flanks."

"It would be our honor!!" said the young guard with a grin.

Seconds later, the first clash of goblin machetes and human longswords rang high and loud across the battlefield.

Seconds before, in the center of the narrow ravine, Vice Commander Fanatio Synthesis Two had prepared to meet the oncoming enemy with a stance that was odd if viewed through the prism of this world's common sense.

She stood in an oblique stance, her left side forward and feet spread apart, the hilt of the Heaven-Piercing Blade held at shoulder height in her right hand. But she held it backhand, the blade level with the ground and the pommel pressed against her shoulder guard.

Her left hand was extended forward, the palm supporting the flat of the blade. If Gabriel or Vassago had seen this, they would have come to the same opinion: She looked like a sniper steadying her rifle.

In a certain sense, this was accurate. Fanatio waited, drawing the enemy closer and closer, keeping her eye on the most effective range for her aim.

Deusolbert could change his method of shooting arrows to attack either a widespread area or a narrow line, but the Heaven-Piercing Blade could only fire its light beam at one slim point. Unleashing it on a swarm of foes would only do so much.

Instead, she wanted to hit a commanding officer—one of the ten lords of the land of darkness.

The forces of the Dark Territory were kept in line with power and fear. Ordinary foot soldiers obeyed their superior officers' orders with total fealty and would do as they were bidden to the last man, regardless of the circumstances. But that also meant that if the commander was struck down, the army would instantly lose its entire command structure.

It was the same for us once, Fanatio reflected.

News of Administrator's death nearly caused the collapse of the knighthood in a single night. Only the calm, wise words of Bercouli could have allowed the Integrity Knights to get back to their feet after the chaos that ensued.

Was our duty, our reason for existence, to follow the orders of the pontifex and the prime senator? No. It was to protect the realm and the people who live in it. As long as we have the will to protect the weak, we remain knights until death.

As a matter of fact, not all the Integrity Knights understood and obeyed their commander. Less than twenty of them had actually gathered to fight in this battle.

But all of those present were prepared to fight to the very last man. The same could probably be said of the five thousand volunteers who'd joined them in this almost certain death. That was their defining distinction from the army of the Dark Territory.

Fanatio pressed her bare cheek against the hilt of her weapon and stared hard at the encroaching enemy. The rumbling advance of the goblins was within a hundred mels now. On the right wing, Deusolbert was attacking with his Perfect Weapon Control art already, red explosions lighting up the dusk.

It was in that momentary flash that Fanatio finally found the target she was searching for.

There were enormous shadows at the very rear of the enemy army, chasing the goblin troops forward: the giants, who stood over twice the height of a human. *The especially large one who stood out among his peers must be their chief*, she reasoned. It was an individual she had seen just once before, named Sigurosig.

The giants were an excessively proud people, if not downright arrogant. Thanks to their superior size, which was the only metric they prized, they secretly looked down on even the darker-skinned humans who were the truly superior class in the dark lands.

So if she defeated their chief in one blow before the battle even began, their alarm, too, would be gigantic.

Fanatio breathed deep, held it, and whispered, "Enhance Armament."

The Heaven-Piercing Blade thrummed and began to glow, shrouded in the brilliant light of Solus. The straight line extending from its sharp point intersected directly with Sigurosig's massive body.

"Pierce him, light!!" she cried.

Schwoo-pah!! The air itself shook as a beam of compressed sunlight shot, blinding, across the battlefield.

"...It's begun...," murmured the Integrity Knight Renly Synthesis Twenty-Seven as the sound of consecutive explosions boomed in the distance.

Renly was one of the seven higher knights who'd declared his dedication to the defense of the realm. That made him one of the central figures of the defensive army, and he was responsible for a significant percentage of its total power.

But he was crouched, huddling over his knees, not at the front line of the Second Regiment's left wing but far behind it, in the corner of a darkened storage tent.

He'd fled from his position.

Less than an hour ago, amid the rush to prepare for the battle, he'd slipped away and found an unoccupied tent to hide in, where he now hunkered down and listened.

The reason for this was the same as his motive for taking part in the defense at all: He was a failure.

Such had the holy pontifex labeled him, and thus he'd spent five years frozen, rather than carrying out any Integrity Knight duties. He had volunteered to fight in this war to repair his honor, but in the end, he could not overcome his fear.

Though Renly did not remember it, he'd once been a boy from Sothercrois Empire to the south who was considered an unparalleled genius with the sword. He'd arrived in Centoria at the age of thirteen, and the very next year, unbelievably, he was crowned champion of the Four-Empire Unification Tournament and ushered into the Integrity Knights.

The Synthesis Ritual robbed him of all his memories, but even after waking again, he showed remarkably keen ability with the sword. He was placed among the elite knights within a very short time and given a divine weapon from the pontifex herself.

When a divine weapon was granted from Central Cathedral's store of weaponry, it was not the pontifex or the knight who chose the weapon, but the opposite: The weapon chose its wielder. There was a kind of resonance that occurred between the soul of the knight and the memory of the holy object.

Renly did indeed resonate strongly with his Divine Objects, a pair of throwing weapons called the Double-Winged Blades. However, most improbably, he was unable to ever activate its Perfect Weapon Control form, the sign of an elite Integrity Knight.

That was all it took for the pontifex to lose interest in him. When Alice Synthesis Thirty entered the knighthood not long after, her incredible ability and potential made Renly's reason for existing questionable.

It would be cruel to lay all of the fault at Renly's feet. Alice's skill was so incredible that she leaped all the way to third among the ranks of the knighthood and received the Osmanthus Blade, the oldest and most powerful of all the divine weapons. Regardless, Renly was branded a failure and sent into a long, long sleep.

When the prime senator placed him under the Deep Freeze art, turning him into an ice sculpture, all that Renly felt was an overwhelming sense of loss and inadequacy.

He was missing something huge and important...and it was why he could resonate with the Double-Winged Blades but not control them.

After a very long time, Renly awoke.

It was, in fact, in the midst of the shocking rebellion that overturned Central Cathedral. All the stationed knights, up to Commander Bercouli himself, had lost in battle, and their secret weapon Alice was missing, dead or alive, so it was at Prime Senator Chudelkin's discretion that Renly was unfrozen.

But again, Renly failed at his duty. Chudelkin and Administrator were felled before he could fully awaken, and when he could move about at last, he found only other Integrity Knights, and they were in a state of utter chaos.

In the position of commander, without the pontifex to give orders, Bercouli asked the others to take part in the desperate, last-ditch attempt to stand up against an organized invasion from the Dark Territory.

Despite suffering recent defeat, the elite knights like Fanatio, Deusolbert, and Alice accepted this duty, and Renly thought them to be even more radiant than he'd remembered.

If he joined them, he might understand at last. He might find what he was missing and learn why the weapon would not respond to him.

Renly had stood up from the corner of the hall where he had huddled, and he timidly raised his hand. Bercouli had nodded with great satisfaction, placed his large hand upon Renly's shoulder, and said simply, *I'm counting on you.*

But now, in his first battle, his first combat, the pressure was more than he could handle. The acrid tang of all the fury, greed, and lethality of those armies just a thousand mels away hung thick over him, and before he knew what he was doing, Renly had run away.

Stand up. Get back to your station. If you don't fight now, you'll be a failure for eternity, he scolded himself over and over as he hid in the tent. But he couldn't even bring himself to undo the grip he had around his knees. Soon the rumbling charge and approaching roars told him that the battle was beginning.

"...It's begun...," he repeated to himself.

He thought he felt his weapons, one on either hip, vibrating with rebuke of their master. But he could not go back. How could he stand again before the commander and the soldiers who looked to him for help?

It will make no difference whether I am there or not. An elite knight who cannot use Perfect Weapon Control is more of an impediment than a boon.

He told himself these excuses and more as he wriggled his face even farther between his knees—when a soft voice from the entrance to the tent caused him to start.

"What about this one, Tiese?"

Have they come looking for me? Renly quaked, unbefitting of a knight, but then he heard another voice. They both sounded like young women.

"Yeah, this tent should work, Ronie. We'll hide him in here and stand guard at the door."

Sigurosig, chief of the giants, was a legendary warrior built like a small mountain, with unkempt copper hair and beard, ferocious features, and countless scars that ran the length of his body.

If anything most purely expressed the one law of the Dark Territory that "strength rules all," it would have to be the giants. From the moment they were conscious, they engaged in competitions of strength, technique, and courage so that they established a pecking order more severe than even the dark knighthood. The giants lived in the highlands in the west of the Dark Territory, but the supposedly ample numbers of huge and magical beasts were always in short supply. The giants used them as targets for every imaginable rite of passage and had hunted them to scarcity.

Why were they so driven to be powerful? Because if they weren't, their very souls, their "fluctlights," would collapse.

The four nonhuman races of the Dark Territory were twisted things, human mental prototypes implanted into nonhuman bodies. They required mental stability to prevent themselves from completely dissociating and collapsing.

The goblins, for example, converted their inferiority complex toward humans into jealous and hateful energy that they used for motivation and self-preservation.

The giants, on the other hand, were the opposite. Their superiority complex over humans gave their human minds inhuman strain.

Every single giant, at least in a one-on-one fight, would always triumph over a human. That was their mental refuge and their ironclad rule. It was why they put their young through such extreme rites of passage, accentuating their individual superiority at the cost of their overall numbers.

So the thousand giant warriors summoned to this battle were silent but harbored great drive to fight. It was the first large-scale war that this generation, born after the Age of Blood and Iron, had ever experienced.

Chief Sigurosig had one serious thought: to flatten the enemy in their initial charge and end the battle altogether.

The dark knights, dark mages, and pugilists were placed in the main force of Emperor Vecta's army, but he would not allow them to shine. By surpassing those troops and claiming victory, he could prove definitively that the giants were supreme among all.

When the little jaw of the slave skull chattered with the emperor's order to charge, Sigurosig felt the old scars crisscrossing his body begin to burn. It felt to him as though he was channeling the strength of all the great beasts he'd torn apart barehanded.

"Crush them!!" he thundered. It was his only order.

And it was enough. He raised his mammoth war hammer alongside his hearty fellows and began to charge, the ground trembling beneath their feet.

The warriors of the Human Empire crammed the space in the ravine ahead. To the giants, who stood at least three and a half mels tall, they were tiny, hardly bigger than goblins. Their swords were smaller than the fangs of newborn rockscale wyrms.

Smash them all, kick them all, tear them all to pieces. Sigurosig's sense of superiority, hard-coded into his soul, flared up and gave off sparks of pleasure. His angular jaw sagged and stretched into a ferocious grin.

Instantly, an alien yet familiar sensation ran up his backbone.

It was cold. It numbed him. He felt pierced by needles of ice.

He had experienced this feeling in the distant past, deep in the Fledgling Valley close to his village. His first trial...

He had gone to snatch the eggs of a snapping bird, and the mother bird had swooped down from overhead...

Sigurosig's eyes flared as he ran, seeking the source of the sensation. At the front of the row of enemy soldiers, right in the center of the ravine, he spotted a tiny, tiny human. Its hair was long, and its frame was slender. A woman—a knight, clad in shining silver armor.

Just once before, he had witnessed one of the dragon riders of the human realm crossing the End Mountains. He had wanted to crush it, but the little creature had merely circled a time or two, then flown back over the mountaintops.

They were nothing to him.

And yet...that she-knight's black eyes.

Despite the distance of over three hundred mels between them, he could feel her gaze keenly on his skin. And there was no amount of fear or mortal terror in those eyes, not even as much as a tiny pinch of salt for a cauldron of stew.

All he sensed was the coldness of identifying a target and taking aim.

...Am I being hunted?

Me, chief of the giants, mightiest warrior of the five tribes of darkness, the great Sigurosig?

"Hurgk..."

A falsetto scream burped out of his throat, completely at odds with his fearsome appearance. The strength went out of his legs, and the great hammer in his hand felt unbearably heavy. Sigurosig toppled and fell onto his face.

An instant later, a rod of light shot from the end of the knight's sword, roaring toward him with a percussive blast the likes of which he had never heard before. It easily pierced the breast of the giant who ran right before Sigurosig.

If he hadn't fallen, the light would have pierced his own breast next. Instead, the white light evaporated a portion of the giant chief's red hair and his right ear, decorated with fangs he'd earned from the hunt.

The light fatally struck through the heads of two more giants behind him before it finally broke into tiny beads and vanished.

Sigurosig was barely conscious of the bodies of the three giants falling lifelessly to the ground like trees. Even the fierce pain burning at the right side of his head was nothing more than a tiny insect bite compared to the overwhelming emotion that assaulted him now.

Fear.

Sigurosig sat helplessly on the ground, his jaw trembling. When Dark General Shasta had led his stunning rebellion, Sigurosig had been surprised but not frightened in the least. After all, the black dragon killed only weakling assassins and goblins. Emperor Vecta's power had to be respected, of course, but he was an ancient god, not a human, so it was not so surprising.

So how was one measly little she-knight able to strike such powerful fear in him? No mere human could possibly bring Sigurosig to his knees in this manner.

"It is a lie...a lie, a lie! It cannot be!" the giant chief groaned as smoke rose from his singed hair. It could not be. He would never allow himself to feel this fear. But the more he repeated it, the more sparks flew deep in his mind, paralyzing him with pain. His mouth and tongue spasmed, causing strange words to spill forth without pause.

"Can't be can't be can't be kill, kill, killkillgilldill, dil-dil-dil-dil-dil..."

In this moment, the subjective identity packed tight in the center of Sigurosig's fluctlight—his self-image as the most powerful warrior—collided unavoidably with the circumstances of his present terror. It was bringing about a collapse of the quantum circuits in his lightcube.

Red light shot from the giant's eyes.

"Dil, dil, dil, dil, di——————"

As the surrounding giants watched, stunned, Sigurosig suddenly leaped to his feet. He swung the huge war hammer around as if it were a twig, and he resumed his mad charge.

Sigurosig bowled over his fellow giants before him and soon caught up to the goblins ahead. He charged through them without slowing, his feet producing wet crunches and high-pitched screams, but the giant, his mind collapsing from within, did not even register them.

All he was conscious of was a single order, resounding and reverberating, to *kill that knight*.

Ultimately, both Chief Shibori of the flatland goblins and Chief Sigurosig of the giants underestimated the power of the Integrity Knights.

Only Chief Kosogi of the mountain goblins, on the right wing of the invaders' spearhead charge, was different. He had just learned, at great cost, of the overwhelming military power of the knights.

It was Kosogi who had designed and arranged the recent invasion of Rulid, re-excavating the cave in the northern End Mountains and leading a great force of goblins and orcs through it. He himself had been tied down to Obsidia Palace, but he'd set up the plan by putting troops under the command of his three brothers and convincing some orcs to join in as well.

But the plan had been a horrific failure. The troops had been wiped out, including all his brothers. The few members who had escaped with their lives reported details he could scarcely believe through the shock.

An invasion force of over two hundred goblins and orcs had been decimated by a single Integrity Knight and dragon mount.

It was difficult to take at face value, but Kosogi was not so foolish that he would allow this bitter lesson to go to waste. He was determined that he would never again repeat the folly of attempting a straightforward attack on the Integrity Knights of the human realm.

But the role that Emperor Vecta had demanded of the mountain goblins in this great invasion was just that. Chancellor Dee Eye Ell of the dark mages guild would be well aware of the Integrity Knights' might. It was why she had advised the emperor to cast forth the goblins, orcs, and giants as sacrificial pawns, throwing the narrow ravine into chaos before they used their dark arts to burn all of them, Integrity Knights included, into ash.

Once the emperor accepted Dee's strategy, there was no choice but to obey. Kosogi spent three days and nights considering it. How could they carry out the order to charge stupidly forward and escape the jaws of death that were the Integrity Knights ahead and dark mages behind? The stunt play he devised involved the little gray spheres he gave out to his troops.

When the emperor gave the orders, and Kosogi sent his forces into the valley floor, he spotted a tall Integrity Knight in gleaming armor far ahead.

It was not Alice Synthesis Thirty, the knight who'd wiped out the invading force at Rulid, but her apprentice, Eldrie Synthesis Thirty-One; however, Kosogi could not make that distinction. In either case, the figure was a demon who meant nothing but merciless death for goblinkind.

"Now...*throw*!!" he ordered when they were within fifty mels of the knight. He crushed the little orb in his left hand.

A small flame licked out of the broken sphere with a crackling sound. It was not some kind of explosive, of course. That would be an artifact of a civilization beyond anything that presently existed in the Underworld.

It was not a flame element generated by arts, either. Embedded in the center of the spheres were tiny insects called flintbugs, found only in the northernmost volcano of the Dark Territory, the sacred ground of the mountain goblins. If crushed, they emitted ferociously hot flames that would scar the palm.

The gray orb around the flintbug was a kind of moss, also from the north, that had been dried, ground, kneaded, and dried again. It then created a great amount of smoke when lit, making it useful for smoke signals. But Kosogi, using methods similar to the assassins guild, had refined the substance until it was dozens of times more potent than its original source.

In essence, what Kosogi and his goblins threw were smoke grenades. When the flintbugs burst into flame, they produced plumes of thick, choking smoke that reduced visibility to zero. Now that curtain covered the northern side of the ravine, which ran east to west.

Even goblins, with their excellent night vision, could not see through this layer of smoke. But Kosogi's plan was not to use the screen to defeat their foes. Before they plunged into the thick plume, he gave his third order.

"Now *run*!!"

He returned his mountain blade to the sheath behind his back and got down on his hands. When a goblin, already small, got down on all fours, he was barely above the knee of a human. Close to the ground, the smoke was just barely thinner, offering them a better chance at spotting the enemy.

Kosogi and his five thousand mountain goblins completely ignored Eldrie and the guardsmen as they rushed deeper through the ravine.

The emperor's order was to charge the enemy army. It did not specify which part. So Kosogi plotted to ignore the main force, meaning the Integrity Knights, and chose to send the goblins toward whatever supply line they had in the rear.

If they could slip beyond the front line, they should be able to avoid the merciless fires of the dark mages and the volleys of the ogre archers. If these attacks succeeded in decimating the knights and guards, the goblins could turn back to finish the job. If not, there was plenty of land ahead in the human realm to which they could escape.

So it was that, of the three "spears" in the hundred-mel-wide ravine, only the northern end produced no bloodshed for the time being.

That was also about the time that the soldiers in the Second Regiment of the Human Guardian Army located behind Eldrie began to realize that their leader, elite Integrity Knight Renly Synthesis Twenty-Seven, was missing.

The first casualty of the guardian army was a middle-aged town guard fighting valiantly beside Deusolbert on the right wing of the First Regiment's line. He failed to adequately block a goblin's thrown hand ax with his shield.

He was a lower noble who had long served as a squad leader for the Imperial Knights of Wesdarath. His skill with the sword was solid, but there was nothing to be done about the downturn of his life value as a whole, and the ax head that bit into his wrinkled, sagging neck proved to be quickly fatal. The healing arts of the priests located behind the fighter were not effective enough to repair the damage caused.

Deusolbert briefly paused in his arrow launching to attempt higher healing arts on the elderly soldier. But the man shook his head, blood spattering from his lips as he cried, "You mustn't! It is a fitting end for this old soldier…The fate of our country rests on your shoulders, Sir…Knight…"

Then the elderly guard passed away, his last remaining life force spilling forth as spatial resources. Deusolbert gritted his teeth, used those resources as fuel to light the Conflagration Bow, and shot the goblin that'd thrown the ax with a flaming arrow.

More soldiers among the Human Guardian Army fell after that, here and there in bursts, but their comrades never stopped their charge. The nonhumans, who outnumbered them over ten to one, ferociously and mercilessly carried out their orders.

The large quantities of life resources that spilled forth onto the battlefield turned to little flecks of light that rose and rose—

—into the sky, far above the narrow ravine, where a single dragon hung in the air, hidden in darkness, and they swirled and condensed toward the Integrity Knight clad in golden armor who stood atop its back.

There was no time nor space for hiding.

Renly simply huddled in the supply tent, clutching his legs, waiting for the approaching figures to find him.

From what little light came through the round port in the canvas, he could see girls who looked to be maybe fifteen or sixteen years old. One had brilliant-red hair, while the other's was dark brown. They had on light armor over gray tunics and skirts, uniforms from some academy. They both had slender longswords on their left side. He did not recognize their faces, and based on the make of their equipment, he took them to be civilian fighters, not knights.

What was much odder was the metal chair that the brown-haired girl was pushing. Instead of legs, the chair had four wheels, and a black-haired young man sat slumped in it. Renly found his eyes drawn to the man's face.

He was about twenty and terribly thin, and he was missing his right arm from the shoulder down. At first glance, he seemed to be weaker than even the girls. But the two swords bundled in their sheaths that his good arm clutched were so incredibly powerful, exuding such force of presence, that it was clear to Renly at a glance that they might even be higher Divine Objects than his own Double-Winged Blades.

What did this mean? Just to carry them across his lap like that, to say nothing of having proper ownership of the weapons, required strength on the level of an Integrity Knight. But the haggard young man with the empty eyes seemed anything but strong.

At this point, the girls had noticed him; they sucked in sharp breaths and froze where they stood. The red-haired one put a hand on her sword hilt with somewhat alarming speed.

Before they could draw their weapons on him, Renly rasped, "I'm not an enemy...Forgive me for startling you. May I stand up? I will show you my hands are empty."

"...Go ahead," the girl said, her voice hard, and Renly slowly lifted himself up. He stepped forward, hands raised, until the light through the canopy revealed his top-level armor and dual weapons. The girls gasped and straightened up. They removed their hands from sword and chair handle and made their salutes across the left breast.

"S-Sir Knight! Forgive the impertinence!" stammered the red-haired girl, her face pale, but Renly just shook his head.

"No...it's my fault for startling you. And besides...I am no longer an Integrity Knight...," he said, his voice nearly vanishing by the end, to the surprise of the girls. They couldn't be blamed—the fringed white cape over his back and combined cross and circle of the Axiom Church gleaming on his breastplate marked him as none other than the highest of knights.

Renly moved his fingers to cover the symbol and wryly admitted, "I abandoned my post and fled to this tent. The battle's already begun at the front. I bet the squad I'm meant to command is in a panic now. People are dying already. And here I am, frozen with fear. I am no knight, and I can claim no integrity."

He bit his lip and finally looked up. He saw his own face reflected in the large orange eyes of the red-haired girl.

Gray-colored hair tufting briefly over his forehead. Rounded cheeks. And big, girlish eyes with long lashes and none of the proud fierceness of his position—a young failure of a knight, just fifteen years old.

He wanted to tear his eyes away from that appearance he hated so much—but the red-haired girl covered her mouth, reeling from some fresh shock.

"...?" He stared at her, puzzlement on his face, and this time it was the girl who averted her eyes and shook her head. "N-nothing, sir. I-I'm sorry..."

She would not look up again, so the previously silent girl with the burnt-brown hair and eyes said, in a faint but firm voice, "Forgive our late introduction. We are Primary Trainee Ronie Arabel and Primary Trainee Tiese Schtrinen of the supply team. And this...is Elite Disciple Kirito."

Kirito.

Recognition of that name brought a gasp to Renly's throat. He knew that name. It belonged to one of the two rebels who'd laid siege to Central Cathedral half a year earlier. The very person whom Renly had been unfrozen to fight, only to fail to reach the battle in time.

This withered young swordsman was responsible for felling the almighty Administrator? Was his missing right arm a scar from the battle?

So intimidated by the presence of this empty-eyed young man was Renly that he drew back his foot. The petite young woman named Ronie did not seem to notice. She pleaded, "Please, Sir Knight...we have no right to comment on your circumstances. We are members of the guardian army, too, but hang in the rear, rather than fighting at the line of battle. But...that is our duty for now. Miss Alice instructed us to dedicate ourselves to his protection..."

Alice. Alice Synthesis Thirty.

The young genius knight who was a foil for Renly in every way. Even in this moment, she would be standing alone at the front line, preparing a mammoth sacred art that would prove to be the linchpin of the guardian army's strategy.

As if to put even more pressure on Renly and his feelings of inferiority, Primary Trainee Arabel desperately insisted, "Sir Knight, I'm afraid to be so rude...but will you please help us? Even the two of us are not certain we can fight off a single goblin. Please...please, we *must* protect Kirito!"

Renly squinted at the pureness of the look in Ronie's eyes. It was the kind of thing found only in those whose duty was carved into their souls and whose determination to achieve said duty would be stopped by nothing, even the loss of their own lives.

If they are primary trainees, then they haven't even graduated yet. And yet, even these girls have something I've misplaced. Or maybe I've been missing it from the moment I awoke in this world as an Integrity Knight...

He heard his own voice issuing from a cracked throat as though it belonged to someone else. "You'll be safe here...I think. Commander Bercouli himself is leading the Second Regiment, and if they break past his guard, then the entire world is done for anyway; the end will come sooner or later. I'm going to sit here until the battle is over. If you want to stay here, too, then I won't bother you..."

His voice was nothing more than warm air by the end. He returned to the back, where he had been, and plopped down again.

Right about that time was when Kosogi and his mountain goblins' smoke bombs began to erupt on the left wing of Eldrie's line. With thick smoke hanging heavy over the battlefield, a swarm of goblins slipped past the defensive barricade like water through a coarsely woven net.

But neither Renly nor the girls could have known that they were plotting to wipe out the supply team at the rear line of the Human Guardian Army.

The collapse of the quantum-light aggregation—the fluctlight—that made up the soul of Chief Sigurosig of the giants happened rapidly.

But because the collapse was not complete and did no more than inflict massive damage on specific areas, it did not immediately reach the level of the fluctlight itself becoming invalid. In fact, the phenomenon brought about a particular side effect.

The result of decades of Sigurosig's hatred and fury toward humankind being unleashed all at once spilled out of his fluctlight and, through the Main Visualizer that interfaced with the Lightcube Cluster, reached the lightcube that contained the soul of Vice Commander Fanatio.

Direct manipulation of events through the sheer power of one's imagination was a power that the Integrity Knights called Incarnation. It briefly stole control of the veteran warrior Fanatio's body.

As the chief of the giants charged, standing a fearsome four mels tall, he held his great hammer high overhead.

Why can't I move?! Fanatio wondered, urging her stubborn legs to obey her, but she couldn't so much as clench a fist. The vice commander of the Integrity Knights must be bold enough to withstand a simple glare from anything, even the fearsome chieftain of the giants.

But it was as if her body was frozen in place, in that sniping position with her knee to the ground.

In practice bouts against Commander Bercouli, she had at times been completely unable to step forward to attack, even with her weapon in hand. But that was against the presence of the commander: heavy but gentle and enveloping. This was more like the pain of being held down all over by many leather straps covered with gouging steel spikes.

Sigurosig charged through his own allies, the goblins and orcs, kicking and stomping them aside as he let out an unearthly bellow. There were just fifty mels of distance left.

In a one-on-one fight, he would be no match for her. Of the lords on the Dark Council, only Commander Shasta of the dark knighthood had earned her respect as an opponent. When she'd fought him before, their thirty-minute battle had ended when he'd split her helmet and seen her face. The way he'd pulled back his blade still stung with humiliation.

But even that fight she did not consider a defeat. By Bercouli's strict order, Perfect Weapon Control arts were forbidden in battle against dark knights. So surely she would not be found lacking against anyone lesser than that. The idea that she would be frozen with fear was simply unthinkable.

And yet, a reality that surpassed Fanatio's understanding was approaching, moment by moment. Less than ten seconds remained until that giant hammer would be lowered on her head.

She had to stand and raise her blade. If she could just strike with it properly, the famed Heaven-Piercing Blade would never be overcome by something as crude as Sigurosig's hammer.

But she couldn't stand. Bound by invisible shackles, Fanatio could only watch as the giant chief, eyes red with raging darkness, screamed incoherently, "*Human kill-gill-dil-dil-dil-di*——"

The hammer hurtled, roaring, toward her.

My lord, Fanatio mouthed.

* * *

Since her awakening as an Integrity Knight, lower knight Dakira Synthesis Twenty-Two had dedicated her entire existence to just one person.

It was not to Administrator the pontifex, absolute ruler of all. It was not to Bercouli, commander of the knighthood.

Her sworn benefactor was Vice Commander Fanatio. Dakira was smitten with Fanatio's ferocity to the cause and with the anguish that she hid beneath that firm exterior. By the standards of the human world, her feelings were nothing short of romantic love.

But for various reasons, Dakira had bottled up her feelings and given up her very face and name to be one of the Four Whirling Blades who served directly under Fanatio. It was joy beyond measure for Dakira simply to work at her hero's side.

The Four Whirling Blades were not some collection of the best and brightest of the lower knights. Instead, Fanatio had collected those knights she had decided were too shaky to carry out frontline missions alone and taught them strategic teamwork to raise their chances of survival. In other words, they were the Loser Squad.

So they were poor in the eyes of the pontifex and the prime senator. In fact, in the rebellion of half a year ago, the Four Whirling Blades had suffered major injuries against the upstarts, just two student swordsmen of common birth. But far more painful than that to Dakira was knowing she had failed to protect Fanatio. Many times in her sickbed, she had wished that she had died in the fight.

But when the four had recovered, Fanatio gave them not admonishment but words of encouragement. She removed the silver helmet that she never took off in public, favored her four followers with her beauty and a smile, and clapped them each on the shoulder.

I nearly died, only for the rebels to save my life. There is nothing for you to be ashamed of, she said. *Instead, you fought bravely. In fact, that was the greatest Cyclic Blade Dance I have ever seen you perform.*

As she shed tears beneath her helmet, Dakira swore to herself that the next time, she would not allow her beloved vice commander to come to harm.

And *this* was that next time.

Despite being ordered to remain at her station until further instructions were given, Dakira leaped from the formation at her own discretion as soon as she sensed something wrong with Fanatio.

She was over twenty mels away from the kneeling knight and the giant chief swinging his tremendous hammer down toward her head. It was an unbridgeable gap for her physical abilities, but Dakira raced at blurring speed, her body becoming a beam of light, until she leaped before Fanatio and met the plunging hammer with her two-handed greatsword.

The earth rumbled from the shock of the impact, and a reddish light burst forth. Dakira's greatsword was a fine weapon in comparison to those of the men-at-arms but was still a far cry from the divine weapons of the elite knights in terms of priority. And Sigurosig's hammer, thanks to his murderous Incarnation, was raised to a tremendous priority level.

The stalemate lasted only half a second, when a number of fissures ran through the blade of the greatsword. The next moment, a faint light spilled forth from where it broke into pieces. Dakira cast the handle aside and held up her empty hands to receive the dropping hammer.

A number of dull sounds rattled throughout her body. Her arms had broken from wrists to elbows. Agony turned her vision white. Blood erupted through the joints of her armor, spraying against the surface of her helmet.

"Hrr...gg...aaah!!"

Through clenched jaws, she struggled to turn her scream into a roar of ferocity and used the brow of her helmet to receive the hammer that her arms could no longer support.

The cruciform helmet of steel instantly crumpled, causing more horrific sounds from her neck, spine, and knees. Searing pain pulsed through her entire being, and her vision went red.

But lower Integrity Knight Dakira Synthesis Twenty-Two did not fall.

Fanatio was right behind her. She would not let this hideous weapon have her.

I must protect her. This time.

"Yaaaah!!" She let loose a high-pitched scream, distorted by her helmet. Blood spurting from wounds all over her body turned to pale flames that wreathed her form.

The flames gathered in her broken arms and pulsed. The hammer shot back and pulled Sigurosig's massive body with it over ten mels backward through the air.

With the sound of the giant crashing to the ground in her ears, Dakira slowly collapsed.

"...Dakira!!" came a shriek.

Oh...Fanatio just called my name. How many years has it been?

Her helmet was gone, and Dakira's exposed freckles and short straw-colored hair framed a little smile as she sank into the vice commander's outstretched arms.

Dakira was born and raised in a little seaside village in Sothercrois. Her parents were poor fishers without even a last name, yet despite that, she grew up strong and healthy and helped out with the family work.

Until she committed a taboo at age sixteen. She fell in love with a friend of the same sex who was one year older.

She couldn't have acted on those feelings, of course. In her anguish, Dakira went before the altar of the empty church late at night and prayed to Stacia for forgiveness. That altar was linked to Central Cathedral's automated senate organ, and Dakira was taken to the Axiom Church for violating a taboo, wiped clean of all memory, and made into an Integrity Knight.

The older girl whom Dakira had fallen in love with, whose name she could no longer remember, looked just a little bit like Vice Commander Fanatio.

Through her cloudy, fading vision, Dakira watched with beatific calmness as Fanatio's beautiful features crumpled and tears fell from her long lashes.

The vice commander is weeping for my sake.

She couldn't imagine a greater bliss. At the end of a very long and painful period of tribulation, she had finally accomplished what she was meant to do, with great satisfaction. Her time to die had arrived.

"Dakira...don't go! I'll tend to you!!" came that pained cry again.

With her last bit of strength, Dakira raised her crushed hand and softly brushed the tears on Fanatio's cheek with a trembling finger. Then she smiled and whispered the feelings that she had kept hidden for so long.

"My lady...Fanatio...I have...always...pined...for you..."

In that moment, Integrity Knight Dakira Synthesis Twenty-Two's life reached its end.

The first member of the knighthood to close her eyes forever.

Wh...what am I doing?! Fanatio demanded of herself as she clutched the mutilated body in her arms.

Through tear-streaked vision, she saw Sigurosig getting to his feet and the remaining three members of the Four Whirling Blades rushing toward him.

Dakira. Jace. Hoveren. Geero. She had placed them under her care to train and protect them. She gave them only harsh words of discipline, but they were her beloved brothers and sisters. And now they were protecting her and losing their lives because of it...

"...It will not happen!!" she swore, to herself, to Sigurosig, to the world.

She would not allow more of them to die. She would keep the other three alive, for Dakira's sake.

This determination became a firm Incarnation of Love that surpassed Sigurosig's churning bloodlust and shot forth from Fanatio's soul.

The thorns of ice that bound her body instantly melted away.

She lay down her charge's body and stood up, the Heaven-Piercing Blade silently rising on its own from the ground to fit into her right palm.

Up ahead, Jace, Hoveren and Geero, their greatswords raised, took no more than a single swipe from Sigurosig's arm to be smashed to the ground. The red light in the giant's eyes was like the fire of the demon realm far below the earth. Even the goblins and orcs around him were pausing in their march out of fear.

"Kill...kill...kiiiill!!" the looming giant bellowed.

But there was no longer any shred of fear or intimidation in Fanatio's mind. She raised the Heaven-Piercing Blade straight up to the sky—and it took on a pure glow, vibrating deeply. The shine of it extended over five mels from the tip of the blade and held its shape.

"Kill humaaaaaaaaaan!!" screeched Sigurosig, holding the hammer over his head with both hands and leaping toward Fanatio.

"...Return to the bowels of the earth," she spat, easily swinging the Heaven-Piercing Blade. The blade of light, well over twice the length of the original weapon, left a brilliant afterimage in the air as it met the massive blunt end of the hammer.

With a crisp *thwik*, the sword cleaved the enormous weapon in two. Flecks of melted iron spattered from the burning-red cut on the hammer. The tremendously long sword of light then made contact with Sigurosig's head and, without losing the tiniest bit of momentum, sliced straight down to the ground.

The sight of the legendary warrior, the largest individual in the world, being sliced into two symmetrical halves in midair left the giants behind him, as well as the humans before him, speechless.

With soggy squelches, the two hunks of meat that had previously been Sigurosig crashed to the earth, while in their midst, Fanatio swung the sword of light with a hum and called out, "First Regiment central unit, advance!! Drive back the enemy!!"

The waves upon waves of flatland goblins that crashed against his side only made Deusolbert more worried as time went on.

In single combat, he could take on any number of goblin soldiers in a row without ever being in danger of losing—and in fact, there was a small hill of corpses before him, pierced with arrows and burned by the flames.

But it was impossible for him to shoot every last enemy soldier on his own when they rushed in a horizontal wave. He would have to leave the majority of the goblins on the sides to the guardian army behind him.

In a direct comparison of ability, it was the guards who were much superior to the enemy soldiers. Their sword techniques, after half a year of fierce training, were much quicker and sharper than those of the goblins, who preferred to rely on brute strength and nothing else when using their crude knives. But that advantage was much less secure than the one the goblins had over the Integrity Knights. Their discipline would be hard-pressed to make up for the sheer disadvantage in numbers.

If only he could share the tremendous power he possessed with all the guardsmen under his command, Deusolbert wished. But there was no such sacred art, of course. The guards fell in battle one by one, whether jumped by several goblins at once or simply reaching peak exhaustion in combat. With each death scream audible over the battle, Deusolbert felt his own life being steadily chipped away.

This was the experience of war.

It was completely unlike the battles he'd been through before, when he'd been wiping out invaders from atop his dragon mount or dueling dark knights one at a time. This was a horrible struggle of attrition, in which the total number of dead was undeniably rising from moment to moment.

An Integrity Knight's pride meant nothing in this situation.

Was there still no command to withdraw yet? He couldn't even tell how much time had passed since the fighting had started. Deusolbert slashed the oncoming hordes with his longsword, and when time and space allowed, he sprayed arrows with the Conflagration Bow. So overwhelmed was he by the action around him that he failed to notice when some of the enemy troops began acting strangely.

Chief Shibori of the flatland goblins was far stupider than his mountain counterpart, Kosogi, and far more cruel.

At first, Shibori considered the Integrity Knight leading the enemy army to be little more than a large magical monster. No matter how strong, he was still just an individual white Ium and, when surrounded, would succumb to the right amount of beating in the end.

But once the fighting began, the Integrity Knight turned out to be far more troublesome than any beast and did not allow himself to be surrounded, no matter how many troops Shibori sent after him. He could blow up a full ten goblins with a single exploding fire arrow, and his ordinary arrows struck the brain and heart with unerring accuracy.

So what could be done about this?

After some thought, Shibori came to an extremely simple and merciless answer: He would continue throwing troops at the enemy knight until his stock of arrows ran out.

But of course, the grunts who were artlessly thrown into battle to their certain death did not appreciate this strategy. More than a few of them were smarter than Shibori, and they orchestrated things to their favor, as far as they could without disobeying an order.

They lifted the corpses of their fellows, hid behind them, and began to circle around the knight laterally, drawing his attention and his arrows.

Under ordinary circumstances, Deusolbert would see through such a simple tactic at once. But the screams of his men-at-arms dying were sapping his ability to stay cool and rational, unbeknownst to him. The goblins were helped by the fact that the battle had begun at sundown.

By the time Deusolbert recognized that the enemies were taking too long to fall, the overly liberal stock of steel arrows he'd prepared was nearly gone.

"There we are. He's finally run out of those wretched arrows."

Shibori chuckled to himself, scratching at his neck with the tips of the battle knives he had resting on his shoulders. The sight of all his fellow warriors' miserable corpses did not seem to bother him in the slightest. He had inherited an incredible resistance to the horrors of war from his ancestors' experience surviving the ghastly Age of Blood and Iron.

About a third of his troops were dead, but he still had over three thousand of them. When they invaded the white Iums' territory and had all the meat and land they wanted, the tribe would quickly repopulate. But in order to gain those spacious lands, they would need to earn them with skill. He had to finish off the knight in the red armor.

"Let's go, you slugs. Surround the archer, grab him, and pull him to the ground. His head will soon belong to Shibori," he instructed the crude and hardy warriors around him as he steadily strode forward.

"...How foolish of me...," Deusolbert groaned.

At last, he realized that the enemy soldiers he saw flitting about in the darkness were merely scarecrows using the bodies of their fallen friends. He shot at the legs, not the heart, of a scarecrow goblin to finish it off for good, then reached over his shoulder for another arrow only to close his hand on empty air.

Even the divine Conflagration Bow was just as vulnerable to running out of arrows as any ordinary longbow. He could create new arrows from steel elements with sacred arts, but that was possible only in singular fights where he had enough time to chant the command. Besides, the atmosphere here was bereft of spatial resources, as all of them were being absorbed by the Integrity Knight hovering above.

Deusolbert clenched his jaw, hung the bow over his left shoulder, and drew his sword again. Then he saw a group of larger goblins approaching fast through the gloom ahead. These were clearly a different type of individual than the rabble he'd been slaying. They had thick metal plates from chest to waist and leather strips covered in tacks over their arms. In their hands were thick cleavers that looked capable of cutting a cow in two.

Behind these seven individuals came one even larger, a goblin that appeared to be taller even than the average orc, by Deusolbert's estimate. Its gleaming cast-iron armor, pair of great axes, and richly colored headdress made it clear that this goblin was an enemy general.

The moment Deusolbert made eye contact with the gleaming red orbs under the goblin's protruding brow, he felt the very air around him squeal. The sound of clanging and slashing swords and knives grew distant until he could not hear them at all. The guards and goblins formed a silent perimeter, watching the face-off of the two leaders breathlessly.

Deusolbert held out his free hand to stay the men-at-arms who tried to rush to his side. With his sword raised and at the ready, he said in a firm but raspy voice, "You must be one of the ten lords…a goblin chief?"

"That's right," said the large goblin, exposing yellowed fangs. "The great Shibori, chief of the flatland goblins."

Deusolbert faced the enemy leader head-on, taking the time to steady his breathing after the long stretch of unbroken combat.

If I defeat this general and his bodyguards, the goblins will lose their will to fight, if only temporarily. If we can use that moment to push the line forward, we will have served our duty as the lead force. Even if I can't use the Conflagration Bow, I have no choice but to defeat eight as one. Every Integrity Knight is worth a thousand, and this is my chance to prove it.

"I am the Integrity Knight Deusolbert Synthesis…," he began, only to be interrupted.

"I don't care what any Ium's name is!" screeched Shibori. "You are *meat*, simply meat attached to the head I mean to take as a trophy! Now...attack him!!"

"Raaaaah!!" the seven elite goblins bellowed, leaping forward.

Deusolbert met them alone.

If they are truly a rabble without the pride of warriors, they ought to have continued that morass of a battle. Instead, they had to pretend to commit to this farce of a duel...

"Laughable!!"

Before they were wielders of the whip or lance or bow, every Integrity Knight was a master of the sword.

Not a single soul present actually saw the motion of Deusolbert raising the longsword and swinging it down. It was just a flash of bright light and an impossibly fast slice. With a pathetic little tinkle, the lead goblin's cleaver split in two pieces.

Then a seam appeared, running down its body from crown to gut. It split apart, gushing blood—but the knight was nowhere near it to suffer the spray.

Deusolbert was on the second goblin before the first even registered that it was dead, and he struck again. This was not the novel, consecutive attack style that Fanatio and the rebels he fought employed—it was the old-fashioned style of single, traditional moves. But Deusolbert's technique was so refined by years upon years of training and use that his movements were practically divine in their purity of form. Only an elite dark knight or pugilist would be capable of handling such blows.

In fact, the second goblin, which was sliced on the left side at nearly the same moment that the first goblin was killed, was only just starting to swing down its knife when the sheet-metal armor gave way for the sword to pierce its heart.

The difference in ability was clear for all to see. But the elite goblin warriors knew no fear. Their chief, Shibori, was also a fearsome higher power to them, and there was no mental structure with which they could consider abandoning his orders.

Two more flanked Deusolbert, bathing in the bloody spray of

their comrades, and attacked him from both sides at once. The practiced knight was not alarmed at all; he promptly swung upward to catch the goblin on the left from below, then followed through in a circle to smite the right-hand goblin from above, all in one smooth motion. It was impeccable.

Three left—four, if you counted the boss.

Would they come together or in a row?

Deusolbert jumped backward to avoid the dark spray of blood and prepared for his next attack. The fifth goblin came swinging straight for him on the left. No shine of a blade from the other direction.

"Hnng!" Deusolbert grunted and swiped his blade flat from the left. A silver arc of light followed the deadly tip, which sank into the goblin's right flank.

Then Deusolbert's eyes bulged. At that very moment, another, larger blade was bursting through the enemy goblin's chest and continuing toward him. The thick slab of metal sent the warm blood of its owner's still-breathing companion flying as it lunged for Deusolbert's throat. He couldn't dodge or block it with his sword.

On a snap judgment, he allowed his left forearm to collide with the dully shining tip of the cleaver.

Pain dulled his senses. The copper-colored gauntlet held up somehow, but the impact jarred him to the bone.

"Kaaah!!" Deusolbert roared back, as much out of shock as anything, and swept the enemy weapon to the left. He heard something crackle inside his body and understood that his left arm had fractured.

It's only one arm!!

It had taken all of Deusolbert's concentration to stop the attack, and now he plunged forward himself. His sword, which was puncturing the fifth—and sacrificial—goblin's belly, caught the sixth behind it.

But it felt too shallow. He had to pull out the sword, gain distance, and prepare for the next attack.

Sweat beading on his forehead, Deusolbert wrenched his sword back to his side. And beyond the now-dead fifth goblin, which toppled over, he saw the sixth and seventh goblins, blades tossed aside, lunging for him with arms outstretched, so low that they nearly crawled on the ground.

And the school of swordsmanship that Deusolbert was trained in had no form to go against a target stance like that one.

The goblins enveloped his legs in the second that he hesitated. Unable to withstand the surprising power of their arms, Deusolbert was promptly flipped onto his back. Through gaping eyes, he caught sight of the sizable Chief Shibori, a cruel smile on his lips, leaping high with a war ax in either hand.

It can't happen like this. Against a goblin. This cannot be how Deusolbert the Integrity Knight meets his end.

"It cannot be."

The firmer the will of the mind that thought it, the more dangerous a poison this idea became. It did not send him into a berserk, unthinking rage as it did Sigurosig, but it did freeze Deusolbert's mind solid and thus stop his body from moving.

All he could do was look upward at the certain doom of those cruel blades—when he heard a fierce shout, ragged with exhaustion.

"Sir Kniiiight!!"

A single human guard was charging at the ferocious goblin leader. It was the young man-at-arms captain. The fellow, whose name Deusolbert never even learned, had his greatsword high overhead, ready to hurl his mightiest slice.

All the enemy did was flick his wrist in annoyance.

There was a deep, loud crash, and the heavily laden—if not as much as the enemy—human warrior shot backward as lightly as if he were made of paper. He bounced again and again. No advantage in technique, speed, or equipment could make up for that devastating gap in strength.

The glowing red eyes of the nonhuman narrowed. He leaped,

as feral as any beast, his hand ax sweeping backward to deliver a finish to the crumpled man-at-arms.

No. As a knight, as a commander, I cannot allow for any more losses!

That thought hit Deusolbert's paralyzed mind like a lightning bolt.

He stood up, briefly kicking off the two clinging goblins, but he didn't have the time to get in front of the fallen guard. He could throw his sword, but that would only delay the inevitable by a few seconds.

Before his mind could conceive of a plan, his hands moved on their own, taking action in a way he had never consciously considered.

He held the Conflagration Bow sideways in one hand and nocked his *sword* against the string as a makeshift arrow. It was so heavy, he felt as if he were pulling a rope tied into the earth. Agony threatened to obliterate his conscious mind.

But Deusolbert groaned through clenched teeth and pulled the string all the way back. When he was in shooting position, he shouted, "Come, flames!!"

The divine weapon heeded his call, even without the proper sacred art command. The force of the conflagration that erupted from the bow was easily superior to any single use of Perfect Weapon Control he'd made before.

The longsword set on the bowstring was not counted among the divine weapons, but it was still a fine model, generated by Administrator herself. It had a much higher priority level than any of the mass-produced steel arrows he normally shot. Every last bit of the sacred power contained in the blade transformed into flames.

Even Deusolbert's armor, which was supposed to be flame-resistant, began to redden under the blistering heat. The two goblins now clinging to his legs again didn't even have time to scream before their eyes and mouths emitted flames of their own.

The enemy leader, finally noticing the anomaly, looked both shocked and furious and made to throw an ax. But before he could…

"Burn it all!!" bellowed Deusolbert, releasing the string. The longsword exploded from the bow, flying in a straight line on wings of scarlet flames. It looked just like the original form of the Conflagration Bow—a phoenix that was said to have lived in the biggest and oldest volcano in the southern empire.

"Gruaah!!" The enemy chief crossed his axes before his body. The fiery phoenix made contact right in the center where they met—and the pig-iron war axes simply melted into nothingness.

In a blink, before he could even catch fire, the matter that made up Chief Shibori of the flatland goblins turned to blackened soot and crumbled into dust on the wind, gone forever.

The goblins that witnessed the horrific death of their leader turned on their heels and fled. But there was little escape from the righteous flames of the phoenix, and all told, three hundred goblins perished, burned entirely to ash.

The battle was already fierce for Fanatio, at the center of the First Regiment, and Deusolbert, at the right wing.

And Bercouli Synthesis One—leader of the Integrity Knights, commander of the Human Guardian Army, and direct officer in charge of the Second Regiment—could clearly see the chaos being caused by the smoke attack on Eldrie's left wing.

But he did not budge.

The primary reason was that he trusted the knights and guards that he had worked so hard to train. The secondary reason was that if the dark knights and pugilists guild that made up the bulk of the enemy's elite forces were not active yet, his own side couldn't start throwing in its rear-line backup troops.

The tertiary reason was that he knew the Dark Territory better than anyone else, and he had to be concerned about a sneak attack—the enemy's flying troops.

In a world without any sacred arts that enabled flight—technically, this was an art only Administrator could peruse, so it had been lost forever when she'd died—the few dragon riders among the Integrity Knights and the dark knighthood loomed large in strategic purpose. They could swoop through the sky, out of the reach of any sword, and lay waste to ground troops with what sacred arts they did have, alongside their dragons' fiery breath.

But because they were so valuable, they couldn't be thrown into battle carelessly. If one side's dragon knight ventured out too early and happened to fall to sacred arts or archers on the ground, it would instantly mean a huge shift in the power balance.

It was why Bercouli had all the dragons aside from Alice's Amayori on call in the rear and was certain that the enemy would do the same. However, the sneak attack he was worried about was not from the dragon riders.

The forces of darkness had their own unique flying unit.

It was a hideous winged monster known as a minion. The dark mages crafted them out of clay and other materials, and although they were not intelligent on their own, they did respond to certain simple commands.

Alice had once told Bercouli that the pontifex had been secretly researching something exactly the same as these minions. But apparently, even she had hesitated to station the horrifying creatures at the Axiom Church. She had passed on before finding a more appropriate appearance for them, which was unfortunate, but there was nothing to be done about it now.

For this reason, Bercouli had to be wary of the skies because of a possible sneak attack from minions. Without the dragons aloft and with the priests entirely occupied with healing the wounded, that left him as the only wide-ranging antiair defensive unit on the battlefield. Or more accurately, his divine weapon, the Time-Splitting Sword.

Bercouli stood in the center of the Second Regiment, both hands resting on the pommel of his sword in its sheath, concentrating hard.

He was aware at all moments of the fierce struggles the three Integrity Knights and men-at-arms of the First Regiment were facing. He could sense the chaos on the left wing and the infiltration of the goblin troops as clearly as if they'd happened in the palm of his own hand.

But he couldn't take a single step from his location. Bercouli already had the Perfect Control art of his weapon active.

Long in the past, there had been a massive clock built into the wall of Central Cathedral to tell the citizens of Centoria the precise time. The long and short hand of the clock were then reforged into the divine Time-Splitting Sword. Its secret power was to "cut the future." Wherever the sword sliced, the power of that swing would remain, suspended in the air, and cut any who touched the space, as though the sword were still there.

Right before the Eastern Gate collapsed, Bercouli had straddled his mount, Hoshigami, and carved out a huge "sliced span" in the air a hundred mels wide, two hundred deep, and a hundred and fifty tall. He'd swept his sword through the air, carefully and deftly moving up and down, back and forth, crisscrossing the empty space. All told, he'd made over three hundred slices.

Maintaining so many Incarnate Swords for dozens of minutes at a time was a first even for Bercouli, a near immortal who had been alive for over three centuries. It was the kind of preposterous feat that could be achieved only by removing one's mind from one's bodily vessel and becoming a being of pure thought. This, more than anything, was why he'd put the First Regiment under Fanatio's command.

Hurry...If you're going to come, do it soon, prayed Bercouli, despite the fact that his presence of mind allowed for no such emotions as haste or anxiety. Mental fatigue was one thing, but the sacred power of the Time-Splitting Sword was limited and already more than half drained. Once Perfect Control was undone, it was impossible to repeat the same action. If he failed to wipe out the enemy's minions and they attacked Alice during her grand sacred arts preparation in the sky above the First Regiment, their one hope would be lost.

Come soon.

Of the seven elite Integrity Knights gathered at the Eastern Gate, it was clearly Renly Synthesis Twenty-Seven who was dealing with the pressure the worst, but despite his actual combat experience, Eldrie Synthesis Thirty-One was not doing much better.

Eldrie was the disciple of Alice, and he worshipped her. It was not the same as the romantic longing that Dakira had felt for her superior officer, Fanatio. He felt two contrary desires at once: to dedicate his all and serve her—and to protect her as her senior in age.

As soon as she'd awoken as an Integrity Knight, Alice had been hailed as the greatest genius in the history of the Church. On top of her ability with sacred arts, which was greater than even the priests' and bishops', she was chosen by the Osmanthus Blade—the oldest divine weapon and a symbol of everlasting permanence—which had refused all knights before her, and she absorbed all the lessons that Commander Bercouli could bestow upon her.

Alice might have looked like a young woman, but to the majority of the knights, she was as distant as a lone star in the northern sky. That isolation was made even worse when rumors spread that she might one day succeed Administrator as pontifex.

So right after his awakening, Eldrie did not attempt to approach Alice. You might even say that he carefully avoided her.

Though the Synthesis Ritual had robbed him of all his earthly memories, Eldrie was, in fact, the heir to Eschdor Woolsburg, a first-rank noble and the greatest general of the Norlangarth Empire. Eldrie was chosen as first representative of the northern empire for the year 380 HE and won the Four-Empire Unification Tournament. Even as an Integrity Knight, the noble-born pride and self-confidence did not leave him.

The idea that a younger girl could be a far greater knight than he was and that she could be the foremost pupil of Commander Bercouli was something he found distasteful, and it did not endear her to him. But late one night, a good deal of time since he'd been made a knight, Eldrie witnessed a side of Alice that he'd never expected to see.

He snuck out deep into the rose garden, intending to get in more sword practice without anyone else knowing, and there he found Alice dressed in a simple nightgown, weeping over a crude little grave marker. It was just a little cross of wood, but carved into it was the name of an elderly dragon that had perished just a few days earlier—the mother of Alice's Amayori and Eldrie's Takiguri.

The dragons were a valuable weapon, to be sure, but they were just dragons—servile beasts. Why was it necessary to build a grave for it and mourn its death so deeply?

But when he tried to snort and turn away, he was stunned to realize that the corners of his own eyes were growing hot and wet.

To this day, Eldrie didn't understand what it was about the sight of Alice mourning the death of the mother dragon that tore his heart apart so. But he did understand, as the tears fell down his cheeks undisturbed, that this tender, graceful vision was indeed the real Alice Synthesis Thirty.

From that day onward, Alice the solitary knight was entirely different in Eldrie's eyes. She was like a crystal flower, bowing her head against the incredible pressures against her but never breaking…

He wanted to protect her, to shelter that girl from the chilling winds that tore at her.

Eldrie's wish only grew stronger by the day. But the idea that *he* would protect *her* was simply arrogant folly. In sacred arts or in swordwork, Alice's talent far outstripped anything Eldrie could do.

The only option available to him was to seek her guidance as a pupil. And since that point, Eldrie had lived for just one hope: that his mentor Alice might accept him as a swordsman and as a man.

This was barely short of impossible. Alice the genius had so much ability that even Commander Bercouli had to admit it, and Eldrie was less trying to catch up than simply desperate to avoid her annoyance.

In the meantime, he spoke to Alice, ate meals with her, and used the confident conversational skills he had somehow picked up—actually, it was just his old personality peeking through—to try to elicit a smile from his mentor.

His efforts gradually produced fruit, as he not only improved with the sword but even caught glimpses of the faint upturn of his mentor's lips every now and then.

Until the worst incident in the history of Central Cathedral occurred.

It should have just been an ordinary mission at the start. A charge of murder for the two sword disciples was a grave one indeed, but the world was a big enough place that every now and then, disagreements led to spontaneous unfortunate events that could coincide with bloodshed. When he saw the students being brought to the cathedral, he didn't sense any danger or evil from them. They were just two normal, dejected young men.

So when Alice threw them in the underground cells and after careful consideration said "Guard the exit to the prison for this one night, just in case," Eldrie was taken aback. He undertook the mission, intent on enjoying the rare all-nighter in the rose garden, and when the sky to the east was beginning to lighten, it was to his great shock that those very prisoners escaped to the surface.

Eldrie was impressed with his mentor's keen judgment and

stood before them to fulfill his duty—and he lost, utterly and completely. He had no excuse for his performance. He had used the Memory Release of his divine Frostscale Whip, while they had just been normal boys with dangling prison chains for weapons.

But he had to accept his defeat. In the end, the two toppled elite knight Deusolbert, Vice Commander Fanatio, his mentor Alice, and even Commander Bercouli, until at last they defeated Administrator herself. Even Alice admitted, in that little shack outside the tiny village to the frozen north, that one of the two criminals was the greatest swordsman alive, beyond even the Integrity Knights.

Eldrie wasn't frustrated that he was inferior to the black-haired youth. Instead, it was the realization that it wasn't *he* who'd pulled off those feats that brought all the pain.

It wasn't Eldrie but that newcomer who'd freed Alice from the cage of ice that had imprisoned her heart. This came as a severe shock to Eldrie's system.

Just hours before the Eastern Gate fell, his mentor had given him the kind of gentle smile he'd never seen in all the hours and days he'd spent with her and said, "It was because of your support that I was able to walk my rocky path to this day. Thank you, Eldrie."

Along with the tears that flooded his eyes came a determination: that he must show Alice how tall her teachings had raised him to stand, here in this battle. This resolve raised the strength of Eldrie's Incarnate power, but it also put him in a corner.

If the mountain goblins that had attacked the left wing of the First Regiment had operated in as orthodox a manner as the goblins on the other side, Eldrie would have fought with a righteous ability every bit as fierce as Deusolbert's. Instead, the mountain goblins had taken away their visibility with smoke screens, slipped through his soldiers' legs, and snuck around to attack from the rear.

He'd been outdone by *goblins*, of all things. As Alice watched from above, he had just disgraced himself. The panic that ensued took away Eldrie's rational decision-making ability. He spun around in the blinding smoke, attempting to give orders to the guards under his command. But all he could tell was that if he ordered them to attack, they were liable to do more damage to one another than to the enemy. He had no idea how to get rid of the smoke.

He bit his lip hard enough to draw blood, his lilac hair wild and unkempt, but Eldrie could do little else but stand still in disbelief.

2

"Um, if you ask me, the left is looking a little dicey," Fizel warned the commander, her voice slow. Her partner, Linel, bobbed her head, braid swaying. But the commander did not respond. Linel looked forward again, noting to herself just how silent he always was.

The apprentice knights Linel Synthesis Twenty-Eight and Fizel Synthesis Twenty-Nine were situated at the front of the right wing of the Human Guardian Army's Second Regiment. Just a hundred mels ahead, the First Regiment was locked in a pitched battle, but no enemies were breaking through the defensive line. Deusolbert the veteran knight was putting up a very good fight so far.

Vice Commander Fanatio was also holding up in the center of the First Regiment. She was the kind of big-sister type who was anathema to Linel and Fizel, but her ability was unquestionable. And since she had taken off her helmet and shown her face to everyone, things hadn't been nearly as strained.

The problem was the left wing.

Eldrie Synthesis Thirty-One was a rookie, just seven months into his time as a knight, and while he had made great improvements lately, this grave duty seemed to be a bit too heavy a burden for him to bear. While it was his desire to lead on the front line, maybe it would have been better to leave it to one of the veterans…

Linel envisioned the layout of the battlefield and the placement of each Integrity Knight.

There were only seven elite knights at the battle. Eldrie was on the left wing of the First Regiment, Vice Commander Fanatio was in the center, and Deusolbert was on the right wing.

Young Renly was on the left wing of the Second Regiment, Commander Bercouli was in the center, and the silent lady knight was on the right wing.

Flying in the air above was Alice Synthesis Thirty.

"…The left wing just looks weaker in general…," Linel muttered, and this time it was Fizel who nodded her head. As a matter of fact, it had been looking strange for several minutes already. There didn't seem to be any damage yet, but the sounds of confused shouting were audible over the heads of the center battalion. If she squinted, she could see what looked like thick smoke flickering amid the darkness of the ravine.

Of course, if Eldrie allowed the enemy to break through the First Regiment, there would still be Renly waiting to lead the Second Regiment…

"I wonder if he's up to the task," Fizel contemplated. Linel nodded and leaned closer to her partner to whisper, "I didn't say anything, because I was sure Uncle Bercouli had good reason, but I still think right and left should be switched in the Second Regiment. It's too worrisome having Eldricchi and Renlicchi lined up together."

In an even more hushed voice, Fizel said, "I've been thinking… I bet he just wants to minimize the chance that our unit has to fight at all…"

"…Ohhh…"

Linel glanced over at the slender figure standing some distance away from them.

She had light armor, with a gray matte finish that was rare for an Integrity Knight. Her dark-gray hair was parted directly in the middle of her white forehead and was pulled into a ponytail at the back of her neck. She looked about twenty years old, her eyelids were long and had a single fold, and she put no rouge on her lips.

It was Sheyta Synthesis Twelve, often referred to as Sheyta the Silent, although the origin of that nickname was unknown. But the girls were painfully aware that she had to be much more dangerous than her unassuming appearance would suggest. This knight was deadly. When she drew the rapier from her left hip, they did not want to be anywhere near it.

Commander Bercouli probably didn't want Sheyta fighting, either, which was why he'd placed her in command behind veteran Deusolbert, rather than the youngster Eldrie. As long as the archer ahead did his job, she would not be called on to fight.

But it was not solely because of this that Linel said to the silent superior officer, "Um, Miss Sheyta?" When the woman glanced back, she continued, "May we go and take a look at the rear?"

The knight's narrow eyebrows rose about two milices. It seemed to be the equivalent of asking why, so she rushed to explain, "Um, it's just, we're worried..."

The brows twitched again. It must have meant *About what?* It was very hard to admit the answer, so Linel struggled to say, "Um...it's the guy with the supply team—you know the one. The rebel...Kirito."

Next to her, Fizel nodded rapidly. Fizel and Linel had fought with the rebels Kirito and Eugeo on the great stairs of Central Cathedral seven months ago. Technically, they had used their hidden poisoned blades to paralyze the two and had intended to drag them to the vice commander before cutting their throats.

It should have been an easy job. But somehow, Kirito the rebel chanted the antidote art, snatched away their daggers, and paralyzed *them* instead. When he lowered the paralyzing dagger toward them where they were lying on the floor, they felt no fear. At most, it was a bit of regret: *Oh, darn, we were nearly out of apprenticeship and made full-fledged Integrity Knights.* Linel awaited the moment that her life would end, hoping only that Kirito would make a clean go of it and ensure she died without too much pain.

But the young man didn't kill them. He stabbed the dagger into the ground, turned his back on them, and faced Vice Commander Fanatio in combat. Then he proceeded to win a fight, ragged and wounded, that he had no business winning.

Before he left, Kirito's partner, the criminal Eugeo, said something that Fizel and Linel still remembered vividly.

"Knowing you two, you might be tempted to think that Fanatio and Kirito are as strong as they are because they have Divine Objects and Perfect Weapon Control at their disposal, but you'd be wrong. They're strong to begin with. Their hearts are strong, not their techniques or weapons, and that's how they can fight through such terrible pain and perform such incredible feats."

Even now, seven months later, they didn't entirely understand it. But it was simply fact that the rebels Kirito and Eugeo had toppled Administrator, the pontifex of the Church. Eugeo had given up his life in the process, and Kirito had lost his mind and an arm.

What was it that the rebels had sought? What made a heart "strong"? It was the search for those answers that had brought Fizel and Linel to take part in the Human Guardian Army, all the way here at the Eastern Gate.

She still didn't have the answers. But when she'd seen Alice pushing that wheelchair with Kirito in it, Linel had felt an unfamiliar emotion cross her breast. It was the first time she had ever been unable to analyze what she was feeling and thinking.

The apprentice knights Linel Synthesis Twenty-Eight and Fizel Synthesis Twenty-Nine were born in Central Cathedral. They were told that their parents were a holy man and woman of the Axiom Church, but they did not know their names or faces.

Their parents had had children on the order of the pontifex and placed the babies in a facility within the tower. There had been a total of thirty children from similar circumstances in that place, but only the two sisters were still alive today. The other

twenty-eight had been unable to withstand the pontifex's "resurrection arts" experiment and died.

Fizel and Linel had survived because they'd studied extremely hard to discover the "best way to die" that caused the least mental and physical damage. They'd pierced each other's hearts as instructed, died, and been revived according to the sacred art. By the time the pontifex had given up on the experiment, they'd been able to kill each other virtually without pain.

To them, strength was the ability to kill efficiently. If the opponent was better, you had to run away. Run, then practice, and if you got better than the opponent, you could kill them next time. So facing a stronger opponent and standing there allowing yourself to be damaged and hurt was a pointless act according to their way of thinking.

The rebels Kirito and Eugeo had been no better than lower knights in terms of sheer battle ability. But they'd given up body and life to fight the pontifex and won.

For what purpose?

What did it gain them?

Linel wanted to ask Kirito on their reunion, but Integrity Knight Alice was at his side at every moment, and they couldn't make contact. She didn't know whether it was possible to have a conversation with him in his current state, but she didn't want him to die before she could try. As long as the Second Regiment didn't get breached, the supply team in the back should be safe, but that unrest on the left wing was concerning.

But they couldn't explain all of that to their commanding officer, Sheyta, so they kept it simple and waited for her answer on pins and needles. The "Silent" knight's gray eyes glanced to the left wing and paused for two seconds, and then she pointed behind them with her left hand.

"Uh...y-you mean we can go?"

Sheyta nodded to them, so Linel and Fizel gave her a compact knight's salute. "Thank you, ma'am! We will return at once if everything is well!"

They turned and began to run along the line of troops.

"Thank you," indeed. We never even said those words to the pontifex.

Linel shared a look and a smirk with her partner and picked up her pace.

Renly Synthesis Twenty-Seven was about to sink to his knees in the back of the supply tent when he heard multiple shouts and breath being drawn sharply from a surprisingly close distance.

Could it be? Had the enemy broken through the ravine's defenses so quickly? No, that was impossible. Less than twenty minutes had passed since the fighting had started.

He was just overagitated, he decided. It was making him hear distant sounds very clearly—that was all. But the reactions of the two girls who had already evacuated to this tent told him that the approaching voices of soldiers were not figments of his imagination.

"No way…Are they already this far back?!"

The red-haired student named Tiese Schtrinen looked up and rushed quickly to the entrance of the tent. She lifted the flap and checked outside. Her whisper came back sharp and quick.

"Smoke…!"

Ronie Arabel stiffened. "Wha…? You can see fire, Tiese?!"

"No, it's just really dark smoke…No, hang on. I can see…a bunch of people coming from the…"

Tiese's words seemed to be swallowed up by the heavy canvas flap as she peered through the gap. In the tense silence that followed, Renly hovered above a crouch, listening intently.

He suddenly realized he could no longer hear the shouting. But while it was quieter now, he sensed that someone was coming closer. There were damp footsteps outside, slapping on firm ground.

Suddenly and awkwardly, Tiese pulled back from the doorway

to the center of the tent. Her trembling hand reached across her body to her waist. No sooner did Renly realize that she was trying to draw her weapon than the hanging door was violently ripped loose.

It was night outside, the only source of light the campfires lit here and there, dim and red, against which stood a figure. It was short and hunched but with unusually thick arms, clutching a crude weapon that looked as if it had been cut straight out of metal plate.

A stench wafted in with the air from the doorway, stinging Renly's nose. Primary Trainee Schtrinen pulled her sword loose, rattling the sheath as she did so. Next to the wheelchair, Primary Trainee Arabel gasped, "A goblin?!"

The alien intruder spoke, its voice hissing and raspy. "Ooh… Little Ium girls…You will be my prey…"

Tiese backed away, repelled by the open, ugly greed in its voice. Though he was an elite Integrity Knight, this was the first time Renly had ever laid eyes on a nonhuman from the Dark Territory. He had been frozen in storage before he could earn the dragon that would have taken him over the End Mountains in the first place.

It's…completely different, he thought, in dull shock.

Through lectures from the older knights and the cathedral's documents, he'd thought he'd learned a fair bit about the four nonhuman races of the Dark Territory. But the goblins he'd imagined to be some mischievous fairies out of legends were nothing at all like the hideous creature standing not eight mels away.

He felt his fingers going numb. The goblin took one heavy step forward. Light gleamed off his dirty armor plates as if they were fish scales.

Tiese held her sword up toward the goblin with both hands, but her knees shook so badly, the tip wouldn't stay still. The faint sound of chattering Renly could pick up must have been her teeth.

"T...Tiese...," Ronie whimpered. She stood before Kirito's wheelchair, protecting it, with her hand on her sword hilt, but her legs were shivering, too.

He had to stand. He had to get to his feet, draw his Double-Winged Blades, and fight the goblin warrior.

And yet, Renly's body was as unresponsive to commands as if it were made of stone. It was just one nonhuman enemy. The Integrity Knight was worth a thousand soldiers; he had been given enough power to take on a thousand such goblins and win.

"Gffh...How tasty you look...," the goblin crowed, licking its lips, only to drool a large, sticky glob of saliva.

"S-stay back! Or else I'll...," Tiese warned, summoning all her courage, but that only enticed the goblin further. The grinning demi-human took another step forward, not even brandishing its weapon yet.

Thuk.

There was a soft, dry sound inside the tent.

The goblin soldier's yellow eyes stared with wonder at its own chest. A piece of sharp, smooth metal jutted out from the crude slab of armor there. Fresh blood gleamed and ran down the surface of the sharp metal object: a sword point. Someone had pierced the goblin's heart from behind.

"...What...is this...?"

They were the goblin's final words. The strength drained from its powerful body, and it fell limp to the floor of the tent.

Standing on the other side was a warrior, or perhaps a priestess, about half a head shorter than even the young students. Her brown hair was tied into a braid, and she wore a silver breastplate over a black habit. The sword in her right hand was short for her size but very fine. She looked no older than a child, but even though she had just slaughtered the fearsome nonhuman soldier, her little face showed no sign of intimidation.

It was at this point that Renly finally snapped to attention. This girl was no swordswoman, nor was she a holy woman.

She was a knight, an apprentice Integrity Knight by the name of

Linel Synthesis Twenty-Eight. She was one of the Terrible Twins, the girl who had dueled and killed the previous twenty-eighth knight and taken the number for herself.

Linel's expression did not change upon seeing Renly and his pathetic posture. She checked on the two students, saw that Kirito was safe where he sat, and turned on her heel. Then another apprentice knight appeared at the doorway of the tent.

Fizel Synthesis Twenty-Nine, her short hair the same color as Linel's, murmured to her partner, "Nel, I cleaned up all the goblins around here, but more will come. Maybe we should move."

"Mm. Got it, Zel," Linel agreed. She stuck the toe of her boot under the body of the goblin that blocked the floor near the entrance and flipped it out of the way. Not much blood spilled in the process, a sign that the blow from behind had been so quick and precise that there hadn't even been time for the goblin to bleed.

She turned back to the speechless trainees and said, "I am Linel, and this is Fizel. We're apprentice knights."

"Y-yes, I know. I saw you during exercises. We're Primary Trainees Tiese Schtrinen and Ronie Arabel. Th…thank you for saving us," Tiese said, her voice still trembling a bit. Ronie bowed her head.

Linel just shrugged, in a very mature way. "You might be getting ahead of yourself. Over a hundred goblins broke through the defensive line along the left wing of the First and Second Regiments thanks to the smoke screen they set up."

She paused then and finally looked right at Renly. Her purplish-gray eyes narrowed.

"What is the elite knight who is supposed to be in command of the Second Regiment's left wing doing in here? Your subordinates are running around in a panic within the smoke."

Renly looked away, avoiding the piercing gaze of the apprentice knight, and grunted, "It has nothing to do with you. Take these two and their sick patient to a safe place."

He was keenly aware of an abrupt change in Linel's manner. A chill brushed his cheek, something no child would be capable of emitting. The little blade gleamed and flickered in the orange campfire light, reflecting off the goblin blood.

Was she going to kill him, as she had the previous Twenty-Eight?

Then let it be quick. He was meant to be stored away as a failure of a knight. It had been a mistake to put him into a real battle in the first place. He couldn't go back to the Second Regiment, and there was no place for him back at the cathedral if he fled there. Being executed by an apprentice knight like Linel was a fitting end for a coward like him.

Renly turned his head away, awaiting the finality of the blade.

But what he heard was not approaching footsteps but a soft voice. "You might be a terrible coward…but you are an elite knight, which means you possess some kind of strength. You ought to be grateful to the swordsman you called a 'sick patient.'"

What does that mean? Renly wondered. By the time he raised his head, he saw only the back of Linel's habit.

"Trainees, bring Kirito and follow me," Linel ordered at the same time that Fizel reported, "Nel, they're here! Eight…no, ten of them!"

There were indeed multiple sets of footsteps approaching from the east. Tiese and Ronie were rooted to the spot, so Linel turned to them and said, "Ignore that command. Stay here for a while. We will go clean up the goblins."

"Y-yes, Miss Knight," Tiese said. Linel slid out of the tent and disappeared with Fizel. Immediately, they heard a goblin yell "There! Ium younglings!" and fading footsteps. They were going to put some distance between them and the tent before they killed their targets.

Facing ten goblins without fear was a bold act, one that seemed out of place for apprentices. But they clearly had the strength to achieve this.

Strength.

Linel had identified Renly as a coward but also said that he had "some kind of strength." And also that he should be grateful to the very rebel, Kirito, who had once been their opponent.

He didn't know what that meant, and he didn't feel the tiniest bit of this strength he supposedly had. He had been within eyesight of the enemy and couldn't even find the bravery to get to his feet. Renly hung his head, unable to even look up at Tiese and Ronie.

But that lasted for only a few seconds. Just to the left of Renly, the thick hemp wall of the tent tore in a straight line. This time, he was startled into lifting off the ground and leaping away from the disturbance.

Standing on the other side of the rip was a goblin in finer armor than the one before, though it was a bit shorter. This leather armor was well crafted and dyed black. Assuming it had slipped past the twins, this one seemed to be an advance scout adept at clandestine actions.

Without realizing it, Renly was reaching for his throwing weapons. But he couldn't draw them; as with the first goblin, the terror that bubbled up from his gut seemed to freeze his fingers.

Renly wasn't clearly aware of this, but the source of his fear was not the sight of his first close-up nonhuman enemy. It was fear of fighting itself. To be precise, fear arising from the knowledge that if he fought with this goblin, it would continue until one of them died.

He was afraid of being killed. And even more afraid of doing the killing.

More feet marched closer as he stood there. This must be a separate unit from the ones Linel and Fizel were drawing away from the tent. More than just ten or twenty goblins had slipped through the defensive line.

The scout saw Renly's fear in the way he stood still, so it grinned and turned to Tiese and Ronie. The girls stepped in front of Kirito and bravely raised their swords. But their faces soon turned to despair—more figures were approaching behind the scout, silhouetted against the smoke.

The scout raised the scythe-like weapon it held and crept closer to the girls.

"S-stop right there! Come any closer, and I'll attack!" the redhead bravely warned. But her voice was thin and wavering.

"..."

The goblin closed the distance. It was clear from the way it kept in motion, rather than wasting time with threats and gloating, that it was a well-trained elite soldier. But Tiese held her ground and pulled back the sword, her face resolute.

You can't. Run away.

But Renly's lips wouldn't move. Even now, his body—his soul—refused to fight.

Then he heard some faint sound, like creaking. His eyes flitted to the right.

In the darkness at the back of the tent, the black-haired young man sat lifeless in his chair, expression blank. The sound was coming from his left hand. A vein rose on the skin where he clutched the two swords, the tendons bulging. There was great strength being expended there.

As though furious that he had no right hand with which to wield a sword.

"Are you...?" Renly whispered, all air and no voice. *Are you trying to save them? When you cannot stand or use your sword or even speak?*

All at once, he understood.

The strength that Linel and Fizel spoke of—it was not about technique or sacred arts or divine weapons or Perfect Control arts.

It was that simple power that everyone, Integrity Knight or common folk alike, possessed but could lose so easily.

Bravery.

Renly's right hand began to move, ever so slowly. His numb fingers brushed the Double-Winged Blades at his waist.

All of a sudden, the feeling returned to them. The Divine Objects were saying something to him.

The goblin pulled back its wicked scythe, preparing to swing it at Tiese.

All at once, there was a swift swishing of air being split, and a pale shine flashed briefly, reflecting throughout the tent.

The light curved from Renly's hand on upward, brushing the roof of the tent before plunging. It swept through the goblin's body, changed angles, and snapped back right between the index and middle fingers of Renly's outstretched right hand.

"...Gr...hg...?"

The goblin's growl sounded more confused than anything. A pale-red line appeared, running through the middle of its face.

Then the top half of the goblin's head slid wetly off the bottom and plopped onto the ground.

The Double-Winged Blades were very thin steel throwing blades that curved at the center. There was no hilt or handle to hold the forty-cen blades. Both ends had sharp tips, which he gripped between his fingers to throw the blades. They then flew, rotating rapidly, changing angles on the fly, before returning to their master for him to catch them between his fingers again.

In other words, even in ordinary use, they required far more concentration than a simple sword did. If he lost any bit of focus, he would fail to catch the returning blade and could easily lose a finger or two.

The fact that he could capably use such a weapon was proof enough of Renly's considerable skill—but he was completely unaware of this. The lack of Perfect Weapon Control was a huge weight on his shoulders, an inadequacy that softened his resolve.

So a single attack that instantly killed its goblin target did not suddenly bring Renly back to his senses, ready to fight.

Cold metal rang faintly in his outstretched fingers. He breathed in and out, shallow and quick. *I killed. I killed it*, he repeated in his head, over and over.

"...Sir Knight."

It was Tiese who broke the silence. There were little tears in her maple-red eyes. "Thank...thank you," she practically whispered. "You...you saved us."

The words were a warm balm on the icy fear that enveloped

Renly's heart. But he didn't have the wherewithal to respond. Multiple figures were approaching from the smoke screen. It looked like more than ten, in fact.

I can't. I can't fight anymore. A single goblin was already too terrifying.

The meager bravery he had summoned from his every fiber was already fleeing him. His breath was quick. His legs felt weak. His eyes swam around, looking for an escape. Once again, they were drawn to the two longswords clutched under the black-haired youth's arm.

One of them, a sword with a beautiful, finely carved rose on its hilt, seemed to be faintly glowing in the gloom. The light was blue but seemed almost warm somehow. It pulsed, beating like a heart. He felt the chilly fear that enveloped him gradually melt.

Renly sucked in a deep breath and said, "You stay here and protect Kirito."

"W-we will!" Tiese and Ronie replied. He nodded to them and left the tent through the rip the goblin scout had made.

Two goblins at the head of the approaching group instantly noticed him and bared their fangs.

His right hand flicked, and the light shot through the air again.

The blade returned to his fingertips at the same moment that two heads fell to the ground. But Renly didn't even register it, his eyes already searching for the next target, at which point he threw the blade from his left side. Two more goblins perished instantly, their bodies crumpling.

In just four seconds, Renly had eliminated four goblins, but more of them approached.

"A knight..."

"It's a leader!"

"*Kill him! Kill him!!*" they screeched. Renly began running toward the front line to draw them away from the tent. The goblins pursued, their armor rattling as they scrambled after him.

Eventually, the rows of supply tents petered out. Just to the left was a vertical rock face, and the visibility ahead was reduced by the thick smoke screen, out of which charged goblin after goblin. Then there were the ten or so following him from behind.

Having charged to his potential death, Renly now stopped and held out his arms, a curved blade in each hand, and shouted, "My name is Renly!! The Integrity Knight Renly Synthesis Twenty-Seven!! If you want my head, you will have to give your life to take it!"

The goblins greeted his speech—containing every last ounce of boldness he had—with ferocious roars. They brandished their crude knives and raced for him, front and back.

Renly hurled his two blades. The one from his right hand went right, and the left blade went left. Each line of approaching goblins was met with a flying, curving projectile.

Numerous heads left their shoulders and toppled to the ground. A second later, filthy black blood spurted from their necks as the bodies flopped over. Rather than pinching the blades as they returned, Renly caught them spinning around his index fingers, keeping the rotation alive, and hurled them again without pause.

The exact same effect resulted. In a head-to-head comparison of regular attack power, this was more powerful than even Deusolbert's Conflagration Bow and Fanatio's Heaven-Piercing Blade. The Double-Winged Blades were thinner than paper and spun with such incredible speed that anything less than the finest armor might as well not even exist.

Two tosses of the pair of blades offed more than ten goblins, and even the fearless goblins' mad charge slowed a bit, as they were stunned by the sudden deaths of their fellows.

He could do this. If he just held out a bit longer, reinforcements would soon come through the line ahead, where the smoke would be thinning out. Stifling the fear he felt toward his own mass slaughter, Renly threw the blades for a third time.

But this time, he did not hear that familiar sound, like a machete slicing through a small branch. Instead, it was a high-pitched clash: *Kshiiing!*

Renly reached out as far as he could to catch the blades, which just barely managed to return, despite being knocked fiercely off their trajectory. He couldn't nimbly catch them on one finger this time and had to gingerly receive the lethal blades on the fly.

Through gaping eyes, he saw a single goblin appear through the hazy smoke.

It was large. In height, it was not far off from Renly, whose physical frame was that of a fifteen-year-old. But the rippling muscles that covered its body and the malevolent look pouring like fire from its yellow eyes were not at all like the other goblins. It wore light armor of studded leather, perhaps for better mobility, and a thick cleaver hung from its right hand.

"...Are you the captain?" Renly asked, his voice low.

"I am. Kosogi, chief of the mountain goblins," the creature replied and made a show of looking around. "Well, well, you've done quite a number here. I didn't think there would be an Integrity Knight stationed back here. So much for my guess."

In addition to its stature, this goblin did not speak like the others, either. While it was just as malicious and hostile, the brutishness was held in check by what was clearly much higher intelligence.

That doesn't matter. Just because it was lucky enough to deflect the Double-Winged Blades once doesn't mean it can keep it up, Renly told himself. He crossed his arms before him and shouted, "Your war ends here!!"

He threw his blades as hard and fast as he could.

The right blade swept down at an angle from above, while the left skimmed the ground and leaped upward, both aiming right for Kosogi's neck.

But again, Renly's attack resulted in a loud, clear ringing noise.

With speed that reduced his weapon to a gray blur, Kosogi had swung it and blocked the attacks coming from both sides in one capable motion. The deflected blades barely made it back to Renly's grasp.

Why?! The blades should be able to slice through any goblin weapon! he thought, scarcely believing it. His eyes were drawn to Kosogi's cleaver.

It was the same crude style of knife that the other goblins carried, but the color of the blade was different. That was not primitive cast iron; it was refined steel that had been forged over a long period of time to increase its quality.

Sensing Renly's shock, Kosogi hefted the blade up close to his face and chuckled. "This? It's a test model. Pretty good, isn't it? Much blood was shed to steal the materials and methods from the dark knighthood. But…this isn't the only reason I was able to block you, boy knight."

"…How about *this*, then?"

Renly hurled his hands upward. The blades vanished out of sight into the darkness of the night sky, then swooped down to attack Kosogi from behind. Surely *that* would be impossible to stop—

"…!!"

But Renly's certainty was proven wrong immediately. To his disbelief, Kosogi swung the cleaver behind his back and struck the high-speed blades that he couldn't possibly see for himself.

The weapons wobbled their way unsteadily back, and Renly just barely failed to catch one of them, cutting the middle finger on his left hand. He didn't have time to register the pain, however.

"They're too light, boy. And they make sound," Kosogi explained simply. He had perfectly identified the weakness of the Double-Winged Blades.

The weight of each blade was almost impossibly light for the weapons known as Divine Objects. It was an inevitable consequence of prioritizing only sharpness and rotation power, and it meant that any enemy with armor of a sufficient priority level who could react in time could not be simply overpowered.

Also, a blade that flew and spun at a high rate of rotation produced a characteristic slicing sound. Someone with good ears listening for that sort of anomaly could predict where it was going if they were skilled enough.

The intelligence that Kosogi showed in identifying and reacting to his attacks after only a handful of chances sent a chill down Renly's spine. How a crude, lesser being like a goblin could be capable of such cleverness was—

"I see that look on your face, boy. It says, 'But you're a goblin...,'" Kosogi quipped, grinning, but with a whiff of mournfulness about it. "And I can turn that phrase around on you. 'But you're a high and mighty knight...' I've heard that the Integrity Knights have the strength of a thousand, but you don't seem to live up to that standard, do you? Is that why you were hiding here in the back?"

"...Yeah, that's right." It was a mistake for him to have looked down on this foe as a mere goblin. Renly decided to abandon his pride and admit the truth. "I am a failure of a knight. But don't take the wrong meaning from that. *I'm* the failure...not these." He held up the silver blades near his face.

The only way to eliminate the inherent weakness of the Double-Winged Blades was the special technique of the Integrity Knight itself: Perfect Weapon Control.

These weapons had once been a pair of holy birds that had each lost a wing, one right and one left. Unable to fly with just one wing each, they'd connected their bodies and risen to a height that other birds could only dream of. They'd flown distances that were nearly infinite.

This legend had inflicted a sharp but tiny wound in his heart, so deep that he did not even realize it was there.

It regarded his loved one, the person removed from his memory by the Synthesis Ritual. It was his best friend growing up, someone whose life he'd taken in an accident during the extreme combat between them in the final of the Four-Empire Unification Tournament.

He and Renly had truly been like a pair of birds. They'd competed with each other from the moment they were self-aware, and after leaving home to travel to Centoria, they became support for one another in their quest to overcome all challenges and reach the very heights of their craft.

But that was where their wings gave way.

Even losing his memory and being made an Integrity Knight did not fill the gaping hole left in Renly's heart. Without the bravery to take his sword and fight, and the joy of having his heart connected to another's, there was no way for Renly to summon the mental image of the holy birds flapping together with one wing each.

However, he had just met this young black-haired man who seemed more damaged than anyone had ever been yet still clutched those two precious swords in his only arm. The faint light that one of those swords emitted seemed to speak to Renly, silently telling him that there was one thing in this world that was never lost, even after death.

It was memory.

Life was passed on from one soul to the next, through personal bonds and connections, in perpetuity, for as long as the world itself existed.

Renly looked away from the approaching goblin chief, who was smiling with the certainty of victory, and closed his eyes. From the body of the boy knight who seemed to have given up all hope, a burst of sword energy like a searing wind suddenly issued forth. His eyes shot open. He crossed his arms in front with the steel blades, hiding the bottom half of his face from view.

"Double Wings, take flight!!"

He flung his arms sideways. Two strips of light leaped upward, arcing, and plunged toward Kosogi from the sides.

"Keep trying it…and you'll only get the same result!!" The goblin chief readied his cleaver and forcefully knocked the blades aside.

Red sparks flew along with metallic screeches. The two flying blades were easily deflected, but they rose into the air again, rather than falling to the ground. Like a pair of birds soaring together, they swept into a spiral formation, growing closer and closer.

The moment that the blades touched, Renly shouted, "Release… Recollection!!"

It was not simply Perfect Weapon Control, but the ultimate secret technique beyond it, the command to unleash the weapon's memories.

Pure, blinding brilliance lit the ravine.

The steel blades drew into the center of that light, where they connected and fused.

It was the unleashed true form of the Double-Winged Blades: a cross-shaped construction that gleamed blue, like the stars of the distant night sky, as it slowly rotated.

Renly lifted a hand toward his counterpart glowing in the far heights.

It's beautiful. Just like me and...

Then he clenched his raised hand.

The cross-shaped blade began to spin with tremendous force. The wind-whistling sound that it normally made rose in pitch until it passed out of the range of hearing and became silent.

With a soft, easy motion, Renly swung his hand downward. The Double-Winged Blades, now just a disc of light, sliced silently toward the goblin.

"This is a waste of time!!" roared Kosogi, swinging his cleaver at the weapon as it descended upon him. But right when the thick steel was about to hit the ultrathin blade, the divine weapon abruptly changed course, bouncing vertically to cause the cleaver to miss, then accelerating straight down once again.

There was a faint, dry sound: *kahk*.

Then a pale shine rippled through the median line of Kosogi's well-muscled body.

"Gaaaaah!!" the goblin bellowed, trying to leap onto Renly. But his left half seemed unable to keep up with his right. After a step or two, the two halves separated entirely and fell heavily to the ground.

At the moment of his death, Kosogi tried to use his excellent mind to figure out how he'd lost.

According to his own values, the weak-looking boy knight

could win only by having a greater will to murder and a greater desire to win than Kosogi. But no matter how he squinted, through eyes quickly separating and losing focus, he could not sense any kind of malice in that knight's childish face.

Then what did I lose to?

He desperately wanted to know but did not find out before everything went black.

When Renly caught the returning Double-Winged Blades, they silently separated into two parts and assumed their former shapes. He stared at the twin blades, which were utterly spotless.

His hidden memories had not returned. In fact, Renly was not aware that some of his own memories had been taken out of his reach at all.

But he was certain now that somewhere within him were faint traces of someone whom he'd once been very close to, whose heart had been connected to his own. For the moment, that was enough for him.

He closed his eyes briefly, then lifted his head. Many goblin warriors waited behind Kosogi, the enemy leader. But it was strangely quiet all around. Through the layer of smoke, which was gradually clearing up, Renly saw that there were hundreds of bodies piled in heaps. They were enemy soldiers who had been alive just minutes before this. He was shocked; who had done this—and when?

"...Well, I suppose you've gotten the tiniest bit more knightly."

He turned, startled, toward the source of the voice. Approaching from the right was the apprentice knight Linel Synthesis Twenty-Eight. Nearby was Fizel Synthesis Twenty-Nine. Clearly, these two were responsible for cleaning up all the enemy troops.

He stood there, dumbfounded. Eventually Linel, the one with the braids, snorted and gave him what seemed like a very forced knight's salute.

"Elder Knight, we beseech thee for orders," she said, probably mostly out of sarcasm, but it beat open derision.

Renly cleared his throat and asked, "Are he and the other girls all right?"

"Yeah. We sent them back to the supply team," Fizel reported.

He sighed in relief. "And the infiltrating enemy soldiers?"

"Entirely wiped out," said Linel this time.

"Then I'm returning to my unit. You should do the same."

"Fine." "Yes, sir."

The girls turned and ran off, not seeming fatigued in any way by the battle. Renly watched them go, then glanced back at the supply tents behind him.

...*Thank you*, he said to the two trainee girls and the young swordsman.

Renly Synthesis Twenty-Seven, elite knight, began running east to rejoin the left wing of the Second Regiment, where he belonged.

3

The very back of the secondary formation of the Dark Territory troops sat about five hundred mels from the ravine, where the fighting was pitched. On the second level of a deluxe four-wheeled carriage (if still inferior to Emperor Vecta's tank) stood a tall woman, arms crossed, with plenty of bare skin showing. It was one of the dark lords, the chancellor of the dark mages guild, Dee Eye Ell.

A messenger mage dressed in black looked up at her master from the side and reported, "Sigurosig, Shibori, and Kosogi have been struck down."

Dee's lips instantly twisted with scorn. "Useless vermin…I shouldn't have expected a nonhuman to do anything right."

She looked down at the necklace charm draped over the skin of her ample breasts. The silver circle with twelve precious stones set around it was a special Divine Object that told time by the changing color of the stones. The six o'clock stone glowed orange, but the seven o'clock stone was still dark. That meant that only about twenty minutes had passed since the start of the hostilities at six o'clock.

"Have you located the Integrity Knights?" she snapped, clearly irritated. The messenger mage uttered a quick command and waited to hear the response of her counterpart lurking somewhere on the battlefield.

"Three sighted on the front line have been targeted. Two others in the rear have been sighted, but their locations are not quite ready."

"Still only five? Perhaps that is all the number they have," Dee snarled to herself, a far cry from the coquettish display she put on in the presence of the emperor. "In either case, we must eliminate those five without fail..."

She thought it over, then ordered, "Send in the minions. My command is..." She narrowed her eyes, judging the distance to the crumbled gate and the battlefield near it. "Fly seven hundred mels, descend to the ground, and lay waste to the enemy."

"At that distance, the nonhuman troops fighting at the front will get caught up in the attack."

"No matter," she replied, unbothered.

The messenger showed no emotion of her own as she nodded her understanding, then asked, "And what number, my lady? All eight hundred currently hatched are at your disposal."

"Let's see..."

Dee considered the question. Minions required considerable resources and time to generate, and they were a far more valuable tool to her than the goblin soldiers. She wished she could be sparing with them, but if her plan to wipe out the enemy's main force with a concentrated dark-arts barrage from a distance failed to do the job, the emperor would be very displeased with her.

"...All eight hundred," she ordered, a cruel smile on her lips.

Dee's secret ambition was to help Dark God Vecta triumph in this battle so he could capture the so-called Priestess of Light and return to the depths of the earth—and then gain the emperor's mantle from him and rule the entire Underworld in the aftermath.

On the day she became empress of the world, she could make thousands upon thousands of minions. Her greatest obstacle, General Shasta, was dead now, and the only power players after him were the merchant who only had interest in money and the pugilist who only had interest in fighting. Ultimate success was nearly at her doorstep.

Once Dee had conquered the entire world, which even the half-god Administrator couldn't do, she would gain the sacred art of everlasting life that was supposedly hidden in the headquarters of the Axiom Church.

Immortality. Eternal youth.

Sweet chills of pleasure ran up Dee's spine at the thought. A red tongue licked over her blue-painted lips.

Just then, the messenger mage's orders reached the brigade of dark mages at the front, and the man-made black monsters took flight all at once, like darkness itself gaining wings. Eight hundred minions rose on command, campfire light reflecting off their shining skin, and flew right for the ravine.

Here they come.

Commander Bercouli's lips, which had been closed as tightly as a statue's since the battle had begun, finally split into a wide grin. He sensed that a large number of flying enemy troops were entering the boundaries of his Perfect Weapon Control power, which he was maintaining in the air over the gate.

These were not dragons bearing dark knights. They were soulless minions, cold as clay.

But he did not activate the art yet. There were plenty more of them yet to be drawn within his giant web of cuts before they were all there.

Bercouli's finely honed senses already told him about the valiant efforts of Fanatio and Deusolbert—and even of Renly's initial escape and subsequent awakening into his power. If they had struck down three of the invading army's advance-line generals, there was no danger of the front line being pushed back upon them at this point.

If they could simply have Alice, waiting high above, use all the resources acquired thus far to nullify the enemy's long-distance sacred arts as planned, then the unharmed Second Regiment of the guardian army would be free to fight with the enemy's main force, which was made up of dark knights and pugilists.

He suspected that his own true part to play would come after that. And not in a one-on-one fight against his rival, Dark General Shasta.

Bercouli was already aware that Shasta's presence was gone from the enemy's camp. Most likely, the snuffing out of the great presence in the far east several days ago had been the final moment of that worthy warrior's life.

As the eldest of the Integrity Knights, Bercouli had lived countless months and years, and he no longer mourned the death of those whose lives met their natural end. But the death of Shasta brought him nothing but bitter disappointment—he was a man who Bercouli had once hoped would one day help draw the land of darkness and the human realm into a peaceful coexistence free of bloodshed.

Now the one out there who'd ended Shasta's life, the owner of that vast, freezing emptiness—whoever he was—likely commanded the entire army of the Dark Territory, and only by cutting that foe down could Bercouli properly mourn his rival.

Or perhaps it would finally be the end of his own life, he sensed. But there was no longer even a shred of him that still clung to living on. If the time had finally come for him to die, then so be it.

When Fanatio's lower knight unleashed her Incarnate power in that final desperate moment, Bercouli was both impressed and even a little jealous. But of course, now was not that time for him. At last, the swarm of minions that tore through the darkness overhead was entirely contained within the prison of his sword's slashes.

Bercouli's eyes flashed, and he slowly, easily lifted the Time-Splitting Sword from its resting point, with the tip against the ground, to an overhead position.

"*...Slice!!*"

His cry cut forth, a naked blade through the void.

At the same time, in the air up ahead, a multitude of white lines formed a three-dimensional lattice pattern and flashed brightly. There was a great chorus of screeching death wails, and filthy black blood poured down on the nonhuman enemy army in torrents. Minion blood was mildly poisonous, and it only brought further chaos to the troops that were already without their commanding officers.

The messenger mage, who had been utterly emotionless the entire time, now let a faint note of fear creep into her voice, giving Dee an ill premonition. That feeling quickly became reality in just a single second.

"My lady, I am afraid...that all eight hundred minions have been eliminated just before they were set to descend."

"Wha—?"

Silence.

A crystal goblet screamed its last as it shattered against the carriage floor.

"But how?! No one told me of any large mage division among the enemy!"

And more importantly, it was nearly impossible to dispatch eight hundred minions with an art command alone. Because they were made mostly of clay, they were highly resistant to burning and freezing. Sharp-bladed attacks were the most effective counter, but the minions were still in the air, far from the soldiers on the ground.

"...And the enemy dragons have not yet made an appearance?" Dee asked, finally controlling her anger somewhat.

The messenger mage hung her head. "Correct. Not a single dragon has been confirmed in the air over the battlefield from the start until now."

"Which would make this…that special bit of Integrity Knight trickery…Perfect Weapon Control arts. But…can they truly have this much…?"

She swallowed the final word of the sentence and let her bared fangs gnash with frustration.

Like Dark General Shasta, Dee had attempted to collect information on the secret technique of the Integrity Knights. But it had been nearly impossible to witness it in action for herself. The only thing she had unveiled was that it combined and amplified the power of the Divine Object and of the knight him- or herself.

"But using the weapon that way should devour a great amount of life. It cannot be utilized in such rapid sequence…," she muttered, her mind racing.

Then the messenger mage, who had been listening to reports from the front, shot upward and said in a voice slightly more composed, "Chancellor, location of two rear Integrity Knights has been found. Identifying all five knights' targets."

"…Good," Dee said, pondering. Should she send in the dark knights and pugilists, who made up the bulk of the Second Army, to force the Integrity Knights to consume more of their Perfect Weapon Control power, the greatest unknown variable on the other side? Or should she use the dark mages guild, her best weapon, and try to finish it all right now?

Dee was normally a very cautious person who plotted obsessively and removed all room for doubt or concern before she finally acted. But the instantaneous destruction of her eight hundred precious minions left her at a loss and filled her with a panic and haste that she wasn't aware she was feeling.

She filled a new crystal glass with more dark-purple liquid and told herself, *I am calm.*

This is the moment when I seize my first true glory.

Dee Eye Ell downed the drink in one go, then held the glass high and commanded, "Ogre archers, dark mages, advance! Proceed into the ravine, then begin preparing the cast of the wide-range incineration projectiles!!"

"*Krururu...*," crooned a lonely voice. Amayori was concerned about its master.

Alice the Integrity Knight managed her best attempt at a smile and whispered, "It's all right. Don't be worried."

But as a matter of fact, she was not all right at all. Her vision was strangely warped, her breathing ragged, and her limbs felt as cold as ice. She might pass out at any moment.

It was not the massive sacred art that Alice had been weaving since before the fighting started—and that even now placed so much pressure on her insides that she felt as if she might explode—that had her so fatigued.

It was the source of the sacred power that the art itself was consuming: all those deaths.

Knights. Guards. Priests. And the enemies: goblins, orcs, giants. So many lives being lost at such an astounding speed—and the fear, sadness, and despair they felt in those final moments all plagued Alice without end.

The old Alice would never have paid any heed to the lives or deaths of the common people of the Human Empire, much less of any who lived in the Dark Territory.

Through half a year of living in Rulid, she understood the divinity of the humble lives of the villagers and realized that it was worth protecting, but she did not find herself caring about the lives of those who dwelled in the dark world. In fact, when the goblins and orcs had attacked Rulid just ten days ago, Alice had slaughtered them without hesitation.

The forces of darkness were pillagers without mercy or compassion and ought to be killed to the very last one, she had always believed without a shred of doubt, until the mission Bercouli had given her.

To her shock…

…the sacred power that arose from the spilled lives of the soldiers on either side of the battlefield below, whether human or nonhuman, was of the exact same nature. They were all warm and vivid and pure, and it was absolutely impossible for her to distinguish which side either of these souls fought on.

At first it shook Alice to her core. But if the people of the human realm and the monsters of the Dark Territory had, in essence, the same souls and differed only in which side of the mountains they were born on…

…then why were they fighting in the first place? *Why are* we *fighting in the first place?*

"…Kirito. If you are still alive and well…"

You might have found another way, she did not say aloud. She had to focus on the sacred art she was still preparing.

At the military council before the battle, Alice had expressed her reservations to Vice Commander Fanatio. Who would actually perform such a massive sacred art that it would devour all the spatial resources that existed within the battlefield—narrow for a ravine but a vast space nonetheless?

Fanatio looked Alice right in the eyes and said, *It is you, Alice Synthesis Thirty. You might not realize it yet, but your present power surpasses the bounds of the Integrity Knight itself. I believe that you are capable of true godly power that splits the heavens and tears the earth asunder.*

At the time, she thought it was an exaggeration, a misunderstanding. But she also felt, in that moment, that it was a duty she needed to give her own life to fulfill, if need be. It was her responsibility, for having turned her sword on the pontifex and shaken the Axiom Church's very power structure.

She stopped thinking about this and tried to focus on nothing but gathering the necessary sacred power and converting it to the sacred words that would further weave the great art.

But the screams never stopped echoing across the ravine, and Alice could not prevent them from affecting her.

They were dying. Someone's father or brother or sister or child.

…*Hurry,* a voice said from deep within her consciousness.

If only that moment would come even a second sooner. The

moment that would invite many times more death, all in one awful instance, to bring this entire atrocity to an end that much sooner…

The nonhuman first wave of the invading army, consisting of mountain goblins, flatland goblins, and giants, was holding fast just one tiny step short of absolute defeat.

The three leaders had died in battle. That meant the knights commanding the enemy force were stronger than any individual among the nonhuman division. And the one rule carved into the souls of the Dark Territory's inhabitants was "the one who is mightiest rules."

If this had been a fight between demi-humans, all of the soldiers would have surrendered completely the moment that their commanders had been struck down. The only thing preventing that outcome now was the existence of Emperor Vecta, the god of darkness, who stepped onto the soil of the Dark Territory in person. The emperor was stronger than any of the ten lords, and it had not yet been determined whether he or the knights of the human realm were stronger.

So they had to stay fixated on their original orders and fight desperately against the guardian army, which was growing bolder with rising morale. The few minutes this ill-fated conflict bought allowed the Dark Territory's secret long-range weapon—the ogre archers and Dee's dark mage brigade—to move into position just short of the collapsed gate.

The plan called for the three thousand ogres to ready their huge war bows in the front, with the three thousand dark mages chanting their attack arts from the rear. It would be not ogre chief Furgr who took overall command but an archmage who also served as Dee's associate.

This mage listened for the orders from the rear and then shouted, "Ogres, prepare to loose greatbows! Mages, begin chanting the command for the wide-range incineration projectiles!! Spotters, begin chanting the command to guide projectiles toward the location of the enemy Integrity Knights!!"

The "wide-range incineration projectiles" were a large-scale eradication art that Dee Eye Ell had designed specifically for this battle. It involved converting all the spatial dark power filling the battlefield into heat elements that could be transferred to the ogres' arrows for extra-long-range attacks.

Because transforming commands like Bird Shape and Arrow Shape did not consume extra dark power, their potency upon landing should be nearly unfathomable. These were the kinds of unprecedented attack arts that were possible only now and not during the Age of Blood and Iron, because all the races were united under Emperor Vecta's rule.

Dee also ordered mages skilled in wielding wind elements to serve as spotters keeping track of the Integrity Knights on the other side. They would set up a "wind path" that would allow for precise aiming at those distant targets. If all of the incineration projectiles landed in one spot, it would result in an ultra-high-priority attack that even the great Administrator would not have been able to defend against without coming to severe harm.

It was that very use of the crude power of numbers to triumph over the power of a great individual that Cardinal the little sage had been so worried about.

Amayori gurgled again. However, this time it was not a worried croon but a sharper sound, wary and full of warning.

Alice summoned her wits, whipping her dazed mind back into shape, and gazed through the darkness to the far distance ahead.

Here they come!!

Beyond the nonhuman enemies, which still fought with the guardian army below, a new army was approaching with care.

She did not see the glint of any metallic armor. This would likely be a long-range regiment—the dark mages guild of the Dark Territory.

They were the ones Bercouli was most careful about, the ones with the potential power to wipe out the entire Human Guardian Army. But the same could be said about Alice herself.

The genesis of the large-scale sacred art she had been preparing this entire time had been an idea from the fight between Vice Commander Fanatio and Kirito, as it was told to others. It might as well be called a "reflective cohesion beam" art.

Using the spatial sacred power released by the countless lives that had been lost in this battle, Alice first generated an enormous glass ball measuring three mels across by transforming crystal elements.

Next, she built a thick silver film out of steel elements and covered the entirety of the glass sphere with it. This created a "locked mirror," as she thought of it. The sphere was kept in a little hollow in Amayori's back, right between its wings. Alice kept her hands pressed to it, locking in the light elements that she continually created with the endless flow of spatial power.

Maintaining elements was a basic but incredibly powerful technique that had tormented greater-arts wielders for generations.

If you didn't keep your focus on whatever flame or ice or wind element you generated, the orbs would float freely, eventually expending the heat or chill they contained, and vanish. The upper limit of elements that could be simultaneously maintained was locked to the number of "terminals" the caster could use—meaning the number of fingers on their hands.

Prime Senator Chudelkin had utilized his unique body type to do a headstand that allowed him to use his toes as output points as well, so he could maintain twenty elements at once. And through some technique known only to her, Administrator had turned her own silver hair into endings, enabling her to maintain over a hundred elements all at once.

But Alice could mimic neither of these things. And neither

ten nor a hundred were even close to enough in this situation. The enemy's dark mages guild boasted three thousand members; assuming each one averaged five elements at once, that meant there would likely be over fifteen thousand in total.

So Alice had tried to come up with a method that would allow her to save the elements she generated, even after letting them drift away from her mind's control. The first idea she'd had was some kind of container. The problem was that the heat and ice elements used in typical attack arts simply affected the temperature of whatever they touched, and then they disappeared.

But in the fight on the fiftieth floor of Central Cathedral, Kirito had used a mirror he'd fashioned from a few steel elements and crystal elements to reflect the light of Fanatio's Heaven-Piercing Blade. When Alice heard that story, she had a flash of inspiration.

If light simply reflected off a mirror, rather than affecting it in any way, and if she could create a mirror that was perfectly closed with no exits and she could generate light elements inside it…

…theoretically, until the life of the mirror itself ran out, she could maintain an infinite number of light elements inside it.

The mighty ogres pulled their great creaking bowstrings and pointed them at the dark sky. Three thousand dark mages raised their hands high, uttering the command that would infuse the rows of gleaming, pointed arrowheads with the power of flame.

""""System Call!!""""

It was a chorus of death, delivered exclusively by female voices. Intoxicated by the sheer size of the power they were channeling, the many mages continued in tandem with """"Generate Thermal Element!!""""

Long, slender fingers blinked with faint red points—but the color promptly dimmed and snuffed out with tiny puffs of smoke.

The archmage in command of the brigade could not tell what

had just happened at first, and she issued the same command again. But the results were the same, to her bafflement.

Then her mages, taken aback, began to shout, "I can't generate the flame elements!"

"It's not going to be possible to execute the wide-range-incineration-projectile art like this!"

She looked around for the source of the phenomenon and heard the aide murmur into her ear, "Ar-Archmage...I think that the spatial dark power might be entirely spent..."

"Th-that cannot be true!!" the commanding officer shouted. Her left hand, knotted with rings, pointed to the front line far in the distance. "Don't you hear the screams?! Everyone is dying there—humans and nonhumans alike! Where could all those lives be going, then?!"

Nobody could answer her question. The ogres were irritated that the order to shoot their arrows was not forthcoming, but they held their strings regardless.

The time had come.

Alice closed her eyes briefly and prayed.

She would accept upon her own shoulders the sin of taking countless lives for the sake of just one.

The silver sphere three mels across resting on Amayori's powerful back was as packed and pressured as it could be on the inside. She pulled her hands off the surface and drew her sword.

"Bloom, my flowers! Enhance Armament!" she called, splitting the Osmanthus Blade into countless tiny pieces, a golden swarm that she could control. "Lower your head, Amayori!"

The dragon obeyed, inclining its body forward. The silver ball rolled silently forth, and by the time it had rotated one full time, it passed the dragon's head and plunged into the void. The little swarm formed by Alice's weapon carefully caught it, cradling the ball and adjusting it so that a particular spot on its surface pointed forward and down.

Aim...steady.

She inhaled until her lungs were full, and she whispered, "...Burst Element."

It was such a short and simple activation for a sacred art that contained such tremendous power.

The silver sphere was fashioned to be thinner in just one spot. The searing luminosity and heat of unlimited light elements focused on that point, melting the layers of silver and glass until they were bright red...

Pow! It burst forth into the outer world.

Fanatio stood in mute shock as she looked up from the surface of the earth at a light beam whose power was thousands of times more potent than what the Heaven-Piercing Blade could create with Perfect Weapon Control.

The other knights and guards simply quaked in fear of what they believed to be the power of Solus herself.

A pillar of light five mels across descended from the sky to the earth at ultra-high speed, plunging into the midst of the demi-human soldiers. Then it changed directions, caressing the ground as it continued farther through the ravine.

With the roar of thousands of bells ringing all at once, waves of heat and light billowed throughout the entire breadth of the ravine. Then the space erupted into a pillar of fire nearly as tall as the End Mountains themselves, lighting the entire night sky red.

When she first saw the incredibly vast explosion, so close she could nearly touch it, Dee Eye Ell smiled, thinking that it was the result of her own strategic masterpiece. But shortly after, the smile vanished from her face as the torrid heat exploded out of the ravine and toward her four-wheeled carriage.

The searing wind brought with it the dying screams of all the nonhumans and the dark mages she had worked so hard to raise into a proud combat force.

She stood still with shock as the messenger mage rasped, "Due to an unidentified drought of spatial dark power, our wide-range incineration projectiles failed to generate...then a large-scale attack of unknown detail issued by the enemy eradicated ninety percent of the nonhuman battalion, seventy percent of the ogre archers, and over... thirty percent of the dark mage battalion..."

"An unidentified drought...?!" Dee raged, trembling at last with the anger bubbling up inside her. "The cause is clear! That monstrous spell on the other side devoured every last bit of magical power in the ravine!! But...it's impossible! Even I could not execute such an art...Not even the late pontifex could do such a thing!! Whose work was this?!"

But none of her screaming earned her the answer to that question. How would she salvage this quandary—and more importantly, how would she report this to Emperor Vecta? Dee Eye Ell was considered to have the sharpest mind in the dark realm, but all she could do now was breathe, rapidly and raggedly.

The blowback from that impossibly huge art and the destruction that it wreaked worked together to crush Alice. As soon as the Osmanthus Blade had returned to her sheath, she crumpled onto Amayori's back.

The dragon gently cushioned her body, slowly descending in a spiral motion toward the front line of the Human Guardian Army. The first to run to the dragon was Vice Commander Fanatio. Her outstretched arms caught Alice as she slid from the dragon's back.

"...That was incredible spellwork and Incarnation, Alice," Fanatio said, overcome with emotion. Alice's eyelids rose, giving her a glimpse of the burning red floor of the ravine and the figures of enemy soldiers fleeing in uncontrolled panic. She couldn't see any bodies, even. Either the initial burst of light had evaporated them instantly, or the explosion had scattered them to pieces.

The sight of such merciless destruction and carnage did not fill her with pride, but soon there came a swelling roar of cheers from the soldiers around her. Individual voices blended and morphed into one great exultation of triumph, repeated over and over.

Praise for the Integrity Knights and the Axiom Church ringing in her ears, Alice finally let out the breath she'd been holding and straightened herself up with Fanatio's help. The vice commander gave her a sympathetic smile and dipped her head.

"The enemy has retreated. You guided us to victory."

Alice smiled back at her, then said severely, "The battle is not yet over, Fanatio. We must consume the sacred power created by that attack for healing arts, lest the enemy reuse it against us."

"You're right...The dark knights and pugilists that make up the core of their army are still in pristine shape," said the beautiful dark-haired woman, though her voice did sound tired. "In that case, everyone on their feet currently, take the wounded and withdraw toward the Second Regiment! All priests and those guardsmen with knowledge of healing arts, focus on curing the wounded as best you can until the power dries up! And keep an eye on the enemy in the meanwhile!"

The guards scrambled to carry out her order. In the rear, the commands for sacred arts could be heard, one after the other.

"I will report to the commander himself. May I leave this in your hands now?"

Alice nodded, and Fanatio gave her another smile before trotting off. The people cleared out of the area, and soon only Alice and Amayori were present at the front line. She watched the vice commander go, then walked to her dragon and scratched under its chin, purring, "You did very well up there, Amayori. I know it must have been tiring to maintain a stationary position for so long. Go back to your bed and eat your fill."

The dragon trilled excitedly, then flapped its wings and rose into the air until it could glide back to its own kind at the rear of the camp.

Alice had just taken her very first step toward aiding the injured when she heard a voice.

".........Mentor."

It was low and soft and belonged to Eldrie.

She turned around to offer encouragement and praise to her only disciple and saw the young man, who was always so carefree and saucy, in a dreadful state. The sword in his right hand and the whip in his left were dyed black with thick dried blood. On top of that, his shining armor and lustrous, curled lilac hair were splattered and hideous. How hard did one have to fight to end up looking like this?

"E...Eldrie! Are you hurt?!" she asked, holding her breath.

With a vacant expression, he shook his head. "No...I did not take any major wounds. But...I ought to have lost my life in the midst of battle..."

"Why would you say that? You have a duty to lead the men-at-arms and fight to the very end of this battle..."

"I could not achieve my duty," the young Integrity Knight murmured, his voice cracking.

What Alice did not know was that after Eldrie had allowed the mountain goblins to slip past the defensive line with their smoke-screen strategy, he'd spent several minutes fruitlessly attempting to clear the smoke without sacred arts, until he'd finally taken his guards and chased after the goblins that had gotten behind them.

But by that point, Chief Kosogi of the goblins had already been defeated by Renly, who was generally known to be a failure of a knight. His chance at regaining face after this failure lost, Eldrie's cool slipped away from him, and he began slaughtering fleeing goblins one after the other. When he stared up into the sky at Alice's godly display, he was already splattered in fresh blood.

"I betrayed…your expectations of me…" He returned the Frostscale Whip to his side and used the empty hand to cover his face. "So stupid…so miserable…so humiliating…A disgrace of a knight…"

And he had wanted to *protect* his mentor?

With the power of that great sacred art to alter the heavens and earth? She was completely beyond his reach in every way.

He was never necessary. What use would a genius have for a half-assed excuse for a knight like him? He excelled in no area—not sword ability nor sacred power nor Perfect Control—and he couldn't even be counted upon to outsmart a bunch of goblins.

The idea that he could be worthy of her heart…of gaining her love…It was laughable.

"I do not have…the right to call myself your disciple!" spat Eldrie, so fiercely that blood nearly flew from his lungs.

"You…you did so well!" Alice stammered, in a daze. It was all she could bring herself to say.

What had happened to Eldrie? There had been confusion at the front line, but they'd defended against the enemy without too much damage so far.

"…I, the guardian army, and the people of the realm need you. Why would you berate yourself so fiercely?" she asked, trying to keep her voice as calm and soothing as possible, but the darkness did not leave Eldrie's eyes. His blood-flecked cheeks twitched, and his voice was barely audible to her ears.

"Need…as a source of power in battle? Or……?"

He did not finish that question. An alien growl rolled through the air at that moment, drawing Alice's and Eldrie's attention.

"Frrrhh…"

It was wet and throaty, like a wolf's warning signal. Alice's eyes were wide and alert as she stared into the darkness down the ravine. The smoldering flames here and there in the valley cast light on some huge shape standing ahead.

It was not human. The lower extremities were folded at an odd angle, the waist was extraordinarily long, and the torso was powerful but slouching forward. The head atop its shoulders was nearly indistinguishable from a wolf. This was the last remaining demi-human race of the Dark Territory, the ogre.

Alice had her hand on the pommel of her sword already, but she noticed that the ogre was unarmed. In fact, the left half of its body was badly burned, even smoking slightly. The burning light attack was responsible for these wounds. But why didn't it flee along with its surviving companions?

She glanced around to see that the other soldiers were all in the back, and only she and Eldrie stood at the front now. Wary of the ogre's movements, Alice asked sharply, "Your life must be nearly down to nothing. Why do you stand there without a weapon?"

The demi-human growled miserably. "*Grrr...*I am...ogre chief, Furgr..." Its long tongue hung out of its open mouth as it panted.

Alice squeezed harder on her sword. If it was chief of the ogres, it was one of the ten dark lords, among the highest rank of the enemy army. It must be expending its last bit of strength to attack.

But the ogre's next words took her aback.

"I...saw. You created...spell of, light. That power...that look... You are Priestess of Light. *Grrr...*If I...take you...war will end. Ogres return...to the plains..."

What...is it saying? Priestess of Light? The war will end...?

It didn't make sense to Alice, but she could tell she was on the verge of obtaining some extremely important information. She had to find out more. What was the Priestess of Light? Where was she to be taken?

But the moment the ogre's words halted, she heard a voice scream, "Why, you...overgrown beast!!"

It was Eldrie. His bloody sword was high overhead, then swooping downward directly toward the ogre chief.

But it did not finish its swing.

Alice leaped so quickly, she practically teleported, pinching the edge of Eldrie's blade between her fingertips and using all her strength to stop his momentum.

"M-Mentor...why?!" he gasped, falling to his knee, but she couldn't take the time to explain it to him. She let go of the sword and turned, approaching the still ogre.

Up close, she could see that the creature's wounds were not just deep, but mortal. It was charred black from its left arm to its chest, and its left eyeball was cloudy. Alice sensed that its consciousness itself was hazy, but she asked her questions anyway.

"Indeed...I am the Priestess of Light. Now, where are you taking me? Who is it that seeks me?"

"*...Grrr...*" The ogre's good eye shone. Blood-flecked spittle ran down its long tongue. "...Emperor...Vecta...said. Only wants... Priestess of Light. Grab priestess...deliverer's wish...comes true. Ogres...return to plains...keep horses...hunt birds...live......"

Emperor Vecta.

The name of the god of darkness, as he was known in the human lands. And that figure was now present in the Dark Territory? And he had started this war for the purpose of gaining this "Priestess of Light" that he wanted?

Alice committed these details to memory as she favored the creature that stood before her with a look of compassion. None of the stink of greed and desire found wafting off the goblins exuded from this wolf-headed warrior. It merely took part in the war as commanded and pulled back its bowstring—and nearly all its people had died out before they could even loose their arrows.

"...Don't you despise me? I was the one who slaughtered your people," Alice said. She couldn't help it, even knowing that nothing would come of it.

The ogre's answer was simple: "The strong...bear as much...as they have strength. I, too...bear chief's duty. So...I capture you... and take...to......!"

Grrrooooo!!

The ogre suddenly bayed ferociously. Its powerful right arm lunged for Alice, quicker than the eye could follow.

Ting.

It was the briefest of sounds: the Osmanthus Blade's hilt hitting the sheath. Alice had drawn it, slashed, and returned it to its scabbard at several times the speed of even the ogre's attack.

The creature's large body froze.

Alice took a step back, and the ogre slowly sank to the ground. There was a fresh bloody line across its burly chest, from which the last bits of its life spilled out as pale dots of light. She reached toward the body of the proud wolf-headed warrior, stopping the sacred power that floated up from it and creating a number of wind elements.

"Let your soul travel across the plains, at least..."

She swept her hand aside, turning the formation of green lights into a little whirlwind that rose up and up into the eastern sky.

4

As her forehead scraped the floor of the dragon tank in obeisance, Dee trembled inwardly at the gaze of Emperor Vecta upon her back.

There was no anger in his ice-blue eyes. He was measuring her value without emotion of any kind. What kind of action would the emperor take against her if he found her to be without skill or use to him? The thought made her very bones shiver.

After an agonizing wait, his deep, smooth voice said, "Hmm. So the failure of your plan and the death of a thousand dark mages were because the enemy absorbed and used the spatial dark power before we could…you say?"

"Y…yes!" she stammered, lifting her face just the tiniest bit. "That is correct, Your Majesty. We had no knowledge that suggested the enemy had a caster so powerful after the pontifex, so…"

"And there is no means of replenishing that power?" he asked, interrupting her excuse. But she could not give him a satisfactory response to that question, either.

"I…I'm afraid…that we will need rich land and ample sunlight to replenish enough spatial dark power to eliminate the enemy Integrity Knights, neither of which is in good supply here. The treasury at Obsidia Palace would have glimstones that can be converted into power, but we would need days to retrieve them now..."

"I see," the emperor said simply, then turned his sharp features toward the distant ravine. "But from what I can see...there are no plants on the land here, and the sun has already set. What source of power were you going to use for this large-scale magic art of yours?"

Dee was in such mortal terror that she never registered how strange it was for Vecta, god of darkness and supposed founder of the dark arts, to ask her such a fundamental question about its workings. It was only the desperate drive for self-preservation that helped her answer the question.

"Well, Majesty, this is a battlefield...so the blood and life shed by the demi-humans and the enemy soldiers becomes dark power that fills the air around them."

"Uh...huh." The emperor stood up from his makeshift throne. Dee's entire body went rigid.

His black leather boots approached, clicking on the floor. She felt terror clenching her guts. The emperor stopped just to the left of Dee, fur cape waving in the wind, and murmured into the night.

"Blood...and life."

"Priestess of Light...?" Commander Bercouli muttered, broad jaw working as he chewed on a flat pastry cooked with dried fruit and nuts.

They used the momentary lull in fighting to rush out some rations from the supply team to the soldiers on the guardian army side. The healing of the wounded was done for now, and thanks to the help of the Integrity Knights, who had considerable healing skill themselves, even the warriors who'd been at death's door were in good enough shape to sit up and sip bowls of soup.

Of course, the dead would never return. Of the two-thousand-plus that had made up the First Regiment, nearly a hundred and fifty soldiers and one lower knight had perished.

Sitting across the folding table from the leader of the knights, Alice said, "Yes. I don't recall that name showing up in any of the history texts, but it seems clear that the enemy commander strongly desires this person."

"Commander...meaning Vecta, god of darkness," Bercouli grunted.

Fanatio poured siral water into his cup and added, "It's very difficult to believe...a god, coming back to walk among us..."

"I suppose so. But some of it does make sense. I know that you, too, must have felt the eerie Incarnation that hangs over the enemy camp."

"Yes...I do sense a chill that seems to suck away the warmth from my bones..."

"For the first time since the creation of the world, there is no Eastern Gate standing there. Perhaps we should understand that anything is possible now. But, Little Miss," he said, staring right at Alice with great intent, "if we presume that Vecta himself has appeared in the Dark Territory, that he wants this 'Priestess of Light,' and that priestess is you—the question is, how does that affect the current status of the battle?"

Indeed. That was the real question. Even if Vecta was satisfied with gaining control of the priestess, the other races of darkness would surely continue their pillaging after that. It did nothing to change the fact that they *must* protect this ravine to the death.

But there was another term that had stuck itself in Alice's brain and refused to leave.

World's End Altar.

It was something the "god of the outer world" had said in conversation with Kirito through the crystal panel, in the aftermath of the battle at the top of Central Cathedral half a year ago.

Head for the World's End Altar. Leave the Eastern Gate and head far to the south.

If she went there, she might be able to bring Kirito's mind back. Yet, no matter how much she might wish to make that happen, she couldn't abandon the defense of the gate.

But what if they chase after me?

What if she went through the gate and Vecta and his armies chased behind her, the Priestess of Light? It might even draw the enemy away from the human world and buy the guardian army enough time to fortify its defenses.

Alice chose to keep the vague topic of the altar a secret for now. She reported crisply to the supreme officer of the guardian army, "Uncle...Lord Bercouli. I will go along, break through the enemy ranks, and head to the distant reaches of the Dark Territory. If the ringleader of the enemy desires the 'Priestess of Light,' he will pursue me with at least some of his troops. Once I've gained some distance and split their forces, strike back at the remaining army and wipe them out."

In a dry voice devoid of all emotion, Emperor Vecta asked, "Dee Eye Ell, would three thousand suffice?"

"Huh...?"

She lifted her head again, uncertain of his meaning. In profile, the emperor's face was smooth, even peaceful, but the way his pale-blue eyes stared down at the armies below filled her veins with ice.

"In order to have the dark power needed to reenact the large-scale dark art that will eliminate the enemy Integrity Knights," he elaborated, "would three thousand lives of that secondary orc battalion suffice?"

Even Dee, who was cruel by the measure of her peers, gaped at this suggestion. A chill crawled up her legs. Fear struck deep.

But as the idea sank into Dee's mind, it all turned to sweet intoxication. "It will be enough." She pressed her forehead to the emperor's boot before she realized what she was doing.

"It will be enough, indeed, Your Majesty. The remaining two thousand mages will pool their efforts to make it happen...The dark mages guild will perform the greatest and most powerful act of terror that anyone has ever seen..."

Whether on the human or the dark side, the Underworld's inhabitants' names did not possess any inherent meaning as defined by their language.

This had happened because the four Rath engineers who'd raised the original artificial fluctlights had not considered the concept of their names too deeply. They'd simply picked out foreign-sounding "fantasy" names and given them to the children and grandchildren under their care.

After the four creators had logged out, the fluctlights continued having children on their own and naturally had to raise them. The first problem that plagued them was the lack of an established naming rule.

Without a better choice, the first parents gave their children meaningless phoneme combinations that were similar to their own. But as time went on and generations passed, eventually there came to be a system for naming, until it evolved into what you might call the Underworld's own unique "naming arts."

In short, each of the individual sounds derived from their names were given meanings, and the combinations that resulted were a way of wishing for that child's future growth.

Specifically, the open vowels meant sincerity. The hard *K* sound indicated liveliness. *S* meant quick-witted. *T* stood for good health. *N* meant generosity. *L* and *R* were markers of beauty, and so on. So as an example, Eugeo was given his name in the hopes that he would be gentle, hardworking, and honest. Tiese was given her name in the hopes that she would be lively, caring, and skilled in the ways of combat. Ronie was cute and empathetic and serious.

Most of these naming arts were shared with the demi-humans of the Dark Territory. Sigurosig, for example, stood for agility, ferocity, fearlessness, and then more agility and ferocity for good measure. Only the highly prolific goblins were an exception, basing many of their names on the roots of Japanese verbs for pillaging, slicing, chopping, and other such menacing activities. The elite families of dark mages, too, saw these naming arts as inferior customs and traditionally took only capital letters from the ancient dark tongue.

As for the chief of the orcs—the final survivor of the nonhuman races' leaders as of the start of the battle—his given name was Lilpilin.

Lilpilin was known, along with the leaders of the dark mages and the goblins, as one of the greatest impediments to the possibility of achieving peace with the human realm, according to Dark General Shasta, owing to his ferocious hostility toward humans as a whole.

But this was not an innate hatred from birth.

When Lilpilin was born to a powerful orc clan, he was praised as the most beautiful baby in the clan's history. They gave him a name with three *L* sounds in it to indicate beauty—a great rarity for an orc.

As his parents wished, Lilpilin grew into a youngling of considerable beauty in both body and mind. He was blessed with skill in battle, and hopes were high for him to become the future chief. One day, he assisted the clan leader at the time on his first-ever trip out of the orcs' marshland domain in the southeast to pay a visit to Obsidia Palace.

When he entered the castle town, back arched with the pride he took in his gleaming armor and sword, Lilpilin saw the thin bodies, lustrous hair, and comely features of the humans who lived there.

It came as an earthshaking revelation to Lilpilin that his own beauty would forever have the phrase "for an orc" appended to the end of it. On this day, he learned that the orcs were mocked by the rest of the dark realm as the ugliest of its races.

A rounded gut, short legs, a huge and flat-ended nose, squashed little eyes, and drooping ears—the only reason other orcs called Lilpilin beautiful for these features was that his face was just barely more human in appearance than theirs.

Lilpilin's soul very nearly reached its breaking point. The only way he could maintain his functioning mind was to cling to one blistering emotion.

It was hostility. The brutal and fierce determination to destroy and enslave all of humanity, crushing all their eyes so they could never again mock orcs for being ugly, was the force that drove Lilpilin into the position of chief.

So he did not have the innate cruelty of someone like Kosogi. His hatred of humanity was simply an imprint of his massive inferiority complex. To his own people, he was a wise and benevolent leader.

"Dis...dis is unfeah!!" shouted Lilpilin when he heard the emperor's orders.

The orcs had already sent a thousand of their number as supplementary troops in the first group, nearly all of whom had been lost. He'd already felt his heart being crushed by the knowledge that his people had fought and died under the orders of goblins and giants, removed from his command. But this order was simply beyond the pale in its cruelty.

Offer three thousand sacrifices to be the cornerstone of the dark mages' attack spell.

It was a death that offered no recognition of a warrior's honor or respect for the wise. They were simply fuel or meat—no different from the long-haired cattle that the provisions troop brought along as a food supply.

"We came heah to fight! Ouwah lives awe not da pwice foh yoh failyah!" Lilpilin argued, his nasal voice high-pitched and strained.

But Chancellor Dee of the dark mages merely stared at the orc with cold eyes and folded arms. She said, "This is by the edict of the emperor!!"

With a grunt, the orc chief's words stuck in his throat. Emperor Vecta's power had been made explicitly clear during the dark general's attempted betrayal. He was almighty, far outclassing any of the Council of Ten.

And the strong must be obeyed. It was the ironclad rule of the land of darkness.

But— But…

Lilpilin stood there, clenched fists trembling. Behind him, a voice that was smoother than usual for an orc said, "Chieftain, we have no choice but to follow da empewah's odahs."

He turned around with a start and saw a female orc who had a comparatively slender build and elegantly long ears. She was from a clan that was distantly related to Lilpilin's, and they had spent time together as children.

With a gentle, comforting smile, she said, "Me and my twee tousand twoops would gladly give up owah lives. Foh da empewah… and foh owah people."

"……"

Speechless, Lilpilin could only gnash his long tusks so hard they nearly broke. The woman stepped closer and whispered, "Lil, I still believe dat it is not just da humans, but also orc souls dat awe summoned to Heaven afta death. We…we can meet again in dat holy place."

He wanted to tell her that she didn't have to give up her life, too. But he also knew that if three thousand soldiers were to accept an unfair order, it would be easier done if they knew their fates were shared by their princess knight, whom they held in a certain esteem even higher than their chieftain.

Lilpilin unclenched his fists, took her hand, and groaned, "I apologize, Len…fohgive me…Fohgive me…"

Dee Eye Ell stared down at the two in obvious disgust. "Pack your three thousand troops together in close formation, a hundred mels before the ravine, within five minutes. That is all!" she ordered.

The orc chief glared at the departing dark mage with burning, squinted eyes. Why did they have to undergo this fate just because they were orcs? It was a question he had asked himself many times, but as usual, no answer was forthcoming.

As three thousand troops lined up, orderly, and marched toward certain death, there was even a kind of pride among them. But from the remaining seven thousand who watched them go came the low rumbling of sobs and comments of loathing.

The princess knight astride her armored boar led the three thousand proudly past the dark knights and pugilists, then arranged their formation a bit before the entrance to the ravine where the battle was taking place.

Almost impatiently, the two thousand dark mages who weren't enveloped in the earlier blast made their ominous appearance and started making a formation. Their chanting, in reflecting the horror of its intended content, set the atmosphere on edge with hideous discordance.

"Aa...aaah...," Lilpilin croaked. The orcs suddenly began to writhe in apparent agony and collapsed to the ground. As they flopped and struggled, little white twinkling lights emerged from their bodies, sucked out by some invisible pressure. As they flew toward the mages' hands, the lights turned black and bunched together, growing sticky and clumping until they took a shape like some eerie, unnatural serpent.

The screams of three thousand soldiers stabbed at Lilpilin's ears, sharp and vivid. He could make out the words, too.

Long live the orcs. Glory to the orcs.

Their bodies began to burst in quick succession. As the blood and flesh went splattering in all directions, the light gushed out of them in great quantities, traveling toward the mages.

Before he knew it, Lilpilin was on his knees, slamming his fist against the ground. The tears that flowed from his eyes trailed down either side of his large nose before falling to the black gravel.

Through stained vision, he watched as the princess knight in her especially conspicuous armor issued blood from all over her body like the petals of a crimson flower.

"......Lenju......!" he gasped as the princess knight slowly toppled toward the ground and out of sight. His jaws clenched so hard that the fangs burst through his lips, dripping blood of his own.

Humans.

Humans!

Damnable humans!!

With each internal scream of fury and loathing, the orc felt his right eye pulse.

Less than twenty minutes earlier, at the camp of the Human Guardian Army, the soldiers who'd been separated into two groups had shared warm handshakes and embraces at their safe reunion.

After the announcement from Alice, Commander Bercouli added a decision of his own. He ordered that the so-called Priestess of Light, Alice, be given half of their number when she diverted the enemy's attention. Alice was strongly against this, of course, and insisted that she would act alone, but the leader of the Integrity Knights would have none of it.

We still have plenty of reinforcements. If you're the only one acting as bait, Little Miss, there won't be many enemies going after ya. Only if you've got a good number with you can the strategy to split up the forces actually work.

She had no rebuttal to that. There was no denying that it was a huge stretch, claiming that she, on her own, would lure the entire enemy army away, based on nothing more than some vague information from the chief of the ogres.

Plus, Alice wanted to take Kirito on Amayori's back with her. Admittedly, she was uncertain about being able to protect both

herself and him against the enemy army. So the idea of military cohorts was reassuring.

When Bercouli announced his splitting of the guardian army, he had another surprise in store. He decided that he, the overall commander of the army, would join the decoy team.

Fanatio and Deusolbert, who were designated the commanding officers of the remaining portion of the army, were vehemently against the idea.

"Hey, you've done enough in this battle already. Gimme a chance to fight, too," Bercouli argued. Fanatio's eyes screwed up in frustration as she said, "You can barely fold your own clothes without me there at your side!!"

That one got a big jeer from the knights and guardsmen who heard it. Bercouli grimaced, leaned over to Fanatio, and whispered something into her ear—and surprisingly enough, the vice commander looked away and backed down.

As for Deusolbert, he had to accept the inevitable, especially when it was pointed out that he had fought to the point of exhausting his arrows earlier. A supply team was heading for the nearest town to get more, but this would take longer than an hour or two.

Concern and nerves were in abundant supply among the soldiers of both the advancing team and the remaining team. In fact, it wasn't clear which assignment posed more danger. How much of the enemy army would pursue the decoy team, and how much would continue attacking the ravine? Only God knew—specifically, Vecta, the god of darkness, commander of the enemy forces.

Eventually, the decoy force was complete: Bercouli, Alice, Renly, Sheyta, the four elite knights' dragons, a thousand guardsmen, two hundred priests, and a fifty-member supply team. Eldrie insisted on joining the decoy team, backing down only after Alice scolded him. The apprentice knights Linel and Fizel threw a fit as well, but when the commander told them to hold down the fort, they didn't have much choice but to accept his order.

To carry their supplies, they set up eight high-mobility four-horse carriages. One of them would contain Kirito in his wheelchair and the two young trainees.

Alice was very conflicted about the idea of allowing Tiese and Ronie to come along. But she would need someone to look after Kirito, and whatever it was that had happened between them, Renly the elite Integrity Knight now insisted that he would protect the girls with his life.

In all honesty, Alice had few memories of Renly. But the determination in his young face and the impressive shine of the Double-Winged Blades on either hip suggested that he was the real deal.

Bercouli's dragon, Hoshigami, began its heavy running start to prepare for flight, giving way to a muted cheer from the guards on the ground. As Alice waited for her turn, clutching Amayori's reins, she looked back to Eldrie below.

Her loquacious disciple had been quiet as she'd prepared to leave, a fact that gnawed at her. But before she could think of something to say, Hoshigami took off into the air. She had to look ahead and gave Amayori's sides a gentle kick. Her dragon mount ran powerfully across the ground and floated up into the air, followed by Renly on Kazenui, and Sheyta on Yoiyobi.

Bercouli, flying slowly up ahead, turned back and shouted, "When we leave the ravine, we use the dragons' breath against the enemy's main force! They should have almost nothing left in the way of long-range attacks, but keep an eye out for their dragon knights!"

She gave him a crisp affirmative response. The sound of the soldiers pursuing them on horseback and foot were audible over her shoulder. When they and the carriage group left the ravine, they would head south, to their right, and it was up to the four knights on their dragons to keep the battle lively and distracted until the ground troops had put good distance behind them.

A multitude of campfires burned in the land beyond the dark, narrow ravine.

There were so many. They had eliminated a ton of enemy soldiers, yet there must have been close to thirty thousand left. But the bulk of that power was concentrated in dark knights and pugilists, both of which were close-range units and had no effective means of attacking airborne Integrity Knights.

No, wait... What is this?

There was a chanting in the air, audible beneath the whistling of the wind, roiling and low.

A...group chant? Of a sacred art command?

Impossible! Alice balked against her own instincts. *There isn't enough sacred power left to carry out any kind of large-scale attack art!!*

But then Bercouli, who was flying ahead of her, gasped, "I...I can't believe what they've done!!"

Ohhh.

What incredible power!!

Dee Eye Ell, chancellor of the dark mages guild, hands outstretched to the sky, shivered in ecstasy.

Had any mage in history ever experienced such rich, saturated dark power as this? The life of intelligent beings was the purest and most potent source of power in the world—even the life of something as low and ugly as an orc. If this potency of power was like fine wine aged a hundred years, then the dark power that came from sunlight and the earth was no more than water.

What they had tried to consume for the wide-range incineration projectiles before had been merely the dregs of the lives expended in battle. But this, now, was power directly and freshly converted from three thousand lives through sorcery.

The misty black substance gathered around the extended hands of Dee and her two thousand cohorts, forming a number of hideous long insects, each with countless writhing legs. They were simulacrums of life, things generated from darkness elements, and were called life-eaters. Nothing with physical form, not even the highest-priority swords and armor, could stop them. It was a less-efficient form of conversion from darkness than fire attacks were, but that didn't matter when the source of power was so rich.

Dee had chosen this particular art as an intentional counterpoint to the pillar of light that the enemy had used to burn a thousand of her precious followers. At this point, the death screams of tormented orcs were almost music to her ears.

"Ready...?" Dee called out on high. "Prepare to unleash the deathworm curse!!"

But as she stared forward, to her shock, she saw a mad rush of four dragon knights approaching through the ravine. Her alarm promptly turned to joy. Now she would be able to wipe out the Integrity Knights and their dragons, the most powerful piece of the enemy army.

"Don't rush it!! Let them come closer!! ...Closer...closer........ Now! Unleash!!"

Zwaaaah!!

Countless black insects thrummed in horrifying fashion as they leaped straight for the oncoming enemy.

The moment they saw the enemy's spell, that great black wave of horror rushing toward them, both the civilian men-at-arms and even the elite Integrity Knights found themselves unable to think for entire seconds at a time.

It was a dark art of an ultra-high priority, even higher than Alice's earlier light attack. A long-range curse art that was impossible to physically defend against and devoured the target's life directly.

How could they produce a dark art of this incredible scale and density when darkness elements had such inefficient conversion to sacred power, and the entire battlefield was barren of resources to begin with? Only Bercouli was capable of spotting the answer.

But even he could not summon the wits to give an immediate order.

Every kind of offensive art carried certain values: its source element, density, range, speed, direction, and so on. In order to defend against a sacred art, you needed to cancel out those elements or utilize them to your own ends. You could snuff out flame attacks with ice elements, confuse a tracking art with a decoy, evade a direct-line attack with enough speed—part of what made a high-level caster was the ability to react and respond appropriately without skipping a beat.

But not in this case.

The enemy's attack was simply beyond the pale.

Only light elements could counteract dark elements. But light, too, was difficult to convert from raw power, and they could not generate enough of it to dispel that kind of curse. Fanatio's Memory Release would certainly be able to punch a hole through the enemy's curse, but the Heaven-Piercing Blade's light was far too thin in its effect, and more importantly, she wasn't in the decoy group.

"Invert!! Pull up!!" shouted Bercouli, about the only thing he could do.

Four dragons turned quickly, spiraling around, heading higher right above the ravine. With a terrible rustling of wings, the swarm of snaking creatures turned accordingly.

But then Bercouli shouted, "No!!"

The worms that chased after them were not even half the total. The rest proceeded straight for the guardsmen and the supply team running along the ground.

"...!!" Alice gasped and turned her dragon into a steep dive. She charged straight for the wriggling mass of dark arts in the lead below.

Shing!! She drew the Osmanthus Blade from its sheath. The blade began to glow a golden color.

"Little Miss!! You can't use that one!!" cried Bercouli, trying to stop his favorite apprentice. The Osmanthus Blade's Perfect

Weapon Control art was tremendously powerful in a battle of one against many, but only with sword against metal. It couldn't cut through a curse that had an ethereal body.

Alice was perfectly aware of that. But there was no way that she could sit there and watch the soldiers be attacked.

Just then, a fifth dragon rocketed forth from the ravine like a shooting star.

It was Takiguri—the dragon of elite Integrity Knight Eldrie Synthesis Thirty-One.

As he gripped the dragon's reins, just one word ran through Eldrie's brain.

Protect.

His mentor. His Alice. He must offer his sword to do whatever it took to safeguard the person whose life he had pledged to protect.

But at the same time, he heard a voice mocking him at exactly the same volume:

How will you protect her? A powerless man like you? Inferior in every conceivable way and yet endlessly seeking validation and attention from your mentor.

The thing that supported Eldrie's skill as a new, junior Integrity Knight was the powerful Incarnation that drove him to serve Alice. It was what made him a higher-ranked knight, but it also meant that when he was hit by doubt, it rocked him to his core.

I don't have the strength to protect my teacher Alice, nor the right to stand at her side, he concluded, which caused a rapid loss in power. Swept up by an unpleasant emotion, he leaped onto Takiguri and chased after the decoy group, though he had no idea what he was going to do.

If it came to it, at least he could die here with his mentor.

As he flew, clinging to this last resort, he thought he heard something, and he glanced down at the ground. The guardsmen below had noticed the oncoming dark magic and were beginning to panic. Behind them, the supply team's carriages were fraying apart the same way.

A pale-blue light flickered in one of the carriages, visible through the covered top.

He heard a strange voice in his head.

Your determination—

—your desire to protect—

—needs no payment in return, does it?

Love is not something you ask for. You just give and give and give it, and it never runs out. Isn't that right...?

Ah, man...

What got me so confused?

That I didn't have enough strength? That I couldn't monopolize her feelings? That I wasn't able to protect her?

What tiny, insignificant things...

Lady Alice has been trying to save all of humanity.

Eldrie whipped Takiguri's reins with one hand and shouted, "Go!!"

The dragon beat its wings powerfully, sensing its master's thoughts, and sped up immediately. The instant they passed the plummeting Amayori, Eldrie heard Alice calling for him to stop. But he did not slow down; he pulled the dragon higher, heading straight for the onslaught of worm creatures.

With his free left hand, he removed the platinum whip from his side.

The Frostscale Whip received its holy power from its core: a great snake that had once lived in the mountains of the eastern empire, known as the god-serpent. Unleashing the power of its memory transformed the whip to many times its original length and gave it free control over its own trajectory.

But this power was nearly meaningless against a curse-type sacred art. Even so, Eldrie continued to pray, filled with absolute conviction.

Serpent!

God-serpent of yore!

If you are indeed the king of the snakes, then devour this swarm of wretched worms!!

"Release Recollection!!" he called out, and the Frostscale Whip shone a brilliant silver.

Amid that light, the whip split into countless ends. Hundreds upon hundreds of beams of light lashed out at the squirming black things.

And then the light turned into glowing snakes. The swarm of reptiles fanning outward from Eldrie's hand opened jaws of sharp, glinting fangs and bit down on the deathworms. There was a horrible *zormp* sound, and the first creature to be bitten in two reverted to darkness elements that promptly scattered into nothing.

Abruptly, the swarm that was heading for the guards and the swarm following the airborne dragons changed directions, recognizing the glowing hydra to be their most urgent foe. The snake heads were soon beset by countless writhing worms. The curse traveled up their length, bearing down on the source.

Eldrie was using the one element of the enemy's dark arts that he could affect, its ability of automatic pursuit, to force all of the spell's attention on himself.

Lady Alice...

He grinned and closed his eyes.

The next moment, darkness engulfed him.

The life value of the Integrity Knight Eldrie Synthesis Thirty-One, which was at slightly over five thousand, instantly plummeted to negative five hundred thousand.

The explosion that rippled outward from a centerpoint in his chest tore his body into tiny, fleeting pieces.

⁂

"Eldrieeeeee!!!" screamed Alice.

Her one apprentice, whose time with her had been short but memorable, slid off his dragon's back, missing over half of his body.

Alice turned Amayori around yet again and plunged through the remnants of the vanishing worms, reaching out with her free hand to grab Eldrie's. Her breath caught in her throat when she felt how light he was, but she gritted her teeth and sent the dragon upward anyway.

Takiguri followed right beside them, concerned for its master. As the dragons shot upward in parallel, Alice shouted again, "Eldrie!! Open...open your eyes!! I won't let you leave me! Not like this!!"

Eldrie had nothing left from the chest downward. His pale eyelids fluttered. Underneath his lashes, his purplish irises shone, weak but firm, as he looked at her.

"...Men...tor...you're...safe..."

"Yes...yes, I'm safe, thanks to you! I told you that I needed you!!"

Her vision went blurry. Droplets landed on Eldrie's cheek. Alice held her disciple tight, not even realizing that they were her own tears.

His voice was barely audible in her ear.

"Lady Alice...you are needed...by...so many more people. I was...such a small person...to think...that I could have you...all for...myself..."

"I will give you whatever you want!! Just come back!! You are my disciple!!"

"I've...had...so much already," he whispered, full of satisfaction. She could sense what little weight there was in her arms rapidly beginning to fade.

"Eldrie!! Eldrieeee!!" she wailed.

His final words were gentle yet heavy.

"Don't...cry......Mo.........ther..........."

And so the soul of Eldrie Synthesis Thirty-One the Integrity

Knight, also known as Eldrie Woolsburg, left the Underworld forever.

Through wet eyes, Alice watched the body of her beloved disciple vanish. It turned into a gentle light that illuminated the night and melted into it, as miraculous as the several seconds she was able to talk with him as he lay dying.

Soon Eldrie was entirely gone, without even a trace of armor. Only the Frostscale Whip remained, falling onto Amayori's back limply. Nearby, Takiguri howled sadly as it flew, sensing its master's death.

Alice breathed in the faint scent of roses and lifted her head.

This is a war.

There was no point in taking any of it personally, no matter how the enemy tried to attack or what damages were suffered from it. Just minutes ago, Alice herself had unleashed a mammoth sacred art that had taken the lives of thousands of enemy soldiers; it could not be described as anything but merciless.

So if she took all this anger, this sadness, and channeled it into power that would allow her to slaughter ever more foes…

"…Let it not be said that you were not ready for me!!" Alice drew the Osmanthus Blade and shouted, "Amayori! Takiguri! Charge at full speed!!"

The dragons, who were pressed into service by a binding art, normally refused all battle orders that did not come from their designated rider. But the two dragons, brother and sister, roared ferociously and beat their wings, rushing forward. The outer end of the ravine, where the charcoal Dark Territory stretched as far as the eye could see, grew closer.

Through the burning rage that threatened to blind her, Alice's blue eyes quickly made out the formation of the enemy's main force.

On the left side, about five hundred mels past the exit of the valley, five thousand dark knights stood in their matching metal armor. To the right, another five thousand pugilists, their hardy bodies wrapped in light leather. These two groups were the bulk of the enemy forces.

Behind them were backup units of orc and goblin infantry and a very large supply team. Somewhere in the midst of them would be the enemy's supreme commander: Vecta, the god of darkness.

And right up front, packed between the rows of dark knights and pugilists, was a group cloaked in black.

That was it. They were the dark mages who had set off that massive curse. There were nearly two thousand of them. And now they were fleeing, those who'd noticed the approaching dragons first among them.

"You're going nowhere!!" shouted Alice, who then ordered the dragons, "Aim for their tail…now! Breathe!!"

The siblings craned their necks and opened their jaws wide. The flames that filled their mouths lit white fangs red.

Two parallel pillars of fire tore through the air and hit the ground right where the fleeing mages were attempting to run. There was an earthshaking blast, and a fireball rose from the spot where the flames struck. The figures caught in its midst flew like leaves.

Their escape route blocked by flames, the mages completely lost order and clumped into one place. Alice held the Osmanthus Blade high overhead. Its body shone a yellow gold brighter than the sun itself.

"Enhance Armament!"

With a crisp metallic ring, the sword split into hundreds of tiny shards. Each one reflected Alice's Incarnation and glinted with sharper edges than they'd ever had before.

Impossible. It cannot be!!

Dee Eye Ell, chancellor of the dark mages guild, stared upward at the oncoming dragon knight, a silent scream tearing through her mind.

Two thousand mages had sacrificed three thousand orcs to prepare the deathworm curse, which had set upon the enemy with even more power than she'd anticipated. The deathworms had a high enough priority level that they should've easily devoured both the Integrity Knights and the soldiers on the ground alike.

But somehow, the deathworms that should've devoured the life of *all* the enemy troops had concentrated only on a single knight and spent themselves on one extravagantly wasteful and redundant kill.

Deathworms were drawn to whatever creature had the greatest amount of life. So if you were to guide them, it would require the creation of some artificial life-form greater than any human or dragon, something along the lines of a magical beast out of legend—but there was no way they could've produced such a thing with a short command. There was no logic that explained this outcome. It was simply *illogical.*

How can there possibly be some power that I, Chancellor Dee Eye Ell of the dark mages guild, center of all the knowledge of the world, do not possess?!

Dee gnashed her teeth and let loose a screech that was all air, no voice. Whatever the answer, the enemy had sacrificed just one person and resumed its charge, and it was now unleashing all hell on her remaining two thousand mages.

"Fall back!! All units retreat!!" Dee called out in a high voice.

But that was when two jets of blazing fire passed overhead and rammed into the ground just a few dozen mels behind her. An explosion erupted from that spot, drawing dozens of screams from her subordinates. A heat wave swept over the second floor of her carriage, singeing the black hair she was so proud of.

"Yeeek...!" screamed Dee, practically falling off the carriage. Standing on it was only turning her into a target. She wanted to flee among the crowd of her followers, but then she caught sight of a bright golden light.

Looking up despite herself, she saw an Integrity Knight atop a dragon, her sword splitting apart into many tiny pieces of light. Each one of them, it was clear, held a frightening level of priority—and there was no element she could generate from the thin layer of dark power hovering around the area that would help her defend against it.

Shit! Dammit! I will not die yet!! Not here!! Not when I am promised to become ruler of the world!!

Dee squinted, features twisted in a rictus of desperation. She swept her hands forward, fingers bent like claws, and jammed them into the backs of two mages running before her. The sharp nails tore through soft skin and flesh until she grabbed round pillars—the very spines of her mages.

"Aaaah! L...Lady Dee...?!"

"What are you...?! S-stop, please...!"

The greatest of mages ignored the pleading screams of her subordinates and began to chant a command, a wicked smile on her face. This, too, was in all ways a curse.

It was an art to change the shape of matter—a secret, forbidden art that used human life force as its energy source to alter the container of flesh that stored it.

Shlurbp.

Two young, healthy individuals melted into uncertain structures, sloughing off flesh and blood in the process. The solution covered Dee entirely where she knelt on the ground, and it hardened into a resilient membrane of living armor around her.

The golden swarm of death descended into their midst.

Alice hardened her heart against the sound of all the screams.

She would not let that art be used ever again. She would remove both the caster and the command from the world.

With each swing of the glowing handle in her right hand, the blindingly sharp little petals followed the movement, slashing at the foes on the ground below. The dark mages, who wore no metal armor, had no physical defense against the metal shards that tore through their bodies.

Alice maintained the Memory Release form of her weapon until she was certain that over 90 percent of the two thousand or so dark mages were wiped out. It used up quite a lot of the sword's life, but she was not in the mood for conservation at this moment.

Two hundred mages fled in terror, not sparing a glance for the stacked corpses of their fellows, but this time, Alice returned the Osmanthus Blade to its original shape and let them go. Out of the corner of her left eye, she spotted about ten dark knights lifting off the ground on dragons from the rear of their formation.

She assumed they would rush for her, but the dragon riders merely formed up and hovered, keeping their distance. She learned why very soon: Bercouli's group was catching up behind her.

"Don't push your luck, Little Miss!" the knight commander called out as soon as he was in range, understanding that she was bereaved after the death of Eldrie.

"I...I know," she managed to stammer. "I'm fine, Uncle. Please watch over the ground troops. I must go and play my role as decoy."

"Sure...just don't go charging too far ahead!" shouted Bercouli, glancing at the enemy dragons. Alice ordered Takiguri to stay airborne where it was, and she had Amayori proceed forward and rise.

She could sense the attention of dark knights, pugilists, orcs, and goblins—and some great, colossal presence, though she could not tell its location—as she rose. Behind her was the low rumble of the soldiers and supply team leaving the ravine, heading south, and proceeding at top speed.

Then she shouted, loud enough to drown out the sound of all those footsteps. Her Incarnate voice, heavily amplified, spread in all directions, crisp and clear.

"My name is Alice!! Integrity Knight Alice Synthesis Thirty!! I am the proxy of the three goddesses who protect the human realm: the Priestess of Light!!"

There was nothing behind this statement. It was, in essence, a bluff.

But the effect it had on the enemy army was immediate. They rumbled and murmured. She sensed the desire to capture her extending toward her like giant invisible tentacles. It seemed true that the enemy was after this "Priestess of Light" at least as much as, if not more than, the actual conquest of the Human Empire and their lands.

The question remained, was that really *her*, or was she merely pretending to own the title?

It didn't matter to Alice. All she needed was for half of the enemy soldiers to follow her. If buying time and getting the enemy to pull away meant that they succeeded in defending the human world, which Eldrie, Dakira, and all those soldiers had given their lives in service of, that was all that mattered.

"Know that any who stand in my way will be struck down by my righteous light!!"

"Ooooh..."

Emperor Vecta, the god of darkness, also known as Gabriel Miller, hunter of souls, stood up from his throne in wonder. "Ooooh."

The apparent failure of the attack that had consumed three thousand orc units, and the destruction of the large majority of the mage units, did not startle or disturb Gabriel in the slightest. Only in this moment did his cold, inert soul feel any kind of rumbling.

From his thin lips, which assumed only the shape of a smile, a quiet voice said, "Alice...Alicia..."

His eyes caught in full detail the sight of the young knight in her shining golden armor, standing on the back of the dragon in the distant night sky.

Straight, long golden hair. Pure-white skin. Blue eyes as cool and crisp as the midwinter sky. In Gabriel's mind, these features perfectly matched the image of a beautifully matured Alicia Clingerman, the very first victim of his desires. He had failed to capture Alicia's soul the first time, but now he knew she had returned to take her place in this virtual world.

This time.

This time she would be his. He would take the lightcube that contained her fluctlight and devour it to his heart's content.

As the knight pulled the dragon's reins and flew to the south, Gabriel poured into her a gaze like blue fire. He leaned toward the master skull and rasped an order, quiet but fierce.

"All troops, prepare to march. Pugilists in front, then dark knights, nonhumans, and supply, in that order. Proceed south. You must capture that knight, the Priestess of Light, unharmed. The commander of the unit that captures her will be given control over the entirety of the human realm."

CHAPTER NINETEEN

PRIESTESS OF LIGHT, EIGHT PM, NOVEMBER 7TH, 380 HE

1

The dust cloud kicked up by the march of the army of darkness was gray against the night sky of the Dark Territory and its red stars.

Commander Bercouli took his eye away from the simple eyeglass made from crystal elements and growled, "Well, this certainly looks like Vecta's got an obsession with you. He's sending their entire army."

"I suppose we should be happy. It's certainly a much better outcome than being ignored entirely," Alice muttered, washing away her nerves with a swig of lukewarm siral water.

After proceeding about five kilors directly south through the uncharted—at least by inhabitants of the human realm—wastes of the Dark Territory, the guardian army's decoy force took its first break on a small hill.

The guards' morale was high. The dreadful magic the enemy had used on them had been briefly terrifying, but the sacrifice of a single Integrity Knight had both relieved them and filled them with determination to succeed in his memory.

But Alice had still not fully registered the fact of Eldrie's death. The time they'd spent together at Central Cathedral had not been long, to be sure, but he had given Alice tastes of his favorite wines and sweets; he'd told silly, charming jokes; and there had never been an entirely dull day with him around.

There had been times when she'd wondered whether the young man really wanted to learn sword techniques and sacred arts, or whether he just wanted to make merry. But only now, in his passing, did she realize how much his presence had lightened her heart and kept it fresh.

...I took him for granted such that I barely noticed when he was around, and it's only after he's gone that I finally realize what he meant to me. Pathetic.

She gazed up at the End Mountains to the northwest jutting up against the stars and touched the coiled whip now fastened behind her waist. Now she understood how Kirito felt, the way he never let go of Eugeo's sword.

Alice closed her eyes, and as if waiting for that very cue, the knights' commander said, "So shall we assume that our plans for now are to continue leading the enemy army onward, chipping away at their numbers until the last of the four remaining Integrity Knights have fallen?"

She turned to the commander, who stood next to her on the northern end of the hilltop, and nodded. "That's what I am thinking. We've eliminated half of the fifty thousand members of the invasion army already, and the dark mages, the most vexing of them all, are essentially wiped out. Next, we fatigue the dark knights and pugilists who make up the bulk of their strength...and if we can topple Vecta, the god of darkness, I think it is highly likely that those who remain will enter stalemate negotiations. What do you think?"

"Yes...the only problem is who the enemy leader will be at that time. If only that Shasta boy were still alive..."

"So is it true, Uncle? The dark general is...gone?"

"From what I could see of the battlefield earlier, he's not around. No sign of Shasta or of his apprentice knight, the woman you fought before..."

He sighed heavily. Alice knew that Bercouli had secretly had high hopes for the general and his disciple. The eldest of knights shook his head and muttered, "All we can do is hope that whichever dark knight took over Shasta's position has inherited some of his mind-set. Though I wouldn't bet on it..."

"You think it unlikely?"

"Aye. The people who live out here in the Dark Territory have no book of laws like the Taboo Index. All they have is an unwritten rule to follow the mighty. And sadly...Vecta's Incarnation is overwhelming...No buffed-up knight will serve as a true counterweight..."

True, when she had announced herself to the enemy army earlier, Alice had keenly felt some terribly cold and unfathomably dark presence reaching and tangling itself around her. She had never felt that sensation since awakening as an Integrity Knight. If the Incarnation of Administrator was fierce lightning, this felt more like an endless black void.

The memory of the sensation brought goose bumps to Alice's biceps. She rubbed her arms and nodded. "You're right...I can't imagine that there are many who would desire to fight back against a god."

The commander chuckled and patted Alice on the back. "And yet, we had three on our side: you, Kirito, and Eugeo. Let's hope that there are some folks with similar backbone on this side."

There was a powerful beating of wings overhead, and they looked up. Kazenui, Renly's dragon, was descending toward them. The boy knight leaped off even before the dragon's talons touched the ground, and he rushed to report to Bercouli, the words practically ejecting themselves from his mouth.

"Report for you, Commander, sir! About one kilor south of this point, there is a shrubland area that might serve for an ambush."

"Good spotting. Get all units ready to move again. And...your dragon must be tired, so give it plenty of food and water."

"Yes, sir!" The small figure saluted and raced off. Alice noticed that there was a faint smile on the commander's lips.

"...Uncle?" she prompted. Bercouli scratched his chin, bashful, and shrugged.

"Just thinking…It's an awful thing to steal someone's memories and freeze their life for the Synthesis Ritual to make them into Integrity Knights…but it's also a shame that we won't get any more young fellows like him anymore."

Alice thought this over and smiled back. "I don't think there's any rule that says you can't be an Integrity Knight without having your memory altered and life frozen, Uncle." She reached back and brushed the Frostscale Whip again. "Even if every last one of us is defeated, our souls…our wills find themselves taking root in fresh minds. This I believe."

"It's about damn time!!" shouted Iskahn, the young leader of the pugilists guild, as he smacked his right fist against his other palm.

They'd been so close to the fighting but forced to sit and wait for what felt like an eternity. The fearsome pillar of light that had burned the demi-human battalions, the freakish worm things that the dark mages had created, and even Emperor Vecta's mysterious order to pursue the Priestess of Light had had no effect on Iskahn's readiness to fight.

The world was split into two things: his body and everything else. Meanwhile, the entirety of Iskahn's interest was in strengthening his own flesh and nothing else. So confident was he in his own ability that if facing down one of those massive dark arts, he was certain he could beat it back with his fists and fighting spirit alone.

His bronzed, muscular body was fixed with leather straps, shorts, and sandals, and that was it. He glanced at the five thousand men and women following his lead and at the dark knighthood behind them. They'd been running for not even five minutes, but the gap between the pugilists and the knights was nearly a thousand mels already.

"For riding horses, those knights sure are damn slow!" he spat.

A large man right next to him, standing a full head taller than Iskahn, opened his cave-like mouth in a pained smile. "They cannot help it, Champion," he said, using the dark-tongue word for that generation's strongest of pugilists. "They *and* their horses are outfitted in armor that is equally heavy."

"Even though it's not doing them any good!" snapped Iskahn. He looked ahead and curled the fingers of his right hand into a tube, then placed it against his eye. In the middle of his fiery iris, his pupil expanded.

"Oh, they're moving again. But…not this way. They're still running," he said, clicking his tongue.

In other words, Iskahn had just accurately read the enemy movements from five thousand mels away, using nothing but starlight. He thought it over and said, "Hey, Dampa. The emperor's orders were simply to chase and capture her, right?"

"That's what he said."

"Okay…" He scratched the bridge of his nose with his thumb and grinned. "Guess we'll try poking the bush. Rabbit Team, move forward!!"

There was an immediate roar at his order. Leaping forward out of the ranks to line up were about a hundred fighters of slim build—not weak, but whip slender and hard. They had matching white string decorations tied around their foreheads.

"We're going to pay our respects to these Integrity Knights! Get pumped!!"

"Yah!"

"Begin Combat Dance Seventeen!!" shouted Iskahn, thrusting his right arm and pounding the ground with both feet. His confidant Dampa and the hundred members of Rabbit Team repeated the motion in perfect synchronization.

"Doom, dah, doom-dah."

"Ooh, rah, ooh-rah."

Amid the rhythmic pounding of feet and chorus of cries,

Iskahn's bronze curls began shining with beads of sweat, and his sunbaked skin began flushing a redder shade. His followers were exhibiting the same symptoms.

When the minute-long combat dance was complete, a hundred and two fighters came to a stop, steam pouring off their bodies.

In fact, that was not all of it. In the darkness, their skin was actually faintly glowing that red shade.

The pugilists were a tribe of people who had spent centuries attempting to learn just what makes up the body.

Swordsmen and mages both ultimately made their pinnacle the use of Incarnation to affect their target. In other words, they used the power of imagination to overwrite external phenomena and information.

But the pugilists were the opposite—they used Incarnation to power up their own bodies. They surpassed their original limitations, making their naked skin stronger than steel and giving their fists the strength to crush boulders.

And their feet, the strength to outrun horses.

"Ooooo, *raaaaah*!!" bellowed Iskahn, beginning to run. Dampa and the hundred fighters followed close behind.

In their wake, the air split, and the earth shook.

"...?!"

Alice took several steps forward, intent on catching up to the guardsmen who had headed toward the shrubland area that would help them set an ambush, then she sensed something off and turned back.

Something was coming.

And fast.

Upon closer examination, the enemy forces that should have been slowly following near the horizon were sending forth a unit of about a hundred that was closing the gap at astonishing speed. It was faster than any cavalry. She almost thought they were dragon knights, but there were too many of them, and they were clearly marching on foot.

"...Those are the pugilists," Commander Bercouli grumbled next to her.

"They are...?"

She'd heard the title before but had never actually seen them for herself. It was usually goblins and orcs that harried the regions around the End Mountains—and very rarely a dark knight. Never before had the pugilists even attempted to invade the human lands.

But as was typical for the eldest of the Integrity Knights, Bercouli had experience with them, and there was a note of concern in his voice. "They're a real pain. They'll happily take an injury from naked fists, but they absolutely refuse to be cut by a sword."

"Huh...? Refuse...?" It seemed to Alice that when it came to a steel blade against flesh, refusal and acceptance shouldn't even enter into the picture.

Bercouli just shrugged. "You'll see when you fight them. It's probably better if the two of us go together."

"..."

Alice swallowed hard. If Bercouli alone wasn't enough for the task, the pugilists had to be dangerous, indeed. But whatever resolution and intensity she had built up was totally wiped out by what the commander said next.

"Uh, by the way...I'm guessing you've got a problem with stripping, Little Miss?"

"What?!" she yelped, crossing her arms in front of her body before she realized it. "Wh-why would you ask that?! Of course I do!"

"No, I didn't mean it like...Well, yes, I suppose I did...but my point is, armor and clothes don't really do anything against their fists, except maybe slow you down, so...," he stammered, rubbing his chin. Finally, he gave up his explanation and shook his head. "At any rate, if you're going to fight dressed like that, you'd better have Perfect Weapon Control ready to go."

"Um...okay."

She felt her nerves creep up her spine again. From what she could see, there were around a hundred enemies approaching. If she needed to use every bit of power she could muster with the Osmanthus Blade to beat them, they were dangerous foes, indeed.

But there was one problem.

She had already used Perfect Weapon Control twice—when she had activated the reflective cohesion beam and when she had wiped out the dark mages—so the life of the Osmanthus Blade was already severely drained. Normal swinging attacks would be fine, but she didn't know how many more minutes it could withstand its own swarming attacks.

The same was true for the commander's Time-Splitting Sword. She had witnessed at close range his wide-ranging trap that instantly dispatched hundreds of minions at once. Both of their swords would normally need to be returned to their sheaths until daybreak to recover.

But even over the seconds of conversation, the pugilists had come close enough that she could make out the details of their imposing bodies. The soldiers weren't done preparing for their ambush. She had to keep them away from the ranks.

Alice nodded to the commander, her lips pursed, and readied herself to slide down the north side of the rock face—until a woman's quiet voice interrupted the two of them.

"I shall go."

Alice turned around in shock and saw that Bercouli was doing the same, eyes wide.

Standing there, to their complete surprise, was the last of the four elite Integrity Knights in the decoy group, after Bercouli, Alice, and Renly.

She was tall and thin, with a dull and drab set of gray armor. Her dark-gray hair was split evenly over her forehead, practically plastered tight to it, and tied into a ponytail behind her neck. Her features were clear and, while not unattractive, utterly emotionless. Like Alice, she appeared to be around twenty years of age.

Her name was Sheyta Synthesis Twelve. The divine weapon at her side was the Black Lily Sword.

But she was almost never referred to by the moniker of her weapon. There was a different nickname that the other knights used on the rare occasion that they spoke about her.

She was known as Sheyta the Silent.

It wasn't Sheyta's volunteering to fight the enemy pugilists alone that had shocked Alice.

It was that she had just heard Sheyta the Silent speak for the very first time.

Iskahn and Dampa and their hundred followers leaped easily over ditches and brooks and even kicked their way through boulders here and there as they raced on. Very soon they would get to fight the Integrity Knights, who were feared as much as demons. The young pugilist felt the corners of his mouth curl with a possessed smile.

As a matter of fact, until the topic of this battle came about, Iskahn had never felt particularly interested in the Integrity Knights of the human lands. He saw them as nothing more than cowards who hid behind swords and armor. The only knight in their own dark tribes whom he truly respected as a gladiator was the now-dead General Shasta.

But the spirit of the enemy knights that he'd sensed while meditating before they got their orders had been no joke. At the very least, they were not just scrubs who relied on fancy weaponry to get themselves out of trouble.

Iskahn placed a bet that if he smashed those ugly swords and suits of armor, he'd find pristinely muscled bodies underneath—and the anticipation of fist meeting fist at full power got him pumped up and ready for battle.

So when he did finally catch a glimpse of one of the knights standing before the hill at which the enemy had been waiting earlier, the pugilist was stunned.

He was too *thin*.

No, not he—it was a woman. So it wasn't surprising that she would be thinner, but this was too much. Even covered in metal armor from head to toe, she was skinnier than any of the female pugilists under Iskahn's lead. Underneath the armor, this woman would look more like a mage. Even the sword at her side looked more like a meat skewer than a weapon.

Iskahn held his troops back with a motion and came to a skidding stop, dust swirling. His eyebrows, which curled up at the ends like flames, rose as he said, "Who the hell are you? What the hell are you doing there?"

The knight inclined her head the tiniest bit, her straight gray hair swaying. It looked as though she was considering how to answer—or more likely, whether there was any need to answer at all. The bridge of her nose was as smooth and small as if it had been carved in a single motion by a very sharp knife, and she betrayed no emotion whatsoever in saying, "I am here to prevent your advance."

Iskahn snorted tremendously, though it wasn't clear whether it was out of mirth or anger. He shrugged. "You couldn't stop a single child from getting past you. Or let me guess...Are you a knight who also casts arts?"

This time, the knight paused just long enough to be irritating. "I am not skilled at sacred arts."

Getting irritated that his finely honed spirit for battle was beginning to wilt, Iskahn spat, "Okay, fine. Whatever." He gestured to one of his followers. "Yotte, deal with her."

"Here we go!!"

Bounding forward out of the formation was a pugilist of slightly smaller build. But while she was smaller, she was at least twice the size of the enemy knight. Her firm muscles bounced and stretched as she stepped forward, light on her feet. If the enemy was without expression, she was the opposite, bearing a fierce, proud smile.

"Hah!"

From five mels away, the pugilist punched the empty air. The wind this movement created rippled the knight's bangs.

Even after this, the knight's thin features betrayed no intention to fight. Instead, she looked almost disappointed and mumbled, "Only…one…?"

"That's what *I'm* sayin', string bean!" shouted Yotte, her thick lips curled back in scorn. "After I've beaten you down, but before I kill you, I'm gonna stuff that tiny mouth of yours full of dried meat! Now draw your damn weapon!!"

The knight gripped the hilt of the sword, looking as if she thought even the idea of replying to that taunt was a waste of time. She pulled her weapon loose without much fanfare.

"…What is *that*?!" shouted Iskahn from his vantage point farther away, arms crossed.

It wasn't just thin. If the sheath itself was as thin as a meat skewer, the blade when drawn was barely even a cen across, no thicker than a child's pinky finger. And it was as thin as a sheet of paper and matte black in color, such that with no light brighter than the stars around, it barely seemed as though there was a weapon there to begin with.

Scarlet fury rippled across Yotte's face.

"…Think I'm some kinda joke…?"

Her feet beat a brief combat dance, more of a tantrum, and the pugilist crossed the gap at once. To Iskahn's eye, it was an excellent lunge. Despite the name Rabbit Team, the pugilists that made up the squad not only were agile but had sharp, deadly fangs, too.

Yotte's fist lunged forward, audibly tearing the air around it. Rather than dodging the punch headed for her face, the knight made to block it with her slender sword.

The resulting sound was high-pitched, like two pieces of metal striking. Orange sparks flashed around them.

Then the needlelike weapon bent, easily and pathetically.

Iskahn smirked. That flimsy little sword would not even split the skin of a hardened pugilist.

When the children of the pugilist clans turned five, they were sent to the guild's training ground. The first training exercise they were assigned there was to break a cast-iron knife with their bare fists.

As they grew, they graduated from cast iron to tempered, from knives to longswords. Not only did the students break the weapons, the instructors swung the blades down on them. It impressed upon the youngsters that they need fear no blade. Their bodies were an inviolable temple to any sharp edge. And that certainty—that Incarnation—turned their bodies to iron, in fact.

Iskahn, the guild leader, could stop a two-cen metal needle with his eyeball. As a member of the guild, Yotte was not at that level, but she was one of the ten group leaders of Rabbit Team, and no sword could possibly stop her fist.

Certainly not a flimsy, paper-thin sword like that one.

Every pugilist there could see it coming next: the black needle bending until it broke with a pathetic snap, then a steel fist driving itself into the knight's face.

But what they heard was an odd *pwipp*, like a leather whip cracking on empty air. Yotte was still, the follow-through of her punch clean. Her fist had just barely grazed the knight's right cheek, and that knight's right hand was fully extended as well.

From where he stood, Iskahn could not see what the black blade was doing. *C'mon—you shouldn't be missing a target that big*, he grumbled to himself. Assuming Yotte won this fight, he would send her to start over from the third-class waiting rooms at the coliseum. *Who cares how strong your punches are if you can't hit the target...?*

Without a sound, a split appeared between the middle and ring finger of Yotte's clenched fist.

"Wha...?"

Before his shocked eyes, Iskahn saw the tear extend from her lower arm to her elbow, then to her biceps and the top of her shoulder. The cut was pristine, absolutely preserving the bone, muscle, and narrow capillaries along its length, until the outer half of Yotte's right arm toppled to the ground. Only then did hot fountains of blood spray like mist from the wound.

"*Aaaaaaah*!!" shrieked Yotte. She fell to the ground, clutching her arm.

The knight stood straight again. A brief sigh escaped her lips.

Sheyta the Silent did not maintain her silence during her stay in Central Cathedral out of some kind of introverted personality or dislike of interacting with others. Instead, she was utterly focused on avoiding the attention of the other Integrity Knights—ensuring that none of them thought to ask her to train or duel with them.

In fact, it was the fear that if she crossed swords with anyone, even Commander Bercouli himself, she might accidentally *cut off his head* that made Sheyta choose to live out her time at the cathedral, over a hundred years, in absolute silence. The only people she spoke to were the personal attendant who saw to her needs and the girl in charge of operating the levitating disc.

Sheyta was a true savant of the sword, synthesized following her victory in the Four-Empire Unification Tournament.

But the results of that year's tournament had been struck from the record. It had been covered up, because instead of stopping at the last possible moment, as custom dictated was most appropriate and graceful, Sheyta had slain every last opponent she'd fought.

In a sense, Integrity Knight Sheyta Synthesis Twelve had a very similar mentality to Iskahn, head of the pugilists guild.

If all Iskahn thought about was punching people, Sheyta had no interests outside of cutting. But it was not something that she enjoyed in the least. It simply happened. Whether it was a person or an object, whenever Sheyta faced off against a target, she had a clear vision of the cross section of what she was meant to cut.

At that point, there was no choice but to make the foreshadowing a reality. Against an immobile training dummy, she could even slice it to a smooth edge with the side of her hand.

Sheyta had always suppressed the side of her that desired the sheer slice; she considered it to be distasteful. It was Administrator who'd first recognized that hidden impulse within her.

Over two centuries ago, Administrator had attempted to master the theory of spatial sacred power, which all who wielded the sacred arts now considered to be common sense. What piqued her interest most of all was the great and final battle that brought about the end of the Age of Blood and Iron in the Dark Territory. At a spot in the wilderness halfway between Obsidia Palace and the human realm, the five tribes of darkness fought to a stalemate, unleashing a nearly infinite amount of spatial power. She desired to use that power for herself.

But being cautious, she could not travel to the Dark Territory. Instead, she summoned Sheyta the Integrity Knight. The pontifex called for Sheyta the Silent, as she was already known, and gave her a tempting message.

You will go to that place alone and look for something in the battlefield. Some kind of living magical beast that would have avoided the slaughter that unfolded there. If not magical, then some kind of large animal. A bird or an insect at minimum. I just want something *that has absorbed that spatial power.*

If you find it for me, I will create a divine weapon from it, just for you.

The highest-priority sword you could imagine. Capable of cutting anything...

Sheyta could not resist the temptation—not that the Integrity Knights could refuse an order from the pontifex to begin with. She scaled the End Mountains on foot, without a dragon, crossed thousands of kilors of charred landscape, and finally reached the gruesome site of that terrible battle.

Nothing moved in the place where the five tribes had so desperately killed one another. No magical beasts, not a mouse, not a single crow lived there. But Sheyta did not give up. The idea of a sword that could cut anything had seized her mind and would not let go.

After three days and three nights of searching, she finally found a single black lily waving limp in the wind. It was the only object that had the ability to absorb spatial resources that had survived the battle.

Administrator generated a sword with the thinnest and smallest of blades from that flower and gave it the name of the Black Lily Sword.

The next year, Sheyta was challenged to a duel by another Integrity Knight, whom she killed with that sword. By her own request, she was put into a long, long sleep.

Sheyta could not tell whether the breath she exhaled upon slicing the pugilist's arm in two was one of lament or of exultation.

For that matter, she also didn't know why she'd broken her long vow of silence minutes earlier, when she'd elected to stay behind and defend this position. She didn't even know what had driven her to raise her hand when the call went out to join the guardian army half a year ago at Central Cathedral.

Did she want to protect the realm, as the other knights did? Or did she just want to cut enemies? Perhaps she really wanted them to cut her?

It didn't matter now. At this point, there was no stopping her sword. All she could do was pray that the number of lives she snuffed out was small.

Sheyta raised her head and glanced at the frozen, shocked pugilists.

The gray knight raised her slender black sword and plunged into the midst of a hundred enemies without a moment's hesitation.

"...She fights with great fury," Alice noted hoarsely.

"Yes...," Commander Bercouli hummed. "Just between you

and me, when we pulled her out of Deep Freeze six months ago, I was actually a bit scared."

"I had no idea that Sheyta was capable of such things..."

Below them, Integrity Knight Sheyta was battling a hundred pugilists. Technically, it was less battling than simply severing. Her sword, so thin its shape was almost difficult to make out, whipped left and right, each high-pitched zip easily cutting off another arm or leg of whatever enemy happened to be nearby.

Despite her wonder at the sight, Alice couldn't help but feel concerned about something she sensed emanating from Sheyta's slender form. There was no hostility coming from her. She didn't seem to be feeling anything at all. So what was it that drove her to fight so fiercely?

"Don't think about it. I've known that girl for more than a hundred years, and I don't understand a single thing about her," the commander grunted. He turned his back. "I think we can leave this to her. The enemy's main force should catch up soon, and we ought to prepare to fight them off."

"...Yes, sir," Alice said. She tore her eyes away from the battle below and hurried after him.

About a kilor south of where Bercouli and Alice were descending the hill, the wasteland of blackened gravel finally began to give way to a region covered in oddly shaped shrubs, where the decoy group was hiding.

The group consisted of a thousand guards, two hundred priests, and fifty supply team members. They would have to fight back five thousand enemy pugilists.

Renly and the guards and priests, split into twenty groups, were hiding among the plants and waiting. There were fresh wheel ruts on the single narrow path winding through the woods, dug by the supply wagons. The enemy would follow the tracks as far as they could lure them in before the ambush pounced from either side.

The commander had already warned Renly that the pugilists would be highly resistant to sword attacks. But he'd also described their weakness: Pugilists were very bad at defending against sacred arts.

To the north, where there was not even a patch of moss growing, there was not enough sacred power to use a higher-level art, but the air was thicker here in the shrubland. The priests hiding in the shrubs would unload sacred arts on the enemy lured into the trap, then evacuate south, protected by the soldiers. With the enemy in disarray, the five dragons would burn them from above.

In the hopes of a speedy escape, the eight supply wagons were situated at the very southern end of the shrubland. Renly decided that the farther they were from the fighting, the safer they'd be. He believed that there was almost no chance that the enemy would slip into the darkness and attack the supply team directly.

But even as Renly busied himself with the coming ambush, the five guards he had placed on the carriages, just in case, were in the process of dying without a sound.

A shadowy figure moved silently, despite the full-body metal armor in unreflective black and the helmet with demonic horns.

It headed for a young guardsman from the Human Guardian Army who was ceaselessly glancing left and right—but never over his shoulder. There should have been other guards looking in that direction.

The shadow slid closer, remaining in the guard's blind spot. There was an excellent longsword hanging from its waist, but it remained there as the figure lifted a tiny dagger.

The figure's left hand reached forward, a black serpent, and covered the guard's mouth and nose. The right hand flashed as the blade slid across the guard's exposed throat.

The body bled out the flicker of life it still contained in absolute silence, then slumped over dead, and the shadow pushed it beneath a nearby shrub.

Through the black fabric that covered its face, the shadow muttered "Five down" and chuckled. It was speaking not in the ancient sacred tongue but in modern English.

This shadow was none other than one of the three current inhabitants of the Underworld who were actually from the real world—subordinate officer to Gabriel Miller, one Vassago Casals.

About an hour before this, Vassago had been chugging yet another glass of red wine in the huge carriage at the rear of the Dark Territory's army when the dark mages' attempt at a grand magic spell had failed. At last, he'd needled Gabriel.

"Hey, Bro. Don't you think we've delegated enough of the work? Why don't we get our own hands dirty already?"

Gabriel glanced at Vassago, a golden eyebrow raised. "You can go first, then."

He ordered Vassago not to invade the ravine that the other army was defending but to move to an empty place far to the south of the battlefield.

From the moment that the nonhuman troops had been zapped by that sci-fi laser attack, Gabriel had predicted that a portion of the enemy forces would slip through into the Dark Territory. Vassago wondered why he guessed they would go south, rather than north, and when Gabriel explained that "there was more room that way," he nearly fell off his seat. But now that the enemy had indeed come this way, he didn't have much choice but to give up and do his job.

No matter how high functioning the human units were, they would come to a stop if their supplies were lost. For the first time since diving into this world, Vassago had a chance to kill time with "killing time." He stared into the dark woods, hoping to make the moment last.

He soon found several wagons camouflaged with branches and

leaves. Under his mask, the assassin licked his lips and continued moving.

There was movement at one of the wagons. He froze, hiding behind a tree trunk.

From out of the wagon canvas poked the face of a young woman with dark-brown hair and the kind of pale skin that none of the darklanders had. She was looking around the area nervously, clearly sensing something was amiss.

As Vassago waited, immobile, the girl carefully stepped down from the wagon, whispered something to someone inside it, and began to walk slowly away. The girl wore gray clothes that looked like a high school uniform with just the flimsiest bits of armor added, and she was heading straight for the place where Vassago was hiding.

He had to stifle the urge to whistle with excitement. His fingers gripped the handle of the dagger, which was still slick with blood.

"Don't...think..."

Iskahn boiled with rage at the sight of the fighters he had personally trained being chopped to pieces before his eyes.

"...you're going...to get away with thiiiis!!"

He barreled forward, his legs working so hard they put cracks in the ground. Flames covered his right fist, a manifestation of the burning fury that consumed him.

Iskahn thrust that fist at the base of the gray Integrity Knight's neck. Sparks spilled over the sides of his hand, leaving a brilliant trail in the air. The knight, who had just finished swinging her sword, made to catch Iskahn's punch with her gauntleted free hand.

Your armor is just paper against my fist!!

His punch, brimming with pure Incarnation, collided with the knight's palm and sprayed a huge wave of sparks outward in all directions. There was an explosive ripping sound, and the gray gauntlet shattered, followed by the metal pieces up to her shoulder.

The knight's exposed left arm showed off a lattice of tiny cuts across the smooth white skin that promptly burst forth with a misting of blood. But to his surprise, he did not register the feedback of breaking bones.

He knew she had to be in intense pain regardless, but the only thing the knight did was lower her eyebrows a bit. With her left hand squeezing his wrist, she whipped the narrow sword with the other.

There was a ringing metallic sound, and sparks shot out from the pugilist's elbow area.

The source of the pugilists' strength was the belief and understanding that it was impossible for any blade edge to violate their bodies. They wore only scant leather straps, leaving the rest of their skin bare, to help feel the certainty of this belief. The moment a pugilist relied on any armor, he revealed the weakness of his heart.

So Iskahn attempted to rebuff the black blade with willpower alone before it could slice through his arm. But the chilling bite of this weapon as it dug into his skin was unlike any blade he'd taken before.

The ultrathin, ultranarrow blade was not simple steel, either, but another manifestation of will. It desired not victory but the sheer thrill of cleaving in twain anything it touched.

On sheer instinct, Iskahn punched with his other arm. It rippled through the air, bursting into the place the knight had stood just an instant before. She was incredibly nimble but did not evade it entirely; his hand made slight contact with her gray breastplate. It cracked and split as she jumped away, just like her gauntlet had.

But Iskahn was not unharmed, either. The inside of his right elbow, which the sword had touched for less than a second, had a very thin cut on the skin. A tiny bead of blood bloomed in the center of the line. One drop of blood—just one.

The young pugilist licked it off and grinned fiercely at her. "Woman…your appearance and what lies underneath it are very different things."

The gray knight did not respond in the way he'd expected.

"But…I'm older than you…"

"Huh? Of course you are. You Integrity Knights are monsters that live for decades without any sign of aging, right? Should I call you Grandma instead?"

"…" The knight's eyelids twitched through her cool gaze. That was all the reaction she showed, however. "I will allow it. You are very hard. I almost cannot find a place to cut."

"Tsk…What's that supposed to mean?"

Iskahn was getting irritated; he could sense that her off-putting attitude was throwing off his will to fight just the tiniest bit. A quick glance at his fellow pugilists defeated around him was enough to rekindle that rage.

Over twenty men and women moaned on the ground, arms and legs severed by that eerie sword. What was worst of all was not that she had hurt them but that she was probably doing her best to hold back and keep from killing them. Not a single pugilist had lost their head. She should have been eminently capable of that, given her knight's training and the excellence of her weapon.

"…How dare you treat us like training dummies. You'll pay for this…I will find a way to crush you!!"

Stomp, sto-stomp!!

The fighters around kicked out a brief combat dance to indicate their ability to fight. They crowed in rhythm with their feet.

"Ooh, rah, ooh-rah-rah! Ooh, rah, ooh-rah-rah!"

With each pounding of the earth and battering of the air, the pugilists' Incarnation strengthened. Sweat began to pour from their bronzed skin, the droplets flying loose and turning into sparks.

The Integrity Knight did not budge. It was as though she was waiting for Iskahn to reach the height of his fervor.

Fine, then.

The king of brawls stopped his combat dance. His dark golden curls stood up with fire, and light began to blaze around his arms. In contrast, the knight was quiet. The narrow black blade in her right hand exuded a frosty cool.

"Here…I…come…womaaaaan!!"

Iskahn closed the gap, the air burning around him. The woman lazily swung the sword up.

Piuw.

Just before the whipping black sword could touch Iskahn's left shoulder, the pugilist hit her left leg, when her sword should have won the battle of distance. He had kicked her, not punched. The toe of his right foot swung low off the ground and hit her gray shin guard directly.

With extraordinary reflexes, the knight stopped her sword and lowered her waist, keeping her from tumbling, but the guard protecting her left leg immediately shattered. The impact ripped the skirt wrapped around her waist, exposing thin but chiseled legs.

"Don't assume that because I'm a pugilist, all I do is punch!" Iskahn smirked. He whipped his left leg into a high kick. The knight turned her wrist so that her sword would meet the kick.

The instant shin and blade connected, a shower of sparks appeared with a roar. The chief of the pugilists felt a piercing pain in his hardy shin and pulled his leg back, throwing a punch instead.

The flaming blow caught the knight directly on the breastplate.

Gagaaang! The resulting explosion threw them in opposite directions. Iskahn did a backflip in the air and landed on his feet. The pain ran through his left shin again, and he glanced at it.

His shin, which was strong enough to break a steel stake in half, had a brilliant line cut right into the skin. Bright-red blood gushed from the wound and dripped onto the black ground.

He snorted—it was only a scratch—and examined the state of his foe.

She had held strong this time, too, but she had her hand to her chest and was coughing quietly. The impact of his fist had completely shattered her breastplate, leaving only the gauntlet on her right arm and the gray cloth around her chest. On her lower half were just the torn skirt and the armor over her right leg.

Iskahn looked at the way her snow-white skin, a feature of the Human Empire, glowed bright even in the dark of night, and he snorted again. "You're looking much more like a gladiator now. But you don't have anywhere near enough muscle. You ought to eat more and train more, woman."

The pugilists around them jeered and taunted, but the knight's expression did not change. She merely grabbed the scrap of cloth hanging from her left shoulder and ripped it loose, then whipped her flexible sword around.

"And I've noticed that you've grown softer."

"...The hell did you just say?" growled Iskahn, the bridge of his nose wrinkling as he exposed his canines. But despite his menacing look, he could tell that his own breathing had gotten just a bit shallower.

It didn't make any sense that his will to fight would weaken just from seeing some bare skin. The women of his tribe exposed their flesh all the time in much greater degree, and only a little kid freshly entered into the training hall would let that unnerve him.

The only thing the world held was opponents waiting to be crushed by a clenched fist. Even if they were exotic foreign women so thin they could snap in the wind, with blindingly white skin.

"You're going to pay for this...I'm going to show you what I'm like at full power," howled Iskahn, wolflike, jabbing a finger at the knight. "So give me all you've got!! Quit lookin' like you're gonna fall asleep from boredom!!"

She looked somewhat troubled by this, brushed her cheek and forehead with her free hand, and tilted her brows just a bit downward. "Then that's what...you'll get."

"...G-good. That's good."

It was these pauses in the action that kept filling his head with strange thoughts. Iskahn sucked in a deep breath, tensing the power in his gut and lowering his center of gravity. He posed with his left fist at his waist and his right fist pointed at the enemy, and he exhaled loudly. With each forceful breath, his firmly planted legs sucked up power from the earth, glowing red, until the heat traveled through his body to gather in his fist.

The glowing flames went from red to yellow, then reached white with blue ends. Iskahn's right fist contained enough heat to char the very atmosphere. It emitted high-pitched pinging sounds.

The knight met this challenge by taking a sideways stance. She extended her left hand straight forward, the fingers lined up, and stretched her ultrathin sword straight backward. The way that her arms were extended straight made her look like a stone-throwing tool that was taut at maximum pressure.

Iskahn grinned. He felt as nervous as if his body had already been split from head to belly.

I've never fought someone like this before. I feel so fired up.

They moved at the same moment.

The knight's sword made a black semicircle.

The pugilist's fist created a bluish-white comet. An ultra-dense shock wave erupted when they met, cracking the earth as it spread. Every last one of the pugilists standing around the duel was thrown backward.

Sword and fist shook for control over an intersection point the size of a needle's eye. Power compressed beyond its limit raged into a pillar of light that burst upward into the night sky.

In terms of Sheyta's skill, she could have defeated her foe without having to rely upon a straightforward contest of strength like this.

The young pugilist's Incarnation was as tough as an elite Integrity Knight's, which was a mild surprise to her, but she could also see that when he concentrated it all into his right fist to attack her, his other parts looked much softer. She could have dodged his straightforward punch and cut off his head, just like that.

But Sheyta did not do that. She chose to stand put and block the shining fist. It was not a conscious decision—it was what her body and sword wanted.

Even Sheyta found her decision surprising. For over a hundred years, she had known that she had nothing in common with the knightly ideals of pride and duty and honor. The only thing she wanted was to cut, because she enjoyed it.

One might as well say that she killed because she wanted to. Only when she was on a guard mission over the End Mountains did Sheyta allow herself to be free. Countless dark knights and goblins had lost their heads and their lives to her sword.

She felt her peculiar nature to be distasteful and chose to live in silence instead. So why did Sheyta choose not to kill in this one battle, out of all the battles she'd been in? It was a mystery.

It was also a waste of time to think about it. The only things that existed in this moment were her, the Black Lily Sword, and the fist before her.

It's so hard and tough. I wonder if I can cut through it.

This is fun.

The enemy knight's small, thin lips actually curled into a tiny smile. Iskahn already understood that she was not mocking him—or this fight. He knew because his own lips formed the exact same smile.

Y'know, for lookin' like a scrawny little wimp from the prissy, soft human lands, you're just like me deep down.

A small crack ran through the inside of his clenched fist. It was not the sound of the enemy's black blade chipping but the sound of a bone in his own hand fracturing, he knew.

Dammit. She's still gonna overpower me, even with this punch? Oh well, then.

If she cut through his fist, that thin black sword would split his entire body in two, his instincts told him. But Iskahn felt no fear. He would never get another chance to face an opponent of this quality. So he supposed it wasn't a bad way to die.

He started to close his eyes, to accept his fate. But then the pressure on his fist gave a little.

All at once, the incredible pent-up force between them was unleashed, and Iskahn and the knight blew backward like leaves in a storm. He understood at once why her Incarnation had weakened. There was a huge figure breaking between the two of them.

Iskahn fell onto his backside and yelled at the man who toppled nearby. "What the hell was that for, Dampa?!"

"Time's up, Champion."

His second-in-command sat up, his normally slit-narrow eyes actually opened wide for once. Dampa lifted a burly arm and pointed to the north. Iskahn followed his gesture and saw the main force of the pugilists and the dark knights behind them, within visual range now. With a full group battle about to begin, it wasn't the time for their leader to be engaged in a personal duel. And yet...

He clicked his tongue and looked forward again. Beyond the swirling dust devils, the enemy knight, nearly all armor and clothing gone, slid her sword into her sheath, seemingly unbothered by any of it.

"Woman! Don't think you've won this fight!!" crowed the young pugilist, momentarily forgetting that he had been expecting to die just a moment ago. The knight glanced at Iskahn, her gray hair shifting, and seemed to search for the right words to say.

"I wish...you would stop calling me 'woman.'"

"Oh yeah? Well...how do you even plan on escaping from this...?"

At that moment, a gust of wind hit them from the south, so powerful that all the pugilists attempting to surround the knight turned their faces away. Iskahn blinked and saw the knight raising her hand high into the sky, and the shape of a huge monster descending rapidly from above. It was a dragon, gray scales glistening in the moonlight.

She threw a leg over the creature, and the dragon swept back

up into the sky. Furious, the king of fighters couldn't help himself from shouting, "At least name yourself before you run away!!"

He could barely hear her voice descending through the beating of the dragon's wings. "I'm…not running away. I am…Sheyta Synthesis Twelve."

Dampa grabbed Iskahn's arm and pulled him away, but he did turn back to stare at the flying dragon as it vanished into the night, and he clicked his tongue again.

If possible, he wished to have a rematch with that mighty foe after another year of training.

He had learned that there was still room to grow. But Iskahn was not so immature that he thought this kind of selfish desire could pass on a battlefield. Once they rejoined the rest of the pugilists, they had to work with the dark knights to wipe out the enemy army. It wasn't clear if there would be another chance to battle that woman.

If I capture that Priestess of Light or whatever…, Iskahn thought for a moment, then clicked his tongue one more time. *How stupid can I be? Asking the emperor to spare that woman's life as my reward? Every last member of my tribe will assume I've gone mad.*

Iskahn spun on his heel and gestured to a subordinate for a jar of ointment to spread on the cut on his leg.

2

That's right.

Keep coming. Straight this way.

Vassago savored the experience of the ambush, rolling the flavor of it on his tongue like a piece of candy. His hiding ability was flawless. Even the negative concealment of his metal armor didn't have an effect on the way he melted into the darkness of the shrubbery.

The dark-brown-haired girl was being cautious, but even her piercing gaze just passed right over his hiding spot. Seven more yards…five…

Nice. Very nice. Oh, it's been too long since I did this.

When she was within ten feet, the girl suddenly turned to her right, moving in the direction of the body Vassago had hidden. He'd been hoping to draw her even closer, but this would have to do.

He slid, silent, out of the darkness, closing in on her, hand reaching for her back. He would cover her mouth, and when her throat convulsed with fear, he would draw his sharp dagger right across it…

The premonition, the anticipation of the moment was so strong and real that Vassago failed to react immediately to the blade that flashed before his eyes.

"...Whoa!"

He darted backward just as the tip of the blade grazed the exposed skin under his chin.

The girl shouldn't have been aware of him at all, but she'd drawn and swung her sword from an away-facing position. It was a brilliant swing—if he'd been one step closer, she would have slit his throat.

When she faced him, sword held in two hands, the girl's navy-blue eyes were full of fear and hostility but not surprise. Vassago had to reluctantly admit that she had seen through his attempt at hiding quite a while ago.

He spun the dagger in his fingers and said "Hey, baby" in English, then recalled that it wasn't spoken here, so he switched to perfectly accentless Japanese instead. "How did you know, Miss?"

The girl kept her sword up, not letting her guard lapse, and said harshly, "My mentor taught me not to rely on my eyes...but to feel with my entire being."

"Y-your mentor...?" Vassago repeated, blinking. He felt some distant memory being triggered, a quote he'd heard years ago...

But before he could travel back to the source of that memory, the girl sucked in a deep breath and shouted, incredibly loud, "Enemy attack!! Enemy attaaack!!"

He clicked his tongue and stashed the dagger at his side. Playtime was over.

Vassago raised his left hand and shouted, "All right, boys... Time to go to work!!"

This time, there was real shock in the girl's eyes.

A hundred or so feet behind Vassago, the brush rustled as people stood up—thirty lightly armored scouts handpicked from the dark knights. A second girl, who'd jumped out of the wagon after the warning, and the ten or so soldiers who'd rushed down from the north all froze in unison.

"Wha—? Enemies in the rear?! Dozens of them?!" Renly shouted back when he received the report from the supply team.

Oh no...Oh no!

If they attacked the wagons and burned all the supplies, the army would be immobilized. Not to mention those three children were in the back. He had sworn to protect the two student girls and the young man they watched over.

He had to send a hundred men—no, two hundred. But if he started sending the main forces now, the enemies approaching from the north might pick up on the ambush being set for them. If that happened, his side would be utterly crushed before the numerical superiority of the enemies.

Or should he assume that they'd seen through the ambush already? Would it be better to send everyone south and hope for another chance to strike back later?

Renly couldn't come to an immediate decision with what he knew.

But just then, he heard a deep voice ask, "So they knew we would be heading south and had forces in place and on the lookout for us...?"

It was Commander Bercouli and Alice, returning from the hill to the north. From Renly's perspective, they might as well be legendary figures, far beyond his level, but they both looked near desperate. Alice in particular seemed ready to rush to the supply team's aid.

Over Bercouli's shoulder, Renly could see the faint outline of a dust cloud to the north, kicked up by the pursuing army beyond the hilly region between them.

The commander briefly closed his eyes, then opened them, the gray-blue portals piercing. "Renly, have the troops retreat. Little Miss, go help the supply team at once. I'll hold off the enemies to the north."

"Hold them off...? But, Uncle, there are over five thousand pugilists among them! And you said that swords don't work on—"

"Look, I'll manage. Just go! Remember that it was your idea to use up every last man to whittle down the enemy's numbers, Little Miss...I mean, Alice!"

And with that, Bercouli spun to the north. His gnarled right hand reached across his body to draw the Time-Splitting Sword. The faded color of the aged blade made it clear at a glance that there was very little life left in it.

Three bursts of sparks lit the darkness in succession.

The dark-brown-haired girl had blocked each of Vassago's swings the first time she saw them. And he had used continuous sword techniques. So when the third blow knocked the sword loose from her hands and caused it to stick into the trunk of a nearby tree, the assassin couldn't help but whistle in appreciation.

The girl bravely put up her fists, but he dropped her to the ground with a sweep kick. She landed hard on her back and grunted in pain.

"Ronieeee!!" screamed the second girl, racing closer.

Vassago put the tip of his sword against the throat of the girl on the ground, forcing the red-haired one to stop. Her skinny legs halted, trembling.

"Heh...heh, heh," he chuckled through his mask, unable to help himself.

This is it. This is the feeling.

The pleasure of having someone's life and everything they possessed balanced on the point of his sword. It was the ultimate pleasure of player killing and why he would never be able to give it up.

"...I'm not going to kill you as long as you stay there and behave," he whispered to the other girl, then leaned over the girl whose name was apparently Ronie. Behind them, thirty blood-starved scouts drew ever closer.

Ronie's big eyes began to fill with tears of fear and humiliation.

All the determination that had rippled through her was turning to despair…

…?

Suddenly, her eyes were focused not on Vassago's face but on the sky above him. Something was reflecting in those wet irises.

Light.

Motes of milky-white light, falling from above. They drifted downward as soft as snowflakes. Vassago looked up slowly, feeling an eerie thrill of dread down his spine.

Black sky. Stars the color of blood.

And floating against them, a small silhouette—but one that radiated an immense power.

A person. A woman.

A breastplate that shone as though made of pearl. Gauntlets and boots of the same color.

Her long skirt was stitched together from countless fine fabrics that hung loose and flapped like wings. Her long hair, trailing in the night breeze, was a shining chestnut brown.

"Lady…Stacia," Ronie mumbled from the ground.

Vassago never heard her say it. The instant that he caught a glimpse of the woman's face descending from the starry sky above, the assassin rose to his feet, drawn to the sight of her.

Free from his threat, Ronie scrambled back to her friend, but he did not even look back at her.

The figure floating in the air reached out her right hand.

Five slender fingers lightly swiped sideways.

Laaaaaaaaah.

A tremendous, rich harmony shook the world, like a chorus of thousands of angels bursting into song. A curtain of light, like the aurora borealis, shot from the figure's fingers and rained down behind Vassago.

Rumbling ensued—and screams.

Vassago spun around to see a yawning, bottomless ravine in the earth—and his thirty followers being swallowed up by it.

Dumbfounded, he turned bulging eyes to the sky. The woman

lifted her right hand again and this time waved it toward the north.

There was another angelic chorus. The aurora that shot down was dozens of times larger than the first, and the effect it had on the ground below was beyond the capacity of his mind to envision.

Lastly, the floating woman looked directly down upon Vassago. Her index finger flicked empty air.

Laaaaaaah.

Rainbow light enveloped him. The ground beneath his feet vanished.

As he plunged into endless darkness below, Vassago thrust his hand upward, trying to grab the tiny figure.

"No way...You gotta be kidding me," he said, his voice tremulous.

That face.

That hair.

That presence.

"Isn't that...the Flash from the KoB?"

Commander Bercouli stood in place, sword dangling from his hand.

An enormous fissure, at least a hundred mels across, yawned before him in the earth. It continued as far as he could see at a glance to his right and left, and it was impossible to gauge its depth. Pieces of rock continually spilled over the lip of the fissure, but he never heard any of them strike the bottom.

And the fissure had not existed just seconds before this moment.

Rainbow light had shone down from the heavens with a tremendous harmony, splitting the earth in two where it touched. Not a thousand—or ten thousand—sacred arts masters working together, not even Administrator herself could achieve the altering of creation itself like this.

It was divine. It was godly power.

First Vecta, and now another god had come to Earth.

Such was Bercouli's first thought, with a deathly chill down his back, but he soon reconsidered.

On the far bank of the massive gouge in the earth, five thousand pugilists stood dumbfounded, their access blocked.

If an all-powerful god with the ability to give and take life had decided to side with the Human Guardian Army, she would have dragged all those pugilists down into the fissure in the earth, too. But she had placed it so they had just enough room to safely come to a stop, despite their sprinting speed.

The knights' commander sensed an emotion in this, a hesitation to take many lives.

He sensed that this was human will at work.

3

Hurry.

Hurry down to the surface. To Kirito.

When Asuna Yuuki had logged in to the Underworld using Super-Account 01, "Goddess of Creation Stacia," she'd floated downward in the slow-fall function enabled only on your first login, as the name of her lover echoed repeatedly in her head.

In the real world, nearly an hour had passed since the marine research megafloat known as the *Ocean Turtle* had been attacked by an unidentified armed group. Asuna had elected to go into the simulation and entered a full dive with Soul Translator Unit Five. According to Takeru Higa's reassurances, he would spawn her directly over Kirito's present location. She knew that where she fell, her beloved would be waiting.

Asuna's mind was racked with almost crazed longing and love-sickness, as well as a sensation like stabbing needles. She winced against the pain.

The admin privileges given to the Stacia account included unlimited landscape manipulation, the side effects of which she had been warned about ahead of time. The massive amalgamation of mnemonic data that made up the landscape, traveling between Asuna's STL and the Main Visualizer, which contained all of the Underworld's data, placed a great amount of strain on her fluctlight.

Higa, the chief engineer of Rath, warned her not to engage in too much manipulation of terrain—and if she felt a headache, to stop doing it at once.

But as soon as Asuna could see about a thousand humans directly below and a huge number of darklanders approaching from north and south, she immediately began reciting the command for altering the landscape.

She stopped the army coming from the north by carving a very long ravine into the ground. But to eliminate the thirty or so in the act of approaching Kirito's location, she had to remove the ground itself.

They were people with real souls. True bottom-up AIs whom Kirito had spent two and a half years in this world fighting to protect. Perhaps it was the fear and hatred from those dying souls that was surging back through her STL and inflicting this pain on her.

She shut her eyes briefly, then yanked them open again, dispelling her moment of hesitation. Her order of priorities had been set in stone years ago. She would commit any sin to protect Kirito—Kazuto Kirigaya. She would accept any punishment.

At last, the few dozen seconds that lasted an eternity came to an end, and the tip of her pearl-white boot touched black earth. She was in the middle of woods featuring oddly twisted shrubs. There was no moon, just eerie red starlight twinkling faintly down.

She shook her head several times to dispel the last bits of her lessening headache, then stretched her back. Directly nearby was the hole that she had created to swallow up the darklanders and their knightlike armor. It was a danger, left that way, but she couldn't bring herself to alter the land again anytime soon.

A horse whinnied nearby. She glanced in the direction of the sound and saw several large carriages parked among the woods in a way that was meant to conceal them.

Where…? Where are you, Kirito?

She was about to shout out the name of her beloved in sheer haste when she heard a quavering voice behind her ask, "Lady… Stacia…?"

Asuna spun around and saw two girls huddled together, dressed in gray jackets and skirts that resembled high school uniforms. Their looks were curious—neither Japanese nor Western. Their skin was smooth and cream-colored, and the girl on the right had red hair like maple leaves, while the girl on the left's was a dark coffee brown.

And on each one's belt, a well-used sword…

The red-haired girl's lips parted, and again she breathed, "Are you…the goddess…?"

It was perfect Japanese—and yet, there was just the slightest bit of foreignness to the pronunciation. Asuna felt as if she were brushing up against three hundred years of the Underworld's own history and cultural evolution, right in that moment.

Mr. Kikuoka, Mr. Higa, what have you created? Maybe this was all just a simulation to you, but this world and the people who live in it are undoubtedly alive.

"…No…I'm sorry. I am not a god," Asuna said, shaking her head.

The girl with the dark-brown hair clutched her hands to her chest and protested, "But…but you worked a miracle and saved my life. You saved everyone from the horrible soldiers of the land of darkness…The soldiers, the priests…and even Kirito."

Asuna gasped at the pulse that tore through her heart at the mention of that name. She struggled to regain her balance before she fell, and while her lips worked to speak, the most she could eventually produce was a whisper.

"I…I only came here…to see him. To see Kirito…," she pleaded, desperately holding back tears. "Please…where is he? Let me see him…Take me to where Kirito is."

The girls seemed stunned by this, but they soon glanced at each other, then nodded together. "Of course…Right this way."

They guided Asuna ahead through the distant circle created by swordsmen wearing matching armor. They soon reached the rear end of one of the carriages. A canopy made of heavy canvas hung over the bed, hiding its contents from view.

"Kirito's in—"

Before the red-haired girl could finish her sentence, Asuna opened the canopy with both hands and leaped into the bed of the wagon, stumbling farther inside.

A small lantern hanging from the canvas ceiling provided dim light, revealing stacked boxes and barrels. She made her way through them, farther and farther back. A familiar scent wafted out.

It smelled like the sun. Like the breeze traveling through forests and meadows.

As her eyes got used to the gloom, they caught sight of light reflecting off silver. The source of the light was a wheelchair built of a metal frame and wooden parts.

And hunched over the seat like a living shadow was a figure dressed in black.

"......!"

A storm of irresistible emotion rooted Asuna to the spot. All the words of reunion she had thought and thought about caught in her throat, refusing to come forth.

Here was the soul of the man she loved more than any other, whose body in the real world lay prone in STL Unit Four on the *Ocean Turtle.*

Battered, incomplete, but living and breathing.

Surely when Kirito had seen Asuna again at the hospital in Tokorozawa, freed from deadly *SAO* at last but still unwaking, he must have felt the same pain, the anguish, and made the same vow that she did now.

It's my turn to save you, to do whatever it takes, pay whatever price to bring you back.

Asuna let out the breath she was holding and whispered, "Kirito..."

His body was painfully thin, and his right arm was missing. His left arm clutched two swords, white and black, and it twitched when she spoke. His downcast face and empty eyes began to tremble and ripple.

"Aa...," his faint voice croaked through a cracked throat and dry lips. "A...aaa...ah..."

The wheelchair began to rattle quietly. His arm was incredibly tense. The tendons in his neck stood out. Two tears tracked down his cheeks and dripped onto the scabbards he clutched to his chest.

"It's all right, Kirito...It's all right now!!" shouted Asuna. She knelt and tenderly, powerfully embraced her beloved.

Hot droplets were spilling from her own eyes now, flowing without end.

It would be a lie to deny that she'd been hoping the moment of their reunion would miraculously heal Kirito's soul and return him to consciousness.

But Asuna was aware that the damage to Kirito's fluctlight was not so easily undone. His subjective sense within the fluctlight, his self-image, was shattered. Unless it was rebuilt somehow, no informational input from the outside was going to restore his proper output.

She recalled what Higa had said: *It turned out that he had a number of helpers—artificial fluctlights, of course...He had friends. Most of them died in the battle against the Church, but when he finally succeeded in opening the circuit to the outside, he was strongly blaming himself. In other words, he was attacking his own fluctlight.*

A massive source of loss, regret, and despair had torn a deep and terrible hole in Kirito's heart.

But I'm going to fill that hole, even if it's a bottomless void. If I can't do it alone, I'll borrow the help of all those people whose hearts he touched. I refuse to believe there's a sense of loss that no amount of love can fill.

Asuna could feel fresh, powerful determination fill her being. She would not let him feel a single further ounce of sadness.

I'm going to protect this world that Kirito loved and lived in. I'll protect it from these mysterious invaders...and from Rath itself.

She hugged her boyfriend tight once more, then got to her feet. When she turned around, the two girls were watching them, tears in their own eyes. She gave them a smile. "Thank you. You must have been keeping him safe."

The girl with the burnt-brown hair let her face droop a bit and asked, voice trembling, "Um...may I ask something...? If you are not Lady Stacia, then who are you...?"

"My name is Asuna. I'm a human being, just like you. Like Kirito, I came from the 'outside world'...to fulfill the same purpose that he did."

4

"I think the only thing I can say is that...this is quite remarkable," offered a relaxed, lazy voice.

Gabriel stood at the edge of his carriage's upper deck, gazing down upon the enormous divide in the earth that had appeared out of nowhere.

After that, he turned to the floor hatch in the corner of the deck, where a middle-aged man was sticking out his portly face. It was the leader of the commerce guild, a fellow named Rengil. He drew his wide sleeves together before his body and bowed deeply.

This was one of the few remaining leader units, but the man himself had very little combat potential. Gabriel inquired as to the reason for his presence by raising an eyebrow. Rengil held his hands up to his face and glanced left and right. He would have seen that Vassago was not on the deck, but he made no mention of it and bowed again.

"Your Majesty, when the moon rises soon...without the presence of an immediate order, I would ask that you allow the troops a break for nourishment and rest."

"Ah."

Gabriel turned back to the yawning fissure. He had sent scouts to either end to see how far it continued to the east and west, but they had not yet returned with reports. It had to be longer than a mile or two, then. And it was obvious at a glance that this was not a hole that could be filled in for passage across.

And Vassago and his helpers, whom he'd sent to the south in anticipation of the enemy's moves, had probably been wiped out by now. In Vassago's case, of course, he would simply wake up again in the real world.

This was the precise situation in which to use his aerial units, of course, but the dragons of the dark knighthood were only ten in number. It would take forever to ferry across twenty thousand infantry. He asked the few remaining dark mages if they could do anything with magic, but they said it was virtually impossible to fashion a bridge that was both long enough to cross the massive gap and strong enough for an army of this size. If a caster on the level of Chancellor Dee Eye Ell used multiple orcs as sacrifices again, maybe that would work, but she was reported dead without a body after the enemy knight's attack.

For having been so motivated and ambitious, she certainly met an ignoble end, Gabriel thought briefly, but it meant nothing more to him than the loss of another AI unit, and she promptly vanished from his mind.

Ultimately, this massive crevice had to be something from outside of the proper "game balance." The AI on the side of the Human Empire would not commit destruction that the units of the Dark Territory could not repair in some way, meaning that this had to be interference from the real world.

The Rath employees trapped in the Upper Shaft were logging in with a super-account the same way that Gabriel was. And they probably had the same goal: retrieve Alice and use the system console to eject her from the Underworld.

This certainly complicated matters, but at least knowing that much gave him options for adjusting. In fact, one might even say things had gotten more interesting.

Gabriel let the ends of his mouth curl into the slightest of smiles, but only for a moment. He turned to Rengil again and said, "Very well. We will camp here for today. Let the soldiers eat their fill. Tomorrow will be busy."

"Yes, Majesty. Your magnanimity does not go unnoticed."

The senior merchant bowed yet again and quickly made himself scarce.

"The same...*world*...as Kirito?" the girls repeated, their red and navy-blue eyes, respectively, big and wide. "D-do you mean...the celestial realm? Where the three goddesses of creation...and the gods who control the elements, and all the angels live...?"

"I don't," Asuna said hastily, shaking her head. "It is a world that exists outside of this place, but it is not a land of gods. I mean...look, do you think Kirito is a god or an angel or anything like that?"

The girls looked at the wheelchair, blinking, then giggled. They quickly regained their composure and bobbed their heads.

"I—I see...I don't think any god would sneak out of school regularly to go buy food, I suppose...," said the red-haired girl, bringing a smile to Asuna's lips this time. He was up to his old tricks in this world, too. She felt her eyes growing hot again with the exasperation and joy of the discovery but kept it under control and smiled for the girls.

Next, the brown-haired one murmured, "Then...what kind of place is this...outside world, as you call it...?"

Asuna considered her answer carefully. "Well...I'm sorry, but I can't describe it in one simple statement. I'd like to give you a full explanation in the presence of the people who are in charge here. Can you guide me there?"

"Y-yes, of course. Come right this way," the girls said, looking serious, and headed for the exit from the carriage bed. Before she chased after them, Asuna stopped and glanced at Kirito. There were drying tear marks on his downcast cheeks.

It's all right. It'll all be okay, Kirito. Just let me handle the rest of this, she told him silently, squeezed his limp hand, and turned away. She made her way through the rows of boxes, lifted the canvas canopy, and leaped down to the ground.

The moment her white boots hit the soil, she saw a golden flash before her.

A sword.

But Asuna's reflexes worked before she recognized what it was. Her right hand was already moving, pulling free her rapier at maximum speed.

A loud, high-pitched clang pierced the night forest.

She succeeded in deflecting the slash of her attacker, but the shock of it numbed her right arm up to the elbow. How heavy was that other sword?

Through the light created by the shower of sparks that resulted, she saw the next swing flashing toward her, giving her no time to breathe.

But if she simply blocked it, she would be battered backward, she knew, so she thrust multiple times with the rapier against the oncoming blade.

Only on the third strike did it stop. Asuna caught the sword on her hilt and pushed, buying her time to at least see who her attacker was.

The breath caught in her throat. It was an incredibly beautiful woman who glared at Asuna with such fury that it brought a flush to her snow-white skin. Her sapphire-blue eyes shone righteously.

Her long hair, the color of molten gold, shook with the pressure of the attack. Her ostentatiously designed armor and the graceful longsword in her right hand were both a deep, bold yellow.

The other girls, who'd been watching this unfold in shocked silence, finally recovered and shrieked, "M-my lady, please stop!!"

"She is not our enemy, Miss Alice!!"

Alice?!

Asuna found herself shocked for a different reason.

So this stunningly beautiful woman with the sword as heavy as rock was none other than the world's first bottom-up AI, the high-functioning intelligence code-named A.L.I.C.E.? The goal of Project Alicization itself, and the core of this entire incident, wanted by both Rath and the invaders?

But why would Alice be attacking her with such hostility? Asuna was desperately seeking the answer as she pushed back against the golden blade when Alice's cherry-blossom lips opened and emitted a voice that, while fierce, was as beautiful as a violin in the hands of a master.

"Who are you?! Why are you trying to approach Kirito?!"

In that moment, everything on Asuna's mind, all the many swirling circumstances, were pushed aside in a reaction that could be described only by a single sound effect: *ka-ching!*

The words that erupted from Asuna's mouth were less of a bucket of water on the enemy's open flame than a bottle of oil.

"Why...? Because Kirito is *mine*!"

"How dare you! Ruffian!!" Alice snarled, baring her pearly white fangs.

Their swords separated, the last friction causing more sparks. The woman in gold floated backward, and as soon as her boots hit the ground, she zipped forward again with a high slash. This time, Asuna was not put on the defensive; she unleashed one of the combination attacks that would forever be a part of her muscle memory.

A huge crescent moon and countless meteors collided in the darkened woods, lighting their surroundings. Again, Asuna was stunned at the shock that ran from her elbow to her shoulder. She had to admit that she was slightly inferior when it came to skill; the only thing keeping her even with her opponent was the fact that the "GM gear" that came with the Stacia account—a rapier named Radiant Light—had a higher priority level than Alice's golden longsword.

Their swords locked at the hilt again, coming to a stop. Amid the silence that followed, a man's voice leisurely cut in: "Well, well, this is quite a sight, I must say. Two beautiful flowers in full bloom. Absolute beauty."

From what should have been empty space emerged two powerful arms. Rough fingers pinched Alice's and Asuna's swords around the sides.

"...?!"

Her rapier went immobile, as though it were held with a vise. Then the arms lifted the swords, combatants and all, and held them apart before setting them back down on the ground.

Standing next to them now was a large man who looked to be in his forties. His clothing was a robe that looked similar to a kimono, with only a minimum amount of armor added to it. The steel-gray longsword in his waist sash and the arms extending from his sleeves were covered with scars. He was every bit the image of a mighty veteran warrior.

His appearance caused Alice to magically appear several years younger. "Why are you stopping me, Uncle?!" She pouted. "I believe she is an enemy spy come to..."

"She is no such thing. It was this young lady who kept me from charging to an early grave, in fact. I'd guess the same goes for you?" he said, addressing the two girls in the back, who were gaping at the proceedings in typical fashion.

They replied very hesitantly, speaking in turn. "Y-yes, Lord Commander. She saved our lives."

"With one swing of her sword, she sent a great number of the enemy to Hell...It was a godly act."

The man they called Commander glanced back in the direction of the great fissure Asuna had created, and he laid a hand on Alice's shoulder. "I saw it happen, too. A rainbow of light rained down from above and opened a gash in the earth a hundred mels wide. The pugilists were shocked that they couldn't jump across it, I bet. It's an undeniable fact that this young lady saved us from being absolutely overrun by the enemy."

"........."

Alice glared at Asuna with obvious suspicion, naked golden blade still dangling from her right hand. "Then are you saying, Uncle...that this woman is neither an enemy spy nor some heretical imposter mimicking the garb depicted in holy art, but the actual Stacia, goddess of creation?"

Asuna bit her lip in silence. If this knight commander, who appeared to be the overall commander of the human army, identified her as a goddess, it was going to cause more trouble than she wanted.

Fortunately, the commander only smirked and shook his head. "I don't think so. If this girl were a true goddess, she'd be scarier than the pontifex, wouldn't she? She might strike down a violent surprise attacker to the depths of the earth, wouldn't you think?"

Alice was unable to mount a response to that. She still glared at Asuna with hostile sparks flying, but she fit the end of her longsword to the mouth of her sheath and clinked it all the way into place.

For her part, Asuna had some comments as well. She wanted to know who this girl thought she was, talking about Kirito that way—but with a deep breath, she was able to stifle that urge for now.

Asuna's duty was to guide Alice to the World's End Altar at the very southern tip of the Underworld and physically eject the lightcube that held Alice's fluctlight from the cluster. In other words, she had to convince this young woman, whom she clearly did not get along with, to leave the side of her army. This was absolutely not the time to bicker.

She stashed her own rapier away and turned to the commander. "Yes...as you say, I am no god. I am as human as the rest of you. I just happen to have some special knowledge about the situation you are in. I know this because I came from a place outside of your world."

"Outside, huh...?" the commander repeated, grinning broadly. He rubbed his fierce, stubbled chin.

Alice, however, sucked in a sharp breath and demanded, "The outside world?! You came from the same place that Kirito did?!"

Asuna was taken aback. He'd explained it to her? At least in some measure? Taking the ratio of the Fluctlight Acceleration currently active into account, Kirito had already spent nearly three years in this simulation. She couldn't help but wonder how much time he had spent together with this golden-haired warrior.

Alice was clearly wondering something along the same lines and took a step closer to Asuna before the commander blocked her path with a thick arm.

"It's probably best if the other knights and the head guards hear the rest of her story. We can discuss this all over tea. The enemy isn't going to be doing anything more tonight."

"I...suppose you're right," Alice said, though her brow was still knitted.

"Good. Then if that's settled...would you girls over there fetch us some hot tea and fire whiskey for me? You can listen in as well."

The uniformed pair gave loud salutes. Asuna wanted to see Kirito one more time before she left the wagons, but before she could do anything else, Alice snapped, "Just so we are clear, you are not to enter that wagon without my permission. It is my duty to secure Kirito's safety."

Asuna felt her scalp burn with anger but held it in.

"And I...will not stand by and listen to you speak about my Kirito as though he means something to you..."

"Did you just say something?!"

"...Nothing at all."

They snorted and looked away from each other, then followed after the commander.

Left behind, Tiese and Ronie exhaled together.

"Things just got really...intense somehow," Tiese murmured.

She clapped her hands together to reset the mood and said, in her usual bright manner, "We'd better go boil the water! And the fire-whiskey jar should be in *that* carriage, right? Let's go, Ronie!"

Before she trotted after her friend, Ronie muttered, to no one at all, "But...he was my mentor first..."

5

Cup of tea in hand, Asuna stared into the campfire, which popped and snapped merrily.

It looked so real. This one was fundamentally different from the fires she'd seen so many times in *SAO* and *ALO*, which were graphical effects generated within the game engine. The brilliance of the sparks that flew out with each burst of the dried logs, the charred tang of the smoke, the radiating heat that warmed the skin of her face and hands—the details stimulated her senses with a reality that even real life failed to deliver.

And it wasn't just the campfire. It was the hard surface of the folding chair they brought her. The smooth finish of the well-worn wooden cup. The calming scent of the tea. The dry sound of the trees around them, rustling in the night breeze.

Since logging in to the Underworld, she hadn't had the time to stop and savor the world like this. Now that she was able to focus on the full sensory experience, she was blown away by the quality of the STL's mnemonic visuals.

If Kirito had logged in to this place without knowing it was a virtual world, it must have taken a great amount of time to figure that out. For one thing, there was no such thing as an NPC in this place.

Asuna tore her eyes off the flickering fire and examined the people gathered at the edge of the little clearing in the midst of the forest. She'd already been given simple introductions to them.

The one just to her left, plopped on the ground with an old-fashioned jar of liquor all to himself, was Commander Bercouli of the Integrity Knights. On his other side was Alice, in her golden armor. Even Asuna had to admire the beauty of that deep-gold hair, enhanced by the orange light of the campfire.

On Alice's left was a boy swordsman of about fifteen or sixteen who seemed to have no real place here. He, too, was an Integrity Knight, which seemed to be the highest class one could obtain in this world. His name was Renly.

Next, Asuna saw a thin knight who sat as quiet as a shadow. Her new armor didn't seem to fit her yet, as she was constantly pulling and loosening its leather straps. It was the kind of thing a VRMMO newbie did, but the moment Asuna was told the woman's name was Sheyta, and she turned her narrow eyes to meet Asuna's gaze, there was an incredible force in them.

On Sheyta's left, now directly across the campfire from Asuna, there were about ten people crammed shoulder to shoulder—they were from the chief man-at-arms class, she was told. They were firm, bold-looking men with chiseled features, with only one woman among the group.

Finally, just on Asuna's right were the uniformed girls, who huddled to themselves and looked quite out of place. The red-haired one was Tiese, and the brown-haired one was Ronie, and they were apparently underclassmen at the academy where Kirito had been until six months ago.

After glancing at each of these dozen-plus warriors in turn, Asuna was left with one very heady conclusion: They were all real human beings.

Nothing about their appearances, actions, and general atmosphere suggested in any way that they had been artificially crafted. It was so seamless that she almost doubted her own secret knowledge: that, of this group, only Alice had surpassed the bounds of the artificial fluctlights that forced them to follow the rules they were given.

Now she could understand why Kirito had damaged his very soul to protect all these people. She had to carry on that spirit for him.

Asuna took a deep breath and said, "It's good to meet you all. My name is Asuna. I came from outside of this world."

Although she had left it only eight days ago, already her short life in the rural village of Rulid filled Alice with a pang of nostalgia. During that time, she'd often wheeled Kirito to a nearby pasture.

Within the bounds of the firm wooden fence, many fluffy sheep sat peacefully grazing, their lambs running and frolicking between the adults. Alice thought their life to be so happy. They had no reason to worry about anything beyond the fence. They spent their days in peace and security, locked inside a protected little world.

To think that she and the others were essentially the same way, inside this world they inhabited...

The otherworld girl named Asuna delivered an earth-shattering shock to the Integrity Knights and chief guards crowded around the campfire. Only Bercouli maintained his usual air of aloofness, but surely he, too, had much to take away from her story.

Asuna referred to their entire world, encompassing both the human lands and the dark lands, by a sacred-tongue title of "the Underworld." And on the outside—not a physical outside but a conceptual one—there was another place called the "real world."

Naturally, the guardsmen questioned whether this was the place they knew as the celestial world. The visitor answered that the real world was full of human beings with emotions, desires, and a limited life span.

And that at this moment, in a very limited space within the real world, two factions were battling for control over the Underworld.

Asuna said that she was an agent of one of those sides. Their goal was to protect the Underworld.

And the goal of the side opposing Asuna's was to pull one individual out of the Underworld, then wipe the slate clean by erasing the entirety of their world...

The leaders of the men-at-arms murmured uneasily when they heard this. It was Bercouli who calmed them down.

"It's the same thing," the three-hundred-year-old hero said. "The human realm is surrounded by the Dark Territory, and hardly anyone, including me, ever gave much thought to the fact that we were all sitting back and waiting for a huge invasion force to reach our doorstep. And now there's another world beyond them? Big difference."

His logic was crude, but when delivered in the commander's firm, reassuring voice, it was convincing. With the audience composed again, Bercouli asked Asuna who it was that the opposing faction wanted to pull out.

The visitor's bright brown eyes drifted away from Bercouli and locked straight onto Alice. Over the following seconds, Alice gradually understood the importance of what was happening, and she pointed at her own face.

"M...me...?"

Renly, Tiese, Ronie, and even Sheyta looked shocked. But once again, it was Bercouli who took this revelation in stride.

"Ah, yes...Hence the 'Priestess of Light' bit..."

Asuna did not seem to recognize the term, as she merely blinked at him. Then she looked back at Alice and said, "There isn't much time left. To prevent the destruction of the Underworld, I'll need Alice to come with me to the real world. Once they know that Alice is no longer here, the enemy should give up on interfering with this world..."

"You...you cannot be serious!!" shouted Alice. She stood up so forcefully that she kicked the chair back and smacked her breastplate with her palm. "Run away? Me?! Give up on this world and all its people, including my comrades in the guardian army, just to go to this so-called 'real world' place?! Absolutely not! I am an Integrity Knight! Protecting the realm is my one and only mission!!"

This time, it was Asuna who shot to her feet. Her hair, brown like the color of platinum-oak nuts, shook as she retorted in a voice like silver bells, "Then it is even more important that you do so! If the enemy—not your darklanders but powerful foes from the real world—capture you, not only the people of this world but its earth, sky, and everything else will be obliterated! They could attack this place at any moment!"

"I think your intel's a bit out of date in that regard, Miss Asuna," interjected Commander Bercouli, his voice calm and controlled. "It would seem that your enemy is already here."

"What...?" she gasped.

He took a slug from his fire whiskey, just to tease her for a moment, before continuing. "It all adds up now. The Priestess of Light...and the god of darkness, Vecta, who seeks her. The Vecta who's leading the enemy army right now is most definitely a person from your 'real world.'"

"God of...darkness," Asuna repeated, her face clearly pale even in the meager light of the campfire. She murmured to herself, voice thick with the accent of the sacred tongue, "Oh no...the super-account for the Dark Territory wasn't password locked after all..."

"Um...m-may I ask something?" said Renly the boy knight, raising his hand to fill the resulting silence. When all eyes were on him, his voice became quiet and timid. "What exactly is the Priestess of Light, anyway? Why would these plunderers from the...'real world'...want Miss Alice so badly?"

The answer to that came not from Asuna or Bercouli but from the previously silent gray knight, Sheyta.

"Because she broke the right-eye seal."

Alice was shocked enough that she momentarily forgot her

anger and unconsciously raised a hand to her eye. "You...you knew about that, Sheyta?! But how...?!"

"There's a thought that makes my right eye hurt. When I think about how much fun it would be...to cut clean through the hardest material in the world...the indestructible Central Cathedral itself."

"......"

Knights and guards alike shared an awkward silence, which Bercouli broke with a cough.

"Well, I wonder if any of the rest of you have had similar experiences before. Feeling any kind of doubt about the pontifex's authority or the Axiom Church's system of rule, causing red light to flicker inside your right eyeball, and a pain that shoots right through your head. So intense, you can't maintain that thought any longer. But if you keep going, the pain just gets stronger and stronger, until the right side of your vision is pure red...and then..."

"Your right eye itself simply bursts into nothingness," Alice finished, recalling in vivid detail that horrible experience. The rest of the campfire party wore expressions of fear to varying degrees.

"Then...Miss Alice, are you saying...?" Renly said with apprehension.

Alice nodded slowly. "I fought against Prime Senator Chudelkin and Administrator. And I had to lose my right eye for a period in order to have the will to go through with it."

"Um...excuse me...," said the trainee girl Tiese from the supply team, who had been listening the entire time, her voice even more timid than Renly's. "Eugeo did it, too...When he drew his sword to protect Ronie and me, blood came from his eye..."

Alice nodded, understanding. The young man, despite his humble origins, had overcome many terrible battles, defeated even Bercouli, and unleashed a brilliant Incarnation against Administrator. Surely he would've been able to overcome the seal of the right eye.

In fact, during the battle on the top floor of the cathedral,

Administrator had looked at Alice and said something about the eye seal. Something like *Code Eight-Seven...*

But before she could recall the full list of words, Bercouli grunted, rubbing his chin. "Hmm...so this enemy that Miss Asuna is talking about is in search of someone who broke through the right-eye seal on their own. Now let me ask you: Do you real-worlders have the same seal on you?"

"...No," she said, shaking her brown hair, after a brief moment of indecision. "I have never experienced such a thing. I believe that the only point of difference between Underworlders and real-worlders is whether one is absolutely forced to obey laws and orders or not."

"So you're saying that there's nothing different between Alice and you folks now? But how does that make sense? Why would Vecta want the same thing as him so much? You'd figure there are plenty of folks living in the real world."

"Well...," Asuna muttered, clearly not sure of how to proceed now. But at that moment, the thorn sticking into Alice's memory at last came loose, and she shouted, "That's it! Code Eight-Seven-One!"

Alice clasped her hands together and continued, "That's what the pontifex called the seal of the right eye. She said that someone had installed Code Eight-Seven-One for her. I didn't understand what the words meant, because they weren't ancient sacred tongue... They were in your real-world language, weren't they?!"

"Code...Eight-Seven-One...?" Asuna repeated, dumbfounded, her brows knitted. "So the seal was...put in place...by someone from Rath...? But...that would only make their mission harder..."

Asuna sat down in her chair and thought this revelation over—until suddenly, profound shock colored her features. Her pale-pink lips trembled, and her voice went hoarse. But Alice did not understand the meaning of what she said.

"......Oh no...There's a mole on Rath's staff! They have someone on *our* side...!"

* * *

Asuna was in a state of shock.

Higa and his team of engineers had taken great pains to try to remove the one flaw of the artificial fluctlights: their blind obedience. At present, the fluctlights were not able to critically examine the orders they were given through logic or morals. If they were loaded onto weapons as an AI system, they could be hacked and given orders to indiscriminately attack civilians or friendlies and would do so without needing confirmation. They could not, as Western militaries defined it, refuse an unlawful order.

Rath had maintained this centuries-long simulation in the Underworld in order to create a true artificial intelligence that could break through this drawback. But what if the seal in the right eye, this "Code Eight-Seven-One"—which seemed specifically designed to prevent the experiment's success—had been secretly installed by someone affiliated with Rath?

That sabotage would likely have been ordered by the invading force that was now taking over the *Ocean Turtle*. They'd wanted to delay the experiment and keep it from succeeding until they were ready to attack the ship.

And the mole was still loose in the *Ocean Turtle*'s Upper Shaft. If he wanted to, he could wait until no one else was looking and sneak into the second STL room, where Asuna and Kirito were lying helpless. She felt her skin crawl with the thought.

Either Higa, Kikuoka, or Dr. Koujiro needed to be told as soon as possible. But since she had logged in to a coordinate far removed from the system console, Asuna had no way of calling them to talk.

She did have one method of getting out—reducing her current avatar's HP to zero—but then she would not be able to log in with this super-account again. With sys-admin privileges currently locked, there was no way for her to reset the account data.

Given that the attackers were using the Vecta account, which had as much power as Stacia, there was no way for her to counteract them with an ordinary civilian-level avatar. She needed this character if she was going to protect Alice and safely log her out.

What should I do? What's the priority? she asked herself, all of the above taking just a split second to run through. She inhaled, exhaled, and made a decision.

For now, she would prioritize the Underworld. This place was running at a thousand times the speed of the regular world. She at least had some wiggle room in terms of time before the mole in the real world did anything.

Until then, she would protect Alice from the Dark Territory army under the enemy's control and eject her into the real world. If she failed and Alice fell into enemy hands, they would shatter the rest of the lightcube cluster to ensure only they could possess a true AI. They would destroy the Underworld that Kirito had risked his life to protect.

The decision that Asuna Yuuki made at this time was absolutely the right one, given the information she currently possessed. But neither she nor Takeru Higa and Seijirou Kikuoka on the *Ocean Turtle* had realized one extremely important fact.

After Gabriel Miller and Vassago Casals had logged in, the FLA ratio had been gradually dropping. It was the work of Critter, the assault team's hacker, on Captain Gabriel's orders.

Twenty hours from now, the Aegis escort ship *Nagato* was going to send in an armed Maritime SDF team, so Rath would not have expected that the attackers would make things harder for themselves by lowering the acceleration ratio and leaving their mission with less time.

For one thing, the purpose of lowering the acceleration ratio was completely outside of their expectations.

But at the present moment, there was *one* person who understood

Gabriel's intentions in doing this. She was collecting information independently through the cell phone that Asuna had brought on board the ship—one of the world's greatest top-down artificial intelligences, now flying through the network on her own secret mission.

"Is something wrong with you?"

When Asuna noticed that Alice's voice didn't have its usual polite formality, she realized that she was the one being addressed. She looked up and shook her head. "No...I'm fine. I'm sorry to have interrupted your conversation."

"You haven't, actually. We're just waiting for your answer," Alice said in the brusque manner she reserved just for Asuna. "Well? Do you have any ideas about what the words *Code Eight-Seven-One* mean?"

"I do. And I'm about to explain it."

Asuna had to wonder at the way that her voice naturally grew snippy when she was talking to Alice. She could barely recall ever fighting with anyone in her life. Things were always fun and lively with Lisbeth, Silica, Leafa, and Sinon, and she got along with everyone at school.

She traced back through her memory, trying to figure out who she'd argued with last before Alice, and she nearly burst out laughing. It had to be Kirito.

After they'd met in the first labyrinth tower of Aincrad, they'd formed a duo for some mysterious reason and started working on the game of death together. In those days, Asuna had glared, yelled, and even smacked Kirito on countless occasions. Only the mystery of human emotions could explain how that relationship had turned into a romantic one.

So would the day come that she got along with Alice, too? *It doesn't seem very likely,* she had to admit.

* * *

"...The one who enabled the right-eye seal known as Code Eight-Seven-One, according to Alice, is a person from the real world...Someone aligned with the enemy."

"Hmm...And is there any way to undo this code without blowing up your eyeball?" Bercouli asked. The otherworld girl shook her head apologetically.

"I'm afraid I don't know...but I suspect that it's not something that can be undone from inside the Underworld."

As she listened to Asuna's pristine voice, Alice wondered what it was about her that made her so irritated.

It was true that her first impression of Asuna had been terrible. Of course she wasn't going to feel good when the young woman approached Kirito without notice of any kind. It was Alice who had protected and cared for him in his wounded state for the past six months.

But Asuna came from the real world, like Kirito did. It was clear from her actions that she had some kind of personal relationship with him there. In other words, she had come all the way to this realm after him. Maybe she had the right to see him. Once.

Was that the source of this irritation? She had believed that the obligation and duty of keeping Kirito safe belonged to her alone, and now there was a new person who laid claim to his past?

Or was it a sense of competition toward Asuna's tremendous skill with the sword? It was the first time Alice had seen consecutive attacks of such speed. Even in terms of speed alone, Vice Commander Fanatio wouldn't stand a chance. The attacks were less consecutive than practically multiple thrusts happening at the same time. If Alice's blade had been deflected in any way, the other girl would have been quicker to hit first. She had never been shocked by a swordswoman of her age like this before.

Or perhaps...

...it was because the very sight of Asuna's beauty caused the breath to leave Alice's lungs. Her features were foreign in a way that personified and exemplified graceful beauty like no one else. Her pale skin was spotless, and her long hair, the color of acorns, looked wavy and soft, like bundles of the finest silk. The admiration on the faces of the head guardsmen was surely not just her imagination. If Asuna had introduced herself as the goddess Stacia, they would have believed her without question.

Alice wanted to *know.*

She wanted to know about Asuna more than about even this strange new world or their new enemy. She wanted to know about Asuna and Kirito.

Suddenly, she realized that her thoughts had been drifting, and she focused her ears again. Asuna was still talking to the commander.

"...was afraid that the one who could break this Underworld seal...the Priestess of Light, to use their words, might fall into enemy hands. They were afraid, because the Priestess of Light has the possibility of becoming an extraordinarily valuable thing in the real world."

"That's the part I don't get," Bercouli grumbled, sloshing his jar of fire whiskey. "This Priestess of Light, little Alice, is the same as a real-worlder, right? Like I asked earlier, why the fixation on the same thing? What are both the enemy and your side trying to pull Alice out into the outer world to do, exactly?"

"Well..."

Asuna hesitated, biting her lip. Her long eyelashes drooped, and her voice went quiet.

"...I'm sorry. I cannot tell you now. I want Alice to see the real world with her own eyes to make her decision. It is no world of the gods out there. It's not a paradise. In fact, it's much uglier and dirtier than this world. The same is true for the motives of the people who want Alice. If I explain them to you right now, Alice would find the real world and the people who live there to be unforgivable. But that's not all there is. There are many good people as well, who want to protect this world and get along with the people here. Just like Kirito, in fact."

Alice listened to her impassioned plea in silence. To her own surprise, she nodded.

"...Very well. I won't ask you more at this time." She spread her hands and shrugged. "In any case, I don't intend to do anything I don't want to do. And I have not decided whether I am going to this 'real world,' either. I'm interested in seeing the outer world, but only after we have broken the invading army of Vecta that is breathing down our necks and have forged a peace with the Dark Territory."

She figured Asuna would offer a harsh rebuttal, but the other girl was briefly silent, too, before agreeing.

"...Yes, knowing that the Vecta leading the Dark Territory army is from my world, it might be dangerous for Alice and me to leave this group on our own. The enemy will be expecting that. I will fight with the rest of you. Please let me handle Vecta."

There was a huge roar from the guardsmen at this. To them, Asuna might as well be Stacia herself, regardless of what she said. If she could wield such high-powered arts that they split the earth beneath their feet, then the enemy army might as well be ten times their current number, for all the good it would do them.

The commander was considering this as well. He crossed his arms and said, "Well, we can leave the circumstances of the real world alone for now. Back to more pressing matters...Are you able to use that earth-splitting trick without limits, Asuna?"

"...I'm afraid I might not be able to fulfill your hope," she replied, shaking her head sadly. "That power places an enormous strain on the mind. I can withstand any kind of pain, but if I'm reckless with it, I might be automatically removed from this world in order to protect my mind. In that case, I won't be able to come back. I would guess that I can only alter the landscape like that one or two more times..."

Given how great their hopes were, the faces of the guards

around the campfire were now crestfallen. Alice sensed their disappointment and spoke a bit louder than she needed to.

"Why would we rely on the help of outsiders to protect our own world? You've done plenty to help already. Now it's time for us knights and soldiers to show these otherworlders what we can do!" she said rousingly, but when she saw the surprise on Asuna's face, Alice began to feel self-conscious.

After Alice was done, it was the youngest person present, Renly, who spoke up next. "Th-that's right! Asuna just told you that she wasn't a god; she's a human being, like us! So we should be able to fight as hard as she does!"

Alice didn't fail to notice that the young knight, hands against his divine weapons, was looking not at Asuna but at the red-haired girl sitting nearby. The discovery brought a mild note of mirth to her mind.

Next, even Sheyta the Silent offered her opinion. "I, too… would like to fight that pugilist again."

The head guardsmen shot each other glances, and it did not take long for them to regain their previous bravado.

"That's right. Let's do this. We're going to protect everyone," they shouted with excitement and purpose, and pretty soon, all the guards stationed in the surrounding meadows were joining in the chorus. Even the campfire seemed to channel the mood, licking higher and burning the night sky red.

Was this the right thing to do?

Asuna sat in the tent she was given, pearl-white breastplate removed, thinking hard.

In the real world, Higa and Kikuoka were hoping that Asuna would bring Alice to the system console as soon as possible so she could be ejected into the sub-control room.

But what would happen after that? From Kikuoka's perspective, once he had Alice's fluctlight, he could just analyze its structure and transfer it to the development of a drone-piloting AI. For these military-industrial men, there was no further merit to the costly maintenance of the lightcube cluster and the thousands of artificial fluctlights contained within it.

And if she saved Alice alone and the other Underworlders got deleted, what would Kirito think when he awoke? And more importantly, would his fluctlight ever be fully whole again…?

But no, she mustn't think that way. She'd seen him again at last, so she needed to find a way to touch him, speak to him, and give him all the chances he needed to heal. Even Higa had said that at some point, they just needed to hope that a miracle within the Underworld would heal his spirit.

She wanted to sneak into his tent, embrace him, and speak to him. She would do it the entire time she spent in the Underworld, if she could. There was no way she wanted to leave him behind to head for this console far to the south.

At least let me spend one night with him…

With her mind made up, Asuna removed her metal armor, changed into a light tunic and skirt, and waited near the entrance of the tent, listening intently.

Despite her repeated claims that she would be just fine, there was still one guard keeping watch outside the small tent the knight commander had given to her. The young man insisted on the honor of keeping watch over the goddess Stacia, and he was diligently patrolling the exterior of the tent. No napping on the job tonight.

His footsteps crunched over the grass underfoot, past the entrance. When he was behind the tent, Asuna slipped quickly out. In three silent bounds, she managed to sneak behind a large tree over thirty feet away.

She glanced back to see the young guard appear from around the rear of the tent and contentedly continue his patrol, unaware that anything had happened. Asuna gave him a silent apology and headed farther through the trees.

The human army's soldiers had gone to sleep quickly, fatigued by the massive battle, and aside from a few lookouts, no one seemed to be awake. Those lookouts kept their focus on the outside of the forest, so Asuna was able to reach the supply team's tents without being discovered.

She closed her eyes and focused her mind. Through either the power of the super-account or her own intuition, she sensed the presence of her beloved at once. Asuna took only a few steps in that direction before she detected a golden light flickering out of the corner of her right eye and froze.

Ugh. She turned, very slowly.

Back against the tent pole, arms crossed, was a person. She wore a dress of the same material as Asuna's tunic, along with a wool shawl. Her long blond hair stirred in the breeze. Her glaring eyes were a deep blue.

"...I figured you would come."

Alice took a step forward, her nostrils flaring.

She stared down the other young woman, who was about her height and barely different in age, intent on unleashing the words she'd been prepared to say.

I warned you to stay away from him. Go back to your own tent.

But the breath she sucked into her lungs refused to exit her throat. She could read the emotions in this otherworlder's eyes far too easily to say those words now. There was deep affection in them—and the anguish and determination that arose from it.

Alice exhaled slowly until her breath was gone. She told herself, *I'm not compromising. This doesn't change the fact that I'm the one with the strongest duty to protect Kirito. We fought together and suffered wounds together, and I was watching when he lost his strength before me.*

So whatever she chose to do, it was part of the effort to bring him back to health.

"...Let's make a deal," she said. Asuna blinked, taken aback. "I'll let you see him. And I'll tell you everything I know. And in return, I want you to tell me everything you know about Kirito."

The brief moment of surprise on Asuna's face melted away, replaced by a smile that almost looked cocky to Alice.

"You've got a deal. But it'll take a while. Might not even finish in one night."

Once again, Alice was reminded that she did not like this person. "How long have you spent with him?"

Asuna turned her light-brown eyes to the night sky, and she began to count, making gestures with her fingers. "Let's see...I fought alongside him as his partner for two years. After that, a year and a half going out with him. And for two weeks, we also lived together."

Does "going out with" mean they were lovers? No, probably not...but then again, "living with him" sounds very serious...

Alice couldn't deny that she was shaken by these facts, but she shrugged it off, determined to stand her ground, and said proudly, "I fought at his side for an entire night. After that, I spent half a year under the same roof, attending to his needs."

This time, it was Asuna who reeled a bit. Then her back straightened again, and she hummed a sound of feigned interest. The two women rippled with hostility, like fighters engaging in a duel. The crisp night air crackled with electricity, such that an unlucky leaf that happened to fall between them at that moment found itself disintegrating into dust in midair.

The battle of wills between Integrity Knight and goddess of creation was interrupted by none other than the frail voice of a third girl.

"Excuse me..."

Startled, Alice looked in the direction of the voice, as did Asuna. Ronie the supply team student, dressed in gray pajamas with her brown hair covered by a loose nightcap, stood between the tents. She had her hands clasped in front of her. "Um, I...I cleaned Kirito's room for about two months, and he taught me some sword techniques, and he brought me honey pies from the Jumping Deer several times! I might not have the length of time that you two do, but...I'd like to trade information, too..."

Alice blinked several times, then looked back at Asuna. They both wore exasperated smiles. "Fine. I guess you're one of us, then, Ronie," Asuna said, and the smaller girl beamed with relief, coming forth from the shadow of the tent. Alice had to admit that it had taken guts for her to do this.

But to her surprise, the cast was not done growing. Another voice emerged from a different patch of shadows. "I don't suppose you'd let me join in your exchange, as well?"

Her tone was boyish, but the voice itself was a cool mezzo-soprano. Appearing under the moonlight without a sound was a rather tall woman. The moment she saw the woman's crisp features, Asuna murmured, "I remember you from before..."

It was definitely her—the lone female senior guard at the campfire meeting earlier. The brown-haired woman with the long ponytail bobbed her head and said, "Norlangarth Imperial Knight Sortiliena Serlut at your service. I was going to wait until the battle was over... but as I, too, have some measure of connection to Kirito, I was unable to withstand my curiosity."

Alice exhaled loudly. She shrugged and asked the tall soldier, "And what kind of connection did you have with him, Chief Guard Serlut?"

"If it pleases you, Lady Knight, call me simply Liena," Sortiliena said. She coughed to clear her throat and made an appreciative gesture. "At the North Centoria Imperial Swordcraft Academy, Kirito spent a year as my page, assisting me in various ways. I believe that, in return, I served as a mentor and taught him some things about the sword."

"......"

The other three went silent, intimidated by this surprising entry.

Asuna shared a look with Alice, and they shook their heads in unison.

"In that case, I suppose you've got plenty you can tell us, too, Liena. Come. Join us."

The four snuck along, all of them feeling awkward, and entered

a small tent off to the side with Alice at the lead. On the leather rug were two travel beds, one of which was empty, the other containing a black-haired young man whose eyes were closed. The handles of two swords stuck out of the end of his blanket.

Alice didn't miss the note of nostalgic longing on Asuna's lips when she saw him.

"...Is something wrong?" she asked.

The otherworld warrior gave her a momentary innocent smile, all hostility briefly forgotten. "Dual-Bladed Kirito. That's what they called him over there."

"...Oh..."

Alice did recall, during the fight against Administrator, how Kirito had fought skillfully with his own black sword in one hand and Eugeo's white sword in the other. So that wasn't some spontaneous idea...

She sat down atop the blanket of the bed next to the sleeping youth and beckoned the other three girls to sit around her.

"Let's start there, shall we?"

Night in the wasteland grew deeper, and the only light upon the earth was from the purple moon. The soldiers of the Human Guardian Army and the dark knights and pugilists of the Dark Territory's army on the other side of the bottomless abyss fell into a deep sleep.

While the forces of both sides recharged for the coming battle, the light from one tiny tent simply refused to go dark. At times, muffled laughter could be heard from under the hemp canvas—but only by a single owl that perched on the branch of a nearby tree.

Eventually, the lamp oil ran out, and four exhausted young women fell asleep, nestled around the object of their interest.

A while later, in distant Centoria, the midnight bells rang peacefully. Naturally, their sound did not penetrate to the distant Dark Territory.

At that very moment, every citizen of the Underworld experienced what could be called a tiny chrono-vibration. It was the effect of the simulation's Fluctlight Acceleration dropping to real-time speed, but hardly anyone who was awake even noticed the shift.

It was midnight on the eighth day of the eleventh month of the year 380 in the Underworld's Human Era.

It was midnight on July 7th, 2026, according to Japan Standard Time.

At this moment, the time of the two worlds was in perfect synchronization.

6

Have you ever sensed your own death?

The phantom voice in his ears caused Integrity Knight Bercouli Synthesis One to awaken.

An eerily colored sunrise was trying to sneak into the dim tent. The air was as cold as ice, and breathing in deep prickled his lungs. He sensed that the time was 4:20 AM. Given the way his mind was melded with the Time-Splitting Sword, which had once been a hand on a great clock, Bercouli had the ability to accurately detect the time. In another ten minutes, he would need to have a messenger blow the morning horn to wake the troops.

The aged swordsman stretched his thick arms behind his head and turned his mind back to the statement that had broken his slumber.

Have you ever sensed your own death?

The owner of that sweet voice had been his only superior, the pontifex, Administrator.

He no longer remembered exactly when the memory had occurred. Somewhere around a hundred years ago or a hundred and fifty. After undergoing treatment that eliminated unneeded memories to prevent the collapse of his soul, Bercouli was no longer able to sense the chronology of his memories the way he used to.

But he *could* remember the scene quite vividly. Seemingly bored by the endless march of time she lived through—by her own desire, it should be mentioned—Administrator chose to invite the next-oldest person in the world, Bercouli, to her chamber for drinks.

The silver-haired ruler of all draped her body, naked save for a sheer scrap of silk, on a long crimson chair and asked him that question as she swirled a wineglass in her fingers. Bercouli was sitting cross-legged on the floor, eating a piece of cheese as he pondered this riddle.

He was used to her whims by this point and so answered honestly, rather than out of some desire to stay on her good side and save his own skin. He said, *Sensed my death? When I was still a lad, and I got smacked down by either the previous dark general or the one before him, I thought that was going to be it for me.*

The pontifex giggled and lifted the crystal glass. *But you brought his head to me quite a while ago, didn't you? I believe I converted it into one of those jewels on the floor. You haven't had any moments since then?*

Well, I can't recall them if I did. Why do you ask? It seems a sensation that would be foreign to you, my lady, he replied.

The girl who lived eternally adjusted her long legs and smiled again. *Hee-hee, you don't understand, Bercouli. Every day...every day I feel death. Every time I awaken in the morning...No, even in my dreams. I feel it because I don't control everything yet. There are still enemies who live. And there is always the possibility that at some point in the future, there will be a new enemy.*

My, my, my. It must be hard to be the pontifex.

A hundred and some years later, in a Dark Territory forest far from the human realm, Bercouli grinned to himself.

I feel like I finally understand what you were talking about. Sensing the approach of your own death is merely the flip side of seeking the possibilities of death. In the end, you were searching for a destination you could accept, a death that was fitting, a foe so powerful that no amount of struggle would bring you to victory...

Just like me, now.

The same way that I can keenly sense impending death approaching by the moment...

Without Administrator, Bercouli was now the oldest human being in the world. He bounced up from the floor and covered his powerful frame with a simple white kimono. He tightened the sash, slipped on his sandals, then stuck his sword on his left side.

Then he stepped through the hanging flap into the chill of early morning and headed for the messengers' tent to give the order to wake the troops.

At about that same moment, from the Dark Territory camp two kilors to the north, ten dragons took flight by the first rays of light peeking over the horizon.

Under the arms of the dark knights riding these steeds were thick bundles of stiff rope. One end of each rope was already fixed to a wooden stake driven into the ground near the edge of the crevice.

The dragons crossed the hundred-mel ravine and landed on the south end, their riders' ropes uncoiling the whole way. When the knights jumped down, they wielded huge hammers rather than swords and began the awkward process of driving new stakes into the ground.

Emperor Vecta's new orders were as follows.

The pugilists and dark knights should travel across ten ropes laid over the crevice to get to the other side.

Enemy interference should be ignored. Crossing the ropes was the top priority.

Those who fell should not be rescued.

Food and other supplies would not be ferried across.

In other words, it was a merciless suicide mission, in which numerous casualties were expected, and there would be no supplies. Iskahn, leader of the pugilists, and the young head of the dark knighthood, who'd taken over after Shasta's death, both ground their teeth at the cruelty and unfairness of it.

But they did not have the option of disobeying the absolute power of their emperor. All they could do was hope that they finished crossing the ropes before the enemy noticed—and contrary to that hope, a Human Guardian Army scout watching the Dark Territory army all night was sprinting down the hill one kilor to the south.

As she ate a simple breakfast of two hard toasted pieces of bread surrounding cheese, dried meat, and dried fruit, Asuna's mind sleepily worked through some calculations.

...If time is accelerated a thousand times here, that means I get to have a thousand meals in the time that people in the real world eat just one. I'm assuming that means I won't get that much fatter...

She glanced up ahead at Alice and Sortiliena, who were equally sluggish in the process of eating their sandwiches. Through the fabric of their dresses, it was clear that the other two had lithe physiques with absolutely no extra meat on them.

Did lifestyle diseases even exist in this world? Or was your physique based on fixed parameters that were assigned at birth? Or perhaps a person's appearance was like a mirror that reflected their mental state?

Next to her, Ronie was cutting a sandwich into little pieces for Kirito to eat. Alice claimed that she had been feeding him enough to maintain his life level, but apparently there was nothing she could do about how scrawny he looked. It was as though he wished that he could simply vanish from the world.

"...Kirito's cheeks are looking less pale this morning," Ronie suddenly said, as though she knew what Asuna was thinking. "And he's eating his food more forcefully than usual."

"Perhaps spending the night with four beautiful women had a positive effect," said Alice, eliciting conflicted smiles from the others.

They had spent the night talking, sitting around Kirito as he slept. It was nowhere near enough time for the four of them to exhaust their anecdotes about Kirito, and they eventually gave in to the temptation of sleep.

The next thing she knew, Asuna was being awakened by a horn, and Ronie had brought breakfast. As she ate, Asuna silently told her lover, *You never change, no matter where you are. You're kind to everyone, and you try to take everything on, and you get hurt in the process. But this time, you've bitten off more than you can chew. You can't take an entire world on your back. You need to rely on me and everyone else. We all love you.*

...But no one more than me.

She felt quiet, strong determination fill her chest. When Kirito woke up, she would smile and tell him, *It's all right. Everything went fine. I and everyone else kept safe what you wanted to protect.*

The other three seemed to feel Asuna's will, too. Alice, Ronie, and Sortiliena looked to Asuna, their eyes sharp and alert, and nodded firmly.

It was moments later that the horn sounded, tensely alerting the camp to an enemy attack.

Alice rushed back to her tent with a scrap of bread in her mouth, quickly slapped her armor on, and grabbed the Osmanthus Blade before heading back outside. She met up with Asuna, who was armed and ready, too, then told Ronie and Tiese to take care of Kirito before setting her sights to the north.

About where the forest gave way, she found Bercouli with his sword drawn. The commander had already gotten the report from the scout, and when he saw Alice and Asuna running up, followed close behind by Renly and Sheyta, his expression went hard.

"Seems like the real-worlder on the enemy side's got quite the bold methodology. Emperor Vecta's played a risky move."

What he said next made Alice bite her lip.

The enemy had run ten thick ropes from bank to bank of the crevice to use as bridges, and they were forcing their way across the hundred-mel-wide gorge. If they fell, they would die. It was an acrobatic act that required great stamina and willpower. If Emperor Vecta was forcing his troops to do this, either he was getting desperate, or their lives were worth less than scraps of paper to him.

But even if one in three of the enemy fell into that crevice, that would still leave nearly seven thousand to deal with. The human army had only a thousand—they didn't stand a chance in a regular fight.

Their original plan, to hide in the woods and use sacred arts to attack, was pointless in the sunlight. They would just have to keep moving south and wait for another chance to lay an ambush.

It was Commander Bercouli who cut through Alice's indecision.

"This is a war," the ancient hero muttered, his pale-blue eyes shining fiercely. "Asuna's from elsewhere and has her own reasons—but there's no reason for *us* to show mercy to the dark army. We've got to make use of this opportunity while we've got it."

"Oppor…tunity?" Alice parroted.

Bercouli gave her a sharp look. "That's right…Renly."

The young Integrity Knight bolted to attention, surprised at the sudden address. "Y-yes, sir!"

"What's the maximum range of your weapons, the Double-Winged Blades?"

"Normally, it's thirty mels, but under Perfect Weapon Control arts, it's seventy…maybe a hundred."

"Good…then, the four of us are going to attack the enemy as they attempt to cross. Alice, Sheyta, and I are going to focus on protection. Renly, you're going to cut down the ropes they've laid across the gorge with your divine weapons."

Alice gasped. The enemy would be desperate to defend their means across, but even if they piled up bodies at the stakes at the end of the ropes, those thrown blades and their curving trajectories could easily fly over their heads and slice through anything. It was a merciless counterstrategy.

But the fifteen-year-old boy knight was firm with resolve and smacked his fist to his chest. "Understood, Commander!"

Next to him, Sheyta the Silent muttered, "It'll be fine. I'll protect him."

Even Asuna stepped forward, though his orders hadn't included her. "I'll go, too. The more defense, the better."

Alice closed her eyes for a moment and thought, *I used my large-scale art to fry ten thousand nonhumans, and my Perfect Control art to slaughter two thousand dark mages. I don't have the right to seek an honorable battle.*

For now, all she could do was fight with everything she had.

"Let's hurry," she said to the four others and turned to the hill north of them. The bloodred rays of the rising sun were already casting the curve of the horizon into black profile.

Hurry.

Hurry, hurry!

Iskahn, leader of the pugilists guild, chanted an inward refrain as he clenched his fists.

The pugilists and dark knights were crossing the ten crude ropes that spanned the crevice, each group using five. They clung upside down with their arms and legs around the ropes, but without any proper training, their movement was awkward and slow. If they had lifelines for everyone and time to distribute them, it would help, but the emperor did not give them that luxury.

On top of that, Iskahn's request to be first had been denied.

Apparently, this was punishment for his fanciful interpretation of last night's orders and for using only a small portion of his troops. He could still hear the emperor's icy voice in his ears: *You will follow my orders and do nothing else.*

While Iskahn worked his jaws with frustration, the quickest of his subordinates was finally getting to the middle of the rope. The man's copper skin was steaming in the chill of the early morning, and even at this distance, his dripping sweat could be seen shining in the light. It was a mad idea.

Just then, a powerful gust of wind ripped through the huge crevice.

Whoooosh! It buffeted the ropes, rocking them back and forth.

"Oh...!" Iskahn murmured. A number of pugilists slipped from the ropes, unable to keep their sweaty palms firm. Their howls echoed off the walls of the gorge.

Those were not screams, the young leader told himself. They were howls of rage that their deaths came not in the glory of battle but in the humiliating failure of forced circus acts.

A single, momentary gust of wind had sent over ten pugilists and dark knights plunging to their inky doom. But those just behind them bravely continued their passage. And from this side, soldiers continued to file onto the ropes at intervals of about three mels apart.

The cruel wind blew again intermittently and cost lives each time. Eventually, Iskahn realized that his clenched fists were emitting a red light that looked very much like flames.

A miserable dog's death.

Even lower than that. At least a dog had bones left to bury.

And the reason for their death was not the long-awaited invasion of the human lands—that fervent hope of the five races of darkness—but merely the capture of this Priestess of Light, because the emperor desired her. Iskahn had no idea how he would apologize to his people back home.

Hurry. Be quick. Let everyone get across before anything else happens, the young leader prayed. Through either divine providence or simple adjustment to the ropes, the lead climbers picked up speed and at last made it to the other side. Five seconds later, the next wave set foot on solid ground.

At this rate, it would easily take over an hour for ten thousand soldiers to cross the ten ropes. It was practically impossible that they'd complete the entire process before the enemy noticed their plan.

But at this moment, they had no choice but to pray for that very slim chance.

The sun rose into the eastern sky with terrifying speed, shining red upon the black earth. In comparison, the crowd of soldiers on the far side who had successfully shimmied across was growing agonizingly slowly. Despite the many who fell along the way, the group went from fifty to a hundred, to two hundred, then at last to over three hundred.

Just then, atop the hillside looming dark on the far side of the crevice appeared five horseback riders. Even with his excellent eyesight, Iskahn could not make out the riders atop the horses.

Just five...Scouts, then. We should still have more time before they marshal their forces.

It took only a moment for this judgment—this hope—to fall to pieces.

The five riders began descending the hill, heading straight for the ravine. With their whipping cloaks, shining armor, and powerful haze-like spirit, Iskahn could no longer deny the obvious.

Integrity Knights! Five of them!!

"Enemy attack!! Defend!! *Defend the ropes!!*" bellowed Iskahn. He didn't know whether his voice even reached the far side, but he had to do it. In possible response, half of the three-hundred-strong soldiers there formed protective circles around the stakes that held the ropes in place. The rest arranged themselves in front of that, preparing to fight back their attackers.

The enemy knights practically flew down the thousand mels from the hilltop to the edge of the cliff. They jumped off their mounts as one and raced for the rope on the right end.

Running in the lead was a large, stout man in foreign-looking dress. To his right was a woman in blazing golden armor. On the left was the woman named Sheyta, whom Iskahn had fought the night before.

They surrounded a smaller knight, and what looked like another one was farther behind, but he couldn't be sure of any details beyond that.

Dozens of pugilists rushed forward to envelop the five knights, beads of sweat flying from their torsos.

"*Raaaah!!*" they roared, fists and feet raining down upon the knights.

There were glints and flashes of metal in quick succession. An enormous geyser of blood erupted into the sky, like some gruesome waterfall rolling backward. At its base, arms, legs, and heads flew helplessly from the bodies they belonged to.

And then, from behind the three lead knights, a silver light rose up high, leaving a bright trail behind it. Amid the red light of the dawn, it arced up and over the heads of the pugilists—and toward the rightmost rope, which was still surrounded by a host of fighters…

"Nooooooo!!"

Iskahn's ears were so sharp that even beneath his own scream, he caught the faint snick of the cut.

The rope split in the middle, and the release of the tension holding it up left the ends writhing loose in the air like serpents. Dozens of warriors helplessly plunged into the depths of the ravine.

The image of them falling burned itself into Iskahn's eyes. Without realizing it, he said aloud, "This…*this* is war? You call this a battle?"

For once, his second-in-command, Dampa, did not have a pithy retort.

Not only were his tribespeople forced to mimic a clown's acrobatics, they were swallowed by the abyss without even having the opportunity to fight. They had not undergone the long and brutal training of the pugilists for *this*.

What would he tell the elderly parents and young children who awaited their return back home? How could he tell them that their loved ones had not stood boldly before the enemy's blades and given their lives as the glorious warriors they were, but fallen to the depths of the earth without a chance to use their mighty fists?

He was helpless to do anything but watch and listen to the spectacle of the overlapping screams of anger and mourning as warriors fell to their deaths.

I will claim your vengeance. Just forgive me. Forgive me.

But such was the cruelty of the situation that Iskahn could not say whom he should defeat to fulfill that vengeance. The Integrity Knights were raising a desperate stand against ten times their number. He could not ask them to wait, pretty please, until all the pugilists had crossed the ropes safely and assumed their battle formations. It was a sign of the knights' courage that they struck with a tiny group of five, knowing that their window of opportunity was limited.

So who was it? Who bore the blame for the undignified deaths of those valiant warriors?

Was it their chief, who could do nothing but stand stock-still like a fool, his fists balled? Or…

Iskahn suddenly felt a sharp pain deep in his right eye. The breath caught in his throat.

Red light pulsed repeatedly through his vision as a second rope was cut, its ends flying through the air.

At the rear of his army's emplacement, Gabriel Miller watched, face propped against his fist, as three of the ten ropes they'd affixed over the gorge were snapped within moments of one another.

It seemed that the human army's artificial intelligences were slightly superior. In fact, taking their adaptability into account, the difference seemed stark. With how quickly they'd identified and countered the Dark Territory army's moves, both last night and today, it was unlike any strategy game's CPU opponent he had ever faced.

The result of the game was that Gabriel had already lost 70 percent of his total units, but he was not yet panicking.

He just watched hundreds of his units die and waited—waited for the moment to arrive.

Critter, who was still manning the desk in the main control room of the *Ocean Turtle*, was as of that point done with the task of matching the Fluctlight Acceleration rate to one, the same as real time. The task had taken as long as it had in order to soften the shock of the shift and prevent the Rath employees logged in to the Underworld from detecting that it was happening.

In parallel, he used the satellite connection to drop a URL into a major online gaming community in America. The link led to a teaser site that Critter had whipped up in short order. It used edgy fonts and blood-splatter effects to announce:

A LIMITED-TIME BETA TEST FOR A NEW VRMMO IN PRODUCTION.

THE BIRTH OF THE WORLD'S FIRST TRUE PvP SLAUGHTER EXPERIENCE.

FULLY HUMAN AVATARS. NO SOFTWARE BOARD RATINGS. NO ETHICS CODE.

The gamers reacted to this bold pitch with equal parts skepticism and excitement. If nothing else, this indie studio had balls.

As of July 2026, VRMMO regulations were evolving in America within the general expansion of anti-terrorism measures, so even indie developers who made games with the free Seed package had to submit to an industry ratings board and implement certain ethical measures, or they would suffer major problems with operating their game.

In particular, depictions of brutal violence suffered a major crackdown. If you really wanted severed limbs to be a major part of the appeal, you had to employ the method of games like *Insectsite* and make the avatars nonhuman in some way. In fact, America's restrictions were even more severe than what existed in Japan, where the first VRMMO was created, a state of affairs that left the American gaming community frustrated...Until this mysterious beta test advertisement, that is.

This was Gabriel's big strategy, which he enacted at the cost of significant valuable time.

He was going to give American VRMMO players the keys to the Dark Territory's dark knight accounts and allow them to dive into the Underworld to serve as his soldiers.

Neither Seijirou Kikuoka, the man in charge of Rath, nor Takeru Higa, who'd designed the Underworld, had ever considered that such a drastic move might be possible.

But the Underworld, on a lower server level, was no more than another VRMMO game that met Seed specifications. If it was presented as a virtual world using 3-D polygon models rather than its original mnemonic visuals—and the time-acceleration aspect were not active—you could use the AmuSphere to log in, touch and interact with the world's objects, and even kill other characters.

And it didn't matter whether those characters were real-world people or Underworld people.

7

Gabriel and Critter's secret plan completely took Rath by surprise. Even if the staff had realized it was happening, they would have had no way of shutting off the satellite connection, since the main control room had been taken over.

But when Critter uploaded the link in question to the Internet, the packet containing the URL was caught and observed by just one person.

It was Yui, the top-down artificial intelligence. Yui had been monitoring the situation on the *Ocean Turtle* from Asuna Yuuki's phone when she detected Critter's message, accessed the teaser site, and accurately assessed and identified Gabriel's plan.

She tried to warn Rath about the situation, but the sub-control room was physically isolated, and with the phone left in Asuna's ship bunk, no one was going to hear its alarm going off, even at maximum volume.

Yui was left with no other option but to focus her senses on distant Japan across the Pacific. She called a number of other phones at the same time.

In the real world, Shino Asada was a junior in high school, but in the virtual world, she was a deadly sniper. As soon as she heard the notification from her cell phone, she bolted upright in bed.

The clock at her bedside said it was three in the morning. Despite the unexpected wake-up at such an odd hour, her sleepiness was instantly gone: The ringtone that awoke her was the one she'd set for calls from Kazuto Kirigaya.

Can it be? A call from Kirito, who's not only unconscious but missing?

When she pressed the device to her ear, however, she heard the stressed voice of a young girl.

"Sinon, this is Yui!"

"Wha…? Y-Yui?!"

She knew about Yui the AI, Kirito and Asuna's "daughter," of course. When she'd talked with Asuna and the other girls about Kirito's whereabouts just a week ago, she'd marveled at Yui's capacity for information processing and emotional expression.

But Shino never expected to receive a phone call directly from the AI and was at a loss for words. Instead, the sweet but faintly electronic voice continued on its own.

"I will explain later. Make preparations to leave the house immediately and take a taxi. I will send the destination and quickest route through your phone. The cost of your fare will be added directly to your electronic cash account."

There was a prompt ringing sound, notifying Shino that her device had received an online deposit. That detail finally banished any thought from her mind that this was a dream or prank of some kind.

"A…taxi? To where…?" She stood up as commanded, pulling her legs out of her pajamas, alarm still blaring in her head. What Yui said next was like a bucket of ice water dumped onto her mind.

"Please hurry. Papa and Mama are in danger!!"

"D-danger?! Big Brother and Asuna?!"

Suguha Kirigaya fastened her jeans button with one hand as she spoke—a high school kendo team member in real life and a sylph magic warrior in the virtual world, as well as Kazuto Kirigaya's younger sister.

"Don't shout too loud, Leafa, or Miss Midori will wake up," Yui instructed calmly from the cell phone. Suguha clammed up.

"Y...you're right. Now that I think of it...this is the first time I've ever snuck out of the house at this hour..."

"Unfortunately, there isn't enough time to explain everything to her and ask for permission to leave. I think that recording a message on the home server about leaving early for a morning training session for your club should be enough."

"A-all right. Wow, you're really clever, Yui," Suguha marveled as she finished dressing. She snuck down the stairs and put her hand on the front door. While it was a fairly old Japanese home, it did have a modern security system active at night, the alarm of which Yui had apparently deactivated.

Since Kazuto had gone missing, their mother had returned home early every day. Suguha felt guilty about leaving without saying anything, so she said a silent message as she passed through the doorway.

I'm sorry, Mom. Don't worry—I'll find a way to save him.

As soon as she made her way through the residential block to the main road, there was a taxi parked on the sidewalk. Yui must have ordered one online. The driver gave her a suspicious look when he saw how young she was, so she gave him an excuse about a sick relative in the hospital and checked her phone for the address.

"Um...take me to Minato Ward of Tokyo."

She felt as though it would be better if she didn't tell him her destination would actually be in Roppongi.

The half-eaten energy bar dropping from Takeru Higa's mouth to his knees was enough to jolt his eyes open. He blinked a few times and checked his smartwatch. It was just before four in the morning by Japan Standard Time. A visual sweep of the room gave him a glimpse of his fellow staffers packed into the sub-control room, looking exhausted.

Dr. Rinko Koujiro was sitting in one of the console chairs, her head nodding in sleep. Even Lieutenant Colonel Kikuoka, though awake, did not have the usual sharp, alert look in his eyes behind his black-framed glasses as he stared at the main monitor.

The only others were four engineers as still as corpses on the mattresses lined up along the wall. There was no eliminating the possibility of an information leaker among the SDF security members, so Kikuoka had them guarding the pressure-resistant barrier a floor below the sub-control room.

It had already—or finally, depending on perspective—been fourteen hours since their unknown attackers had infiltrated the craft. It would be ten more hours until the *Nagato* defense ship assigned to guard the *Ocean Turtle* rushed in to neutralize the threat. Given the circumstances, it was a devastating length of time. Especially for the Underworld, where time was drastically accelerated to stretch it out.

Ten hours had passed since Asuna Yuuki had logged in with Super-Account 01. Since the FLA ratio was normally set to its limit of times one thousand, that meant ten thousand hours had passed inside the simulation—over an entire year of subjective time. Yet there was still no report from within the Underworld of success or failure in the mission to capture Alice.

"Was the World's End Altar really that far from the human settlements...?" Higa muttered to himself, envisioning the full map of the Underworld, which was designed to look very much like Rath's logo.

Just then, the receiver on the console made a series of connected, shrill beeps, nearly causing him to jump out of his seat. "K-Kiku, phone call," he said to the man seated next to him, assuming it was regarding something on the lower floor.

The Hawaiian-shirt-wearing commander bolted upright with

the same kind of surprise and lunged for the receiver, losing a wooden sandal from his toes' grasp.

"Sub Control! Kikuoka!" he said, hoarse but still commanding. After a few moments, the speaker emitted the voice of not Lieutenant Nakanishi downstairs but a young man, audibly bewildered and overwhelmed.

"Um...you're in the STL Development Lab at Rath headquarters... right? My name is Hiraki from the Rath Roppongi office..."

"Huh? R...Roppongi?" Kikuoka repeated, his voice squawking at this unexpected communication. Higa was just as startled.

Why would the Roppongi office be contacting them at this moment? The employees there didn't know that Rath itself was just a mock venture capital firm secretly funded by the national defense budget or that its real headquarters was not in Japan at all but floating in the sea to the south in the form of the *Ocean Turtle* or even that the title of their research was Project Alicization.

And of course, they didn't know that Rath was currently under attack by an unknown enemy force. The Roppongi office was just a lab for STL research and development.

That's right...STL...

Suddenly, there was a brief glimpse of some kind of epiphany in Higa's mind, but before he could seize and identify it, Kikuoka distracted him by clearing his throat loudly.

"Ah, y-yes. This is Kikuoka, STL Development."

"Oh! Hello, sir! I met you once before. I'm Chief Hiraki of the Roppongi development team!"

Enough of the workplace formalities! Just get to the point!! Higa wanted to scream. Kikuoka had the same expression on his face, but he did a very good job of assuming his business persona verbally.

"Ah, yes, I see, Chief Hiraki. Are you really working overtime this late?"

"Actually, I was out drinking after work and missed the last train. Roppongi's a terrible place for an office, I tell you! Oh, and please keep that comment off the record, heh-heh."

You're talking to the boss, *you idiot! The head honcho! Just get to the damn point!!* screamed Higa. Thankfully, his psychic message seemed to sink in, as Hiraki tightened up and got down to business.

"Well, uh, the reason I'm calling is...I guess you could call it a problem...Whatever it is, it's strange. We've just had a cold call from some outside people with no appointment..."

"Outside? A partner?"

"No, someone completely unrelated to the company...In fact, it just looks like two teenage girls..."

"Huh?!" Kikuoka, Higa, and even Dr. Koujiro, who had awoken from her light slumber, gaped. "T...teenage...girls?"

"Yes. I tried to send them away, of course. We have a very confidential arrangement here, after all. But the things that they're saying, I just can't dismiss out of hand..."

Higa was getting sick of Hiraki's reticence and stood up, placing both hands on the console. Kikuoka exhibited more patience as he gently asked, "What exactly did they say?"

"Well, sir, they told me to contact Seijirou Kikuoka at Rath headquarters right away and confirm the FLA ratio of the Underworld immediately..."

"Wh-whaaaat?!" the entire room screamed in unison.

How did some random teenage girls know those terms? You would never in a million years stumble across that series of words unless you knew the entire workings of Project Alicization.

Higa shared an openmouthed look with Kikuoka, then turned to the console in an automatic daze and began typing commands on the keyboard. The current acceleration rate appeared on the dark monitor: x1.00.

"Wha—? We're in real time?! Since when?!" Higa gasped. Kikuoka tore his eyes away and shouted into the phone receiver, "N-names! Did the girls name themselves?!"

"Er, they did. But it seemed like a joke...They clearly aren't their real names. They said that if I told you they were named Sinon and

Leafa, you would understand. But they looked perfectly Japanese to me..."

Thonk.

Kikuoka's other wooden sandal fell to the floor.

When Yui confirmed through the phone that the lock on the building containing Rath's Roppongi office had opened and allowed Shino Asada and Suguha Kirigaya to rush inside, the artificial intelligence exhibited signs of relief. Specifically, that meant that she exhaled and dedicated the majority of her processing ability to a parallel task she was dealing with.

Yui expected that great trouble would interfere with the potential success of their mission. It was something that she on her own could never hope to achieve. But at the same time, she knew that failing would mean exposing her beloved Kirito and Asuna to great danger.

She pulled her attention away from Shino's cell phone and focused her large eyes on four fairies sitting before her.

They were in the living room of Kirito and Asuna's in-game home on the twenty-second floor of New Aincrad in the VRMMORPG known as *ALfheim Online*.

Yui flitted about in the form of a tiny navigation pixie. Sitting across from her on the sofa was Silica the cait sith, with her triangular ears, little fangs, and long tail.

Next to her was Lisbeth the leprechaun, her puffed-out hair a metallic pink color.

Leaning against the table farther away was the salamander Klein, a flashy bandana spiking his red hair upward. Standing by him with arms folded was Agil the imposing gnome.

All of them were experienced VRMMO players who had survived the incredible gauntlet that was *Sword Art Online*, the original game of death, and they were lifelong friends of Kirito and Asuna. They had logged in to *ALO* in the middle of the night upon Yui's summons and had just gotten a briefing on the situation.

Klein scratched his forehead through the bandana. With the gravest tone he could muster in his normally aloof voice, he said, "Man...he's really gotten himself wrapped up in a crazy one this time...A virtual world created by the military, with a true AI named Alice? We're way beyond the bounds of video games at this point."

"So this AI isn't like an NPC in a game but is pretty much...the same as us human beings?" Lisbeth asked.

Yui bobbed her head. "Yes, that's right. It's fundamentally different from traditional AIs like me. This is a true soul. Within Rath, they call that an artificial fluctlight instead."

"And they want to take that AI and put it on fighter jets...," murmured Silica, who looked away from Yui to the little dragon pet curled up on her knees, Pina.

"Rath seems to hope to use that technology for demonstrations both domestically and internationally," Yui explained, "but the attackers in control of the *Ocean Turtle* right now have a much more direct application in mind, I suspect."

Klein spread his arms. "So who the hell are these guys sieging the ship?"

"There is a very high possibility that American military or intelligence is involved."

"M...military?! The United States?!" Lisbeth gasped, pulling her head back.

Yui nodded. "If Alice falls into the American military's hands, she'll be placed on combat drones as an AI pilot in the not-too-distant future, I am certain. And Papa and Mama would do anything to keep that from happening. Because...because..."

The little pixie stopped, alarmed. She was getting an unexpected reaction from her own emotional modeling program. Large droplets of water began to spill down her cheeks.

Tears.

I'm crying. But why...?

But even this question was shoved aside by the unfamiliar sensation pushing her onward. Yui clasped her little hands before her chest and continued, "Because Alice is the evidence of the existence of all the VRMMO worlds, beginning with *SAO*, and the many people who lived in them. She is the fruit of all the time, material, and mental resources that were expended there. I am certain that the purpose of the Seed package in the first place was none other than the birth of Alice."

The four people listened to her in silence. Yui went on, the tears still streaming from her eyes. "Through all those countless linked worlds, the laughter, tears, sadness, and love of all those many people…the feedback of all those souls glimmering with life brought about the birth of a new humanity in the Underworld. Papa, Mama, Leafa, Klein, Lisbeth, Silica, Agil, Sinon…It was from the cradle woven of your hearts and so many, many more people in one great tapestry that Alice was born!"

She stopped there, but not one of them rushed to fill the ensuing silence.

Yui had no means of knowing the thoughts and emotions happening in the minds of the humans congregated around her. It was she most of all who understood that, being a top-down AI and an amalgamation of information, she had no true emotions and could not understand them in the realest sense.

Even this powerful urge to help Kirito, Asuna, and those people she loved was nothing more than a part of the source code that someone had compiled so she could function as a mental health counseling program. Even before this conversation began, Yui had been afraid that the things she said might not register a real difference in the hearts of the human beings across from her.

So when clear liquid sprang from Lisbeth's eyes and ran down her cheeks, Yui was taken aback.

"Yes…you're right. It's connected. It's all connected. Time, people, hearts…It's all one big river."

Silica leaped to her feet, eyes watery, and enveloped Yui in her arms. "It's all right, Yui. We're going to go rescue Kirito

and Asuna. We're going to see to it that they make it out of this safely...so don't cry."

"You bet. Don't be so distant with us, Yuippe. You know we'd never abandon Kirito like that," said Klein, voice hoarse, pulling his bandana lower, over his eyes.

Agil bobbed his head deeply and pronounced, "I owe him a whole hell of a lot. This is a chance for me to make up just a little bit of that."

"...Everyone...," Yui squeaked, wrapped in Silica's arms. It was all that she could utter; the mysterious tears from an unknown source kept coming and coming and refused to stop.

But we don't have time. There are so many things I still need to explain. My priority should be to calmly and effectively relay information. I wonder if my emotion-mimicking circuits have broken down.

But in the thrall of a single bit of code that dominated her priority system, Yui could do nothing but sob and hiccup, repeating the same words over and over.

"...Thank...you...Thank you...everyone..."

Minutes later, her tears stopped at last, and Yui told the four the current situation as she understood it and her expectations for what would happen in the near future.

The situation: The attackers on board the *Ocean Turtle* with Kirito and Asuna had uploaded a fake game teaser site in an attempt to recruit players to their cause. The expectation: Players drawn to the site would soon appear in the Underworld in great numbers.

There was a deep furrow on Klein's brow. He growled, "So that's thirty thousand VRMMO players diving from America, at minimum, possibly up to a hundred thousand...and to them, the human army soldiers with Kirito and Asuna are nothing more than PvP targets?"

"Why don't *we* post on those American VRMMO sites, too, then?" suggested Lisbeth. "We could tell them about the experiment and the ongoing attack and ask them not to take part in this fake beta test…"

But Yui just shook her head. "At the root of all of this is a struggle for military secrets between Japan and America. If we let them sense even a bit of that, it will only have the opposite effect of what we want."

"So saying that they're real people and you shouldn't kill them…is only going to make matters worse…," Silica murmured, looking downcast.

Klein broke the heavy silence that followed. "Heh! Then we'll just do the same thing! We've got at least as many shut-in game addicts as the US does. If we whip up our own beta test page and spread it around, and the Rath folks set up as many accounts as we need, I bet we could get thirty or forty thousand, no problem!"

"Actually, there *is* one big problem," Agil warned, crossing his massive arms.

"What's that?"

"The time difference. It's four thirty in the morning in Japan, the least active part of the day. While in America, it's twelve thirty in the middle of the day in LA and three thirty PM in New York. They're going to have way more active players right now."

"Hrrng…," Klein groaned. It was true.

Yui was already concerned about that very thing. She said, "Agil is correct. After the difference in VRMMO population itself, we're also lagging in time zone, and they have a big head start in promotion. I don't think we will be able to recruit anywhere near ten thousand people from Japan. If we use accounts of the same level as the enemy side, our chances of fighting them back are exceedingly slim."

"But there aren't any more god accounts like the one Asuna used, right? And there's no time to build up from nothing the way that Kirito did," Lisbeth murmured, concerned, "so I guess we'll just have to make do with the strongest accounts we have available…"

Yui stared at her. "Actually…there are accounts. They are much more powerful in level and gear than the defaults that the enemy side will be utilizing."

"Huh...? Wh-where?"

"You already have them. They are the very accounts you're logged in with at this moment," Yui said, revealing the true core of what was being asked of them—and received four dumbfounded looks in return.

She knew that she was suggesting a tremendous price—the sacrifice of their alter egos, the personas they spent half their lives enriching—but she also knew with all of her being that these people, especially, would rise to the occasion.

"You must convert! You and many other VRMMO players must take the characters you've built up through all of the many Seed worlds that exist—and convert them to the Underworld!"

(To be continued)

AFTERWORD

It's been an entire year since the last time, but I would like to thank you for reading the sixteenth volume of *Sword Art Online*, titled *Alicization Exploding.*

The battle in Central Cathedral wrapped up, the focus of the story expanded from the human realm to the entire Underworld... and then I left you hanging for much longer than usual. I'm sorry for that. In this volume, Asuna finally touches down on the battlefield, and there are hints that the old familiar gang is about to get involved, so I'm hoping that I can get back to the usual pace and rush through the end of the Alicization arc. Kirito is under protection in this volume, just as he was in the last one, but I have a feeling that he's about to break out and play a huge role again!

The subtitle *Exploding* was appropriate for the content of the story in a variety of ways. The first few titles, like *Beginning* and *Turning*, were nice and punchy, but I feel as if these English terms are getting longer and more difficult to pronounce, so I'll try to find a shorter one next time. As for the content, as the chapter title "Battle for the Underworld" suggests, the first half of the book is almost like an ensemble war story, with characters jumping in and out of the fray. So I tried switching from my usual third-person-limited narrative style to a third-person-omniscient style instead. Hopefully no one was too surprised by information popping up that the viewpoint characters couldn't have known!

I was thinking of writing a bit of a personal update, but my life continues to be a very predictable one, with no real new topics to discuss…I haven't seriously played an MMORPG in a few years, but I don't have the time to pick one up, so instead, I tried out a bit of one of the modern open-world Western RPGs on PS4. All I can say is that it's awe-inspiring. The map's so huge, and there's so much freedom to do stuff that I waste my time on frivolous things until I forget what I was supposed to be doing in the main quest. Once they get head-mounted VR displays and motion controllers going, I'll never come back! It makes the dream of a game like *SAO* more real to me. I told Futami, a game producer with Bandai Namco Entertainment, to make a game where you can adventure "throughout the entire Underworld!" He just gave me a smile and stared into empty space.

And now it's time for the usual acknowledgments. To my illustrator abec, who made Asuna's cutting-edge Stacia design so beautiful and cute (and Sheyta, Renly, and the goblin chieftains are great!), and to my editor Miki, who stayed up late listening to me chuckle over drinks, despite being the editor in chief, thank you so much! See you again for the next volume!

Reki Kawahara—June 2015